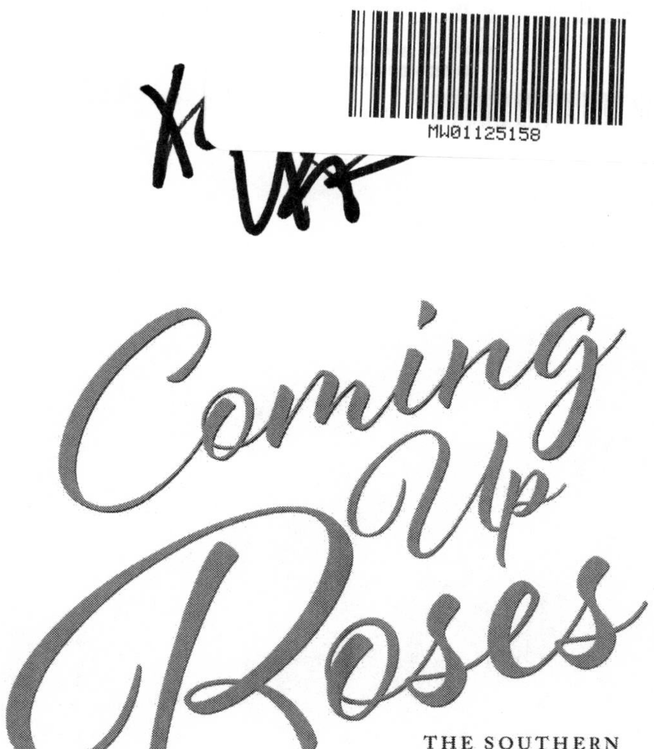

THE SOUTHERN ROOTS SERIES

LK FARLOW

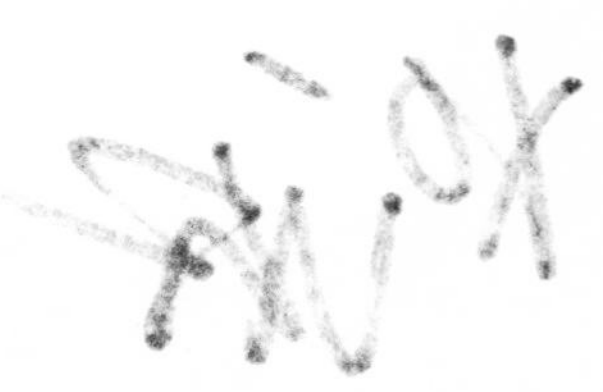

Coming Up Roses (The Southern Roots Series)

This book is a work of fiction. Names, characters, businesses, organizations, places, events and incidents either are the product of the author's imagination or are used fictitiously. Any resemblance to actual persons, living or dead, events, or locales is entirely coincidental.

The author acknowledges the trademark status and trademark owners of various products referred to in this work of fiction, which have been used without permission. The publication/use of these trademarks is not authorized, associated with, or sponsored by the trademark owners.

For information contact: *www.authorlkfarlow.com*

Cover Design & Interior Formatting: Jersey Girl Design | Juliana Cabrera
Editing: Librum Artis Editorial Services | Valorie Clifton
Proofreading: Keyanna Butler/The Indie Author's Apprentice | Karin Enders

ISBN-10: 1986436586
ISBN-13: 978-1986436588

Second Edition: March 2018

10 9 8 7 6 5 4 3 2 1

To my Phoobs, because with you by my side, everything is coming up roses.

Chapter One

Cash

Tonight's the night. I've got everything planned to a T. I made sure to take off early from work so that I could get to the house before she did to set everything up. I've got her favorite Italian food from Luigi's riding shotgun. I have candles and her favorite flowers, lilies, to place all around the dining room table—and the bed.

But more important than any of that is the black velvet box—you know, the ring-holding kind—that's tucked into my front pocket.

I park my truck down the street so that if she happens to come home early, she won't know I'm here. Gathering everything up, I head toward the house, my arms full and a spring in my step.

It's so damn gorgeous this time of year—cool October mornings and just a hair past warm at midday. Maybe Kayla will want to plan the wedding for this time next year. I pause at the sound of my phone ringing in my pocket. Shuffling the items I'm hauling, I carefully slide my phone from my pocket. Seeing that it's my brother, I swipe to answer the call.

"Jake, what's up?"

"Cash." He sighs. "Are you sure you want to do this?" He's never been very pro-Kayla. Come to think of it, none of my family is. Friends either, for that matter.

"I'm sure. She's been so off lately. Distant. This'll get us back on the right path."

"Bro, don't rush into something just because you *think* she wants it. You're smarter than that."

"Jake, I got this." I huff, and my annoyance comes through loud and clear. "I'm not rushing shit. We've been together six years. She's probably just pissy because I've taken so damn long to ask." His reply is nothing more than a grumble.

My steps falter when I see Kayla's car in the driveway. What's she doing home already? "Hey, Jake? Let me call you back," I mumble as I slide my key into the lock.

"Kayla?" I call out. No answer. *What the hell?* I hear noise coming from the back of the house—in the direction of our bedroom—and my heart drops like lead into my stomach. I can feel it, soul-fucking-deep. Something's not right.

I shoulder the door open, and there she is. In *our* bed, head thrown back in ecstasy, someone else's hands gripping her thick hips as she cries out his name. This *can't* be real. This *can't* be happening. They're so into each other, they don't even notice me.

"What the fuck?" I shout. Kayla's head whips toward me, and Kevin—assuming the name she was chanting is his—sits up so fast that she falls back onto her ass. "WHAT THE FUCK?" I roar again. Because, really, what else is there to say?

Kevin's eyes slide from Kayla to me and back again. "Kay, what's your brother doing here?" *Kay? Dude has a nickname for MY girlfriend?* She just blinks, tears welling.

"Your brother?" I grit out. "Your fucking brother?" Kevin looks genuinely confused. "I'm here, Kevin, because this is my house. That's what I'm doing here."

"Babes, I had no clue your brother was in town, or I would have suggested my place." Kayla looks a little green, her eyes darting rapidly around the room like she's looking for an exit. Tough luck, *babes.*

"I'm not her brother," I hiss at Kevin, who is clearly not the sharpest tool in the shed.

Kayla's given up on her escape plan and has devolved to crying. You know, that raccoon eyes, ugly kind of crying.

"Bro, just chill." The douche tries to pacify me. "I'll be on my way, and you guys can talk."

I shake my head, my face a mask of cool indifference. "Nah, *bro,* nothing to talk about." Storming over to the closet, I fling open the door and grab my overnight bag, throwing God knows what into it. Hopefully, enough shit to last me the weekend. "I'm outta here."

She's sobbing uncontrollably into the sheets, refusing to look at either of us. But I have this nagging feeling that it's all for show. "Ca–Cash. K–Kevin, I c–can explain—"

"Nothin' to explain, Kayla. Dinner's on the table. Enjoy it." *Or choke on it.* I keep that thought to myself, though. "We'll deal with shit when I'm ready. Don't call." I snatch my bag up off the floor and head back the way I came, slamming the front door as I go, leaving my house—*our house.* The house I'd spent the last three years in, with her. The house we talked about raising kids in. Jesus. How did I miss this? I was ready to get down on one fucking knee. Guess she saved me the trouble by getting on both of hers.

After hours of aimless driving, I finally decide to grab a room at King's Motor Lodge. A lumpy mattress sounds better than hearing the inevitable 'I told you so' I'd get crashing on a friend's couch. The room is the size of a large closet, with dingy brown carpet and faded, peeling wallpaper. A mothball mixed with air freshener scent surrounds me as I drop down onto the bed and check my phone—two missed calls from my mom and three from Jake, along with a slew of text messages. Not a thing from Kayla. I know I told her not to call, but damn. I swipe away the notifications and dial my brother. It's time to face the music.

"Cashmere," Jake chirps into the phone. *Goddamn, I hate that nickname.* "So, did the tr—I mean Kayla—say 'yes'?"

"Nope," I offer, knowing how much he hates single-word replies. Serves the asshole right for calling me Cashmere.

"Seriously, bro. I've been trying to reach you for hours. Don't leave me hangin'."

I inhale deeply through my nose, trying to gather my thoughts, and then launch into a play-by-play of everything that went down tonight.

"I'm so sorry, Cash. Never did like her, but I didn't think she was that..."

"Man, I didn't even see it coming," I whisper into the phone. My voice breaks, utterly defeated. "I don't know what I'm supposed to do now."

"What do you mean, you don't know what to do? Pack your shit and head to Dogwood. Come home, Cash."

"Right, because it's just that easy. I can totally just throw my shit into the back of my truck and move. I have obligations here, Jake. I can't just up and move because Kayla fucked me over."

"Wasn't you she was fucking, Cash."

"Thanks, Jake. Because that isn't still fresh in my mind," I snarl.

"Check yourself. I know you're pissed, but don't take it out on me."

I huff out a harsh breath. "I know. I'm sorry. I'm so damn angry."

We both know he isn't the problem. Kayla is. And maybe I am too. How could I have been so blind? I jump up from the bed and start pacing the small room, trying to get a grip on the rage building inside me.

"I bet you are. If Paige ever...Jesus. Do you know how long? Not like that matters. Once is enough."

"It was definitely more than once. I can feel it." My eyes are watering, but I refuse to let the tears spill. *Man up, Cash.* "I wasted all this time. I had plans, a vision, and she shot it all to hell. What am I gonna do, Jake?" I fish the ring box out of my pocket and just stare at it. I was so damn convinced this little box was the key to my future—our future. What a joke. I slam it down onto the small table by the door and zone back in on my brother's words.

"Listen, here's the plan. You're gonna talk to her." I start to interrupt him, but he just keeps on. "Sucks, I know, but it has to be done. Y'all are going to get shit sorted with the house and the lease. Then you're going to pack up and come home. Stay here, or at Mom's, or Drake's, until you figure out a plan. You have options. Use them. You know you can do some work from here. That's the joy of self-employment. Stop overthinking. You can't change what happened, you hear me?"

"Yeah, I hear you. I'll call you in a few days and let you know what's up. Thanks, brother."

I know I need to call my mom. And Kayla. I rub my hand down my face, the full weight of my exhaustion settling in. I toss my phone down beside the little black box and collapse into the rickety chair next to it as a cloud of dust floats up around me.

Tomorrow. I'll call them tomorrow.

The sound of someone knocking wakes me, and I stumble as I walk to check the door, my muscles stiff from sleeping in that damn chair all night. I look through the peephole and there she is. Kayla. How in the hell did she know where to find me?

"Cash, I know you're in there!" Seriously, how does she know I'm here? "Open the door, Cash. We need to talk." She sounds angry, and that's just fuel to my fire. What right does *she* have to be mad?

"How the hell did you know where to find me?" I whisper-shout at her through the crack in the door.

"Open up and I'll tell you, Cash."

"You can tell me now."

"I checked your bank account. Your room here was the last charge."

"You've got some nerve." I throw open the door, ready to tear into her. My outrage over her checking my bank account takes a backseat when I see what looks like all of my belongings shoved into garbage bags piled around her feet. "What the fuck is all of this?"

"Your stuff from the house," she says slowly. Like saying it slow clarifies anything. So, I ask her again, and she sighs like she's being inconvenienced. "Look, Cash, obviously, we weren't working out. I've been meaning to talk to you about it." Her tone is so fucking nonchalant, like she's telling me the goddamn weather.

"You've been meaning to talk to me about us...'not working out'? Are you kidding me right now?" I pinch the bridge of my nose in an effort to control my temper. A few people are staring at us from the parking lot, so I usher her inside, not in the mood to carry this conversation out in front of an audience.

I park myself back in the chair I slept in while she perches on the edge of the bed. "Cash, I'm not happy. I haven't been for a long time."

I stare at her in disbelief. "So, you cheated?"

"I met Kevin, and he just sparked something in me. I–I don't know how to explain it, and even if I could, I doubt you'd understand. He just has this passion for me, and it—"

"Stop!" I cut her off, not wanting to hear any more. "Almost seven damn years down the drain. How long have you been seeing him?"

"Three years." I stare at her in disbelief. *Who is this girl in front of me?*

"You know what? Fuck this, you, all of it. You can go." She doesn't move an inch. "Get out, Kayla!"

"Cash, be reasonable, we still need to talk."

"Be reasonable? REASONABLE? I'm about three years past reasonable," I roar, my temples throbbing from the adrenaline rushing through me. "I bought a goddamn ring, Kayla. I was going to propose. We had an entire life planned together, and y–you blindside me with this—*with him*." It's then she notices the ring box on the table. Her eyes flick from it, then over to me, from me to her left hand, and then back to me. My eyes follow hers, guiding me straight to the ring on her left hand. A ring I didn't put there. My brain can't seem to catch up with what's happening.

"I love him. We're getting married, Cash. I already talked to our landlord, and he's allowing us to break the lease. Something about a commercial offer on the house. It's over. We're over."

My fucking world implodes. I drop my head into my hands to hide the tears trailing down my cheeks. "Just go."

Chapter Two

Myla Rose

"No, no, no. This isn't..." I glance down at the test, at the two glaring pink lines. The results haven't changed—it's still positive. I slump back against the bathroom wall and slide to the floor. How did this happen? This wasn't supposed to happen—at least, not for a few more years.

We were careful. *Except New Year's Eve*, my brain practically shouts at me as I sob, clutching the little stick that just changed my entire life.

I've never missed my Grams more than I do right now. She'd know what to do, what to say.

Everything I have, everything I am can be attributed to her—Marjorie Rose McGraw was the strongest damn woman I've ever been graced with the pleasure of knowing. She gave birth to my mama right in the middle of Hurricane Karin and swore it cast a mark on the child, said someone brought about amid all that destruction was bound to be a bad egg. Even though Grams tried her damnedest to keep my mama on the straight and narrow, she always strayed. *Some people just have hearts wired for trouble, Myla Rose*—I can't tell you how many times I've heard my Grams say that phrase throughout my life.

Mama was young when she had me, only nineteen. I never knew my daddy, and I doubt she really knew him either. Mama was all about fun, always flying by the seat of her pants. While she was never abusive, she wasn't nurturing either. Someone or something always came before me. I was seven when my mama decided she didn't want me anymore. I remember it like it was yesterday.

"Come on, Myla Rose, grab your shit and get in the car. Mama has to go," she urged, directing me toward the car with a little push to my back. I stumbled a little, my untied shoelace sealing my fate—I still hadn't learned how to tie them. Down I went, right to my knees, scraping them on the driveway. It stung, but her words stung worse. "Myla Rose! Get up off the ground, girl, and get in the damn car. How many damn times do I need to repeat myself?" She teetered in her high heels, drunk. She was always drunk. I pulled myself up off the ground, dusted off my knees, and climbed into the back seat. She dropped me off at Grams' and never looked back.

Thankfully, Grams welcomed me with open arms and a smile on her face. Until the day she left this earth, she was my rock. My foundation.

Now, here I am, just a year older than Mama was when she had me, and pregnant. *Mirror, mirror on the wall, I am my mother after all.*

"Five minutes, Myla Rose. You can cry for five minutes," I tell myself, "then you gotta get up, girl. Cryin' isn't gonna change nothin'." I hear Grams' voice in my mind, echoing the words I spoke aloud to myself. That's exactly what she'd have said if she were here, and it's damn sure what I need to hear.

With a newfound resolve, I force myself from the bathroom floor and head into my bedroom. I crawl into my bed, blindly fumbling around for my phone so that I can call AzzyJo. If I can't have my Grams, she's the next best thing. Azalea Josephine Barnes—AzzyJo for short—is my best friend and my biggest supporter. We've been inseparable since the third grade when we decided to sit together at lunch because we both had flower names. It was fate, y'all. That girl...she just gets me.

She answers on the first ring, all but singing into the phone.

"Good mornin', Myla Rose."

"A–Azalea." My voice trembles with fear and uncertainty.

"Are you okay? No, don't answer that. I'm on my way, sweet girl." She hangs up before I can even respond.

I'm not sure how long I've been lying here. Could've been just minutes—or maybe hours—when I hear my front door unlatching.

"Myla, I'm here," Azalea calls out.

"In my room," I call back, my voice hoarse from crying. I hear her shuffle into the room, and I can only imagine how pathetic I look with my tear-stained cheeks and matted auburn hair curled up in a ball on my bed. Azalea, though, doesn't even blink at the sight before her. She just kicks off her shoes and snuggles in behind me, offering silent comfort.

Finally, she breaks the silence. "Myla Rose, you wanna tell me what's got you in such a tizzy?" I don't even bother to respond. I just point to the damning little stick. "Oh, sweet girl, it'll be okay. Have you talked to Taylor?"

I shake my head. "No. Not yet. You're the first person I thought to call."

"Okay, it's okay. Just call him. Tell him you want to meet and talk. He's—"

"AzzyJo, I don't even know if he wants kids. We've never talked about the future! Hell, I can hardly get him to commit to a date these days." I can feel myself starting to panic.

"I know y'all's relationship is still new, but you've known him forever. Plus, what's done is done. He'll either man up and help you raise this baby or he won't, simple as that. One thing I know for sure—you'll be right as rain either way."

Her words are like a balm, and she's right—I can't change the past. It is what it is. Maybe he'll be a good dad. Maybe he'll love this baby. Only one way to find out.

Chapter Three

Myla Rose

Seeing no sense in delaying the inevitable, I grab my cell and dial Taylor. It goes to voicemail. So, I hang up and call him again. Voicemail. Now, I'm not the kind of girlfriend who goes all crazy when her man doesn't pick up, but I really need to talk to him before I lose my damn nerve. I try his number one more time. He declines the call, sending me once again to voicemail. *You've reached Taylor Mills. Sorry I can't take your call right now...*I drown out the rest of the recording and leave a message after the beep.

"Hey, Tay, I know you're really busy with school, but if you could call me as soon as possible, I'd love it. I have some stuff...just call me, 'kay?"

"He didn't answer?" Azalea runs her fingers through my messy hair, pulling the tangles free as she goes.

"Nope. Guess all there is to do now is wait."

"Myla Rose, I know this is tough and unexpected, but

sister-girl, this isn't you."

I open my mouth to defend myself but close it just as quickly. She's right, this *isn't* me. "You're right. I got myself into this, and even if it sucks, I need to own it. Also, I need to call the doctor." I pale at that realization, and Azalea notices.

"It'll be okay. They have laws and ethics and oaths. That's the last thing you need to worry about."

"You really think so?"

"I know so. The law is the law. Now, go on and give them a call. I'll be right here with you."

I Google the number to the OB-GYN's office and tap the *Call* button. My stomach churns with each ring. After the third, the automated greeting picks up.

Thank you for calling Dogwood Obstetrics and Gynecology. Please listen closely, as our menu has recently changed. I wait for the recorded voice to tell me the number to press to speak to the receptionist.

After a few more rings, it connects. "This is Tina, how may I help you?"

"Yes ma'am, hello. I just got a p–positive pregnancy test. So, I was calling to make an appointment."

"First day of your last period?"

"Um, maybe right before Christmas?"

"Okay, so due in September. You don't need to come in until you're eight weeks. Dr. Mills can see you February thirteenth at eight A.M. Does that work for you?"

"Yes ma'am, that'll be great." I disconnect the call and make note of the appointment in my calendar.

"Well?" Azalea asks.

"Apparently, I don't go until I'm eight weeks. So, next month, just before Valentine's Day."

"Huh. Guess you learn something new every day. Do you want me to come with you?"

"As much as I'd love it, we can't both take off."

"True. Well, maybe Taylor will want to go with you." She sounds a hell of a lot more hopeful than I feel.

"Thanks for rushin' over. I think I'm gonna lie down for a bit," I tell her as I crawl under my fluffy duvet.

"Always, Myles. Anytime and every time." She draws the covers up to my chin and plants a kiss on my forehead before showing herself out.

I wake to the sound of my phone alerting me to a missed call. From Taylor. I bolt upright, hitting *Redial.*

"Good God, Myla Rose. Three missed calls—is the world ending?" The irony of his words isn't lost on me.

"No, Tay, just need to talk to you."

"You wanted to talk, so you called me three times, back-to-back?" His voice has this tone to it. I can't quite put my finger on what I'm hearing, but I don't like it.

"I–I'm sorry. Like I said, I know you're busy. But if we could meet up—soon—that'd be really great."

"How soon?" I can hear his eye roll through the phone. This attitude of his is getting worse and worse every time we talk. This isn't the boy I crushed on all throughout middle and high school.

"I was hoping within the next day or two."

"Jesus," he mutters so quietly that I might have imagined it. "I guess meet me for brunch tomorrow. But I won't be able to stay long. I need to study."

"See you—" He hangs up before I even finish my sentence.

The following morning, I sleep through my alarm, favoring the *Snooze* button instead. I fly through getting ready, throwing on the first dress I see. It's a pale mint maxi with a scoop neck and long sleeves. Perfect for brunch. I quickly twist my long hair into a braid, swipe on some lip gloss, and rush out the door.

I fly into the diner at 10:45, fifteen minutes late. I instantly spot Taylor. He's seated right where he always sits, in the back left booth.

"Hey, Tay! Sorry I'm late," I tell him as I slide into the booth across from him.

"Are you, Myla Rose?"

"Am I what?"

"Sorry. Are you sorry?" He steeples his fingers together and rests his chin on them.

"Of course. Yes. Why wouldn't I be?"

"I just figured you'd be on time, with how much you went on and on about us needing to talk." I really hate the way he's speaking to me. Like I'm somehow less than him.

"Taylor, it was fifteen minutes. The world's still spinning. Can we move on to more pressing matters?"

"Right, because my time isn't pressing."

I have to bite down on my cheek to keep from snapping at him. This holier-than-thou shit isn't gonna fly with me. "Taylor, listen. I don't know what crawled up your ass, but put it on hold, 'kay?" I don't dare take my eyes off him. When he nods his agreement, I continue. "Good. Now, look. I need to tell you something—"

"Well, out with it, then," he says in a bored tone.

Deep breath in. *Here goes nothing...*"I'm pregnant."

"And you think it's mine?"

"Excuse me? I *know* it's yours."

"You know? How?"

"Taylor, you're the only person I've been with."

"Have you even been to the doctor?"

"No, I go on the thirteenth."

He scoffs. "So, you might not even be pregnant."

"No, I'm pregnant. And it's yours," I tell him, my voice firm.

"Look, it's fairly obvious we're not on the same page. We aren't..." he pauses. "This has been fun. But that's all it's ever gonna be. And having some brat call me 'Dad' isn't my idea of fun. We weren't serious—you have to know that."

"Wait. What?" My words come out raspy, and my eyes shine with tears, but I refuse to cry in front of him.

He cracks his knuckles, like he's prepping for a hard

hit or two. "This" —he gestures between us— "was only ever meant to be a bit of fun, a good time now and then. Sowing my oats. You're just not a 'forever girl', Myla. And I really don't even want kids."

"Tay—"

"Sorry," he says, but he doesn't sound sorry, not even a little. "You should go."

"What would your mother say if she could hear you right now?" I say as I rise from the booth. I almost laugh at the absurdity of my question. His mother would probably be proud—because that tone I couldn't place earlier...it's all Kathy Mills.

I feel a tap on my shoulder and turn to investigate. Like a devil summoned, there stands Mrs. Mills, her face as pinched as ever. "If I could hear what, Ms. McGraw?" She shuffles past me and arranges herself into the seat I was just in.

"Mother, Myla here was just informing me that she's...with child."

Mrs. Mills entire body tightens. "Are you now? And my Taylor needed to know why?"

"Because he's the father," I tell her honestly. Some stupid part of me is holding out that the thought of becoming a grandmother will make her knock some sense into him.

She looks down her nose at me. "Oh, Myla Rose. You poor, poor thing. You're certainly turning out to be just like your mother."

I suck in a breath through my teeth. The nerve of this

woman. I'm done playing nice. *Finished.*

Leaning down, I press my palms into the end of the table top. "Well, I'm sorry y'all feel this way. A baby is always a blessing, and I've got this with or without you, Taylor Mills. Not only will I raise *our* baby on my own, I'll thrive while doing it." Taylor makes to interrupt me, but I stand to my full height and place my hands on my hips, silencing him with a sharp look. "If there's one thing my Grams has taught me, it's that from shit, flowers grow. So, y'all can sit back and watch me fucking blossom."

Chapter Four

Myla Rose

I'M GOING ON ALMOST TWO MONTHS OF LITTLE-TO-no sleep. At first, I was heartsick over the way things ended with Taylor. It wasn't so much that he only saw me as a fling. I mean, did it hurt my pride? You bet. Did it break my heart? Maybe, a little. But nothing hurt more than the fact that he was trying to act like he wasn't this baby's father. His mother's willingness to play along is a whole 'nother story.

I moped and moped over the fact that my little bean would never know its daddy until Azalea whipped me into shape with a "What would Grams say if she could see you now?" That girl knows just how to get to me. Thank God.

Now, it's morning sickness keeping me awake. Morning sickness, my ass—I swear the son of a bitch who thought up that name had a perverse sense of humor. After spending all *night* throwing up, I would kill for five more minutes of sleep, but *beauty calls*.

I've got back-to-back clients at the salon today, with none other than Kathy Mills to start me off. "Thinks she's so much better than me...sure loves the way I do her damn hair though." I bitch and grumble as I kick back the covers and head for the shower.

As the hot water and suds wash away any lingering nausea, my mind wanders. I imagine a different future for me and my little bean. In my mind, we're a family of three instead of two. I'm not still hung up on Taylor. I just wish like hell my baby had a daddy who loved him—or her, but I'm hoping for a boy—a daddy who would coach his T-ball team. A daddy who would read him bedtime stories and take him camping. If only...

"Ain't no sense in wallowing, Myla Rose. Pull up them bootstraps, girl," I chide myself, just like Grams would've done.

I guide my car into a parking spot in front of Southern Roots, the salon I own with Azalea. With a quick check of the time, I see that I'm earlier than I thought, so I pop into Dream Beans, Dogwood's local coffee shop.

It's a cozy little place, with stained concrete floors covered in gorgeous Oriental rugs, mismatched antique furniture, and funky industrial lighting.

I step up to the reclaimed wood bar to order, hoping that caffeine will knock out that last bit of sluggishness my shower missed.

"Good mornin'. Whatcha drinking today?" Hazel, the barista, asks with a small smile.

"A large coffee with room for cream," I tell her through a yawn.

As I'm pulling out my wallet to pay, I hear a hushed voice behind me. "Well, my goodness, drinking coffee while pregnant. Hmph." I glance over my shoulder as Mrs. Mills continues griping to herself. "A good mother would never subject her baby to anything that could cause harm." *God bless it, I swear she thinks the sun comes up just to hear her crow.*

I look back to Hazel, roll my eyes, and move down the counter to fix up my coffee. I take a sip of the steamy beverage and release a dramatic sigh as I make my way to the door. I pause as I pass Mrs. Mills, look her dead in the eye, and take another big gulp of coffee.

"Now, Mrs. Mills, I figured you'd know that expectin' women can have up to two hundred milligrams of caffeine a day, what with your husband being an obstetrician and all." With a big fake smile and a wave, I continue on my way out the door. I pause once more, holding the door with my hip, and call over my shoulder, "Looking forward to your appointment, as always."

I hop across the street to the salon, fighting my frustration with every step. That woman knows just how to push my buttons—always has—and now I have to spend the next two hours with her. I should have just kept my mouth shut, but who the hell is she to judge me? I roll my shoulders back and crack my neck before heading into the salon. "Mornin', y'all." I greet Azalea and Seraphine—our receptionist—trying my hardest to check my attitude at the door.

"Good mornin' to you too, Myla Rose. Wanna tell me about that sour look you're wearing?" Azalea asks, her perfectly arched brows dipped in worry.

"Nothin' major. I just let Mrs. Mills get under my skin."

"Well, bad news then," Seraphine interjects. "She called to say she was gonna be late." Her dark chocolate eyes asses me, waiting to see my reaction. These pregnancy hormones have made me a tad more emotional than usual.

"Great. Of course she is." I fume, angrier than a wet cat. "Obviously, I have nothing better to do than wait for Kathy fucking Mills to finish her coffee. Now my entire day is going to be one big game of catch up." Azalea and Seraphine both look at me with sympathetic expressions.

With a huff and a few more muttered curses, I set to work pulling foils and gathering the color I'll need for her hair—she *never* changes it. Apparently, consistency is key.

By the time she arrives, I've been waiting for fifteen minutes. Seraphine walks her to my chair, and without a word, I get straight to work applying her color.

"Myla Rose, aren't you going to ask me what we're doing today?" She turns her head, causing the lightener on my brush to almost miss the foil.

"Damnit," I hiss under my breath. "Did you want to do something different, Mrs. Mills?" I struggle to keep my annoyance to myself. I glance up, and AzzyJo's brilliant green eyes catch mine in the mirror. She shoots me a look that screams *calm down, Myla.*

"No, but I may have, and that is my point." Her voice is like nails on a chalkboard. *Doesn't she know that self-righteousness is an ugly color*?

"You're absolutely right, Mrs. Mills. I apologize." My cheeks ache from holding my oh-so-fake smile. All of my smiles around this woman are fake.

You'd think knowing her most of my life would dull her effect on me, but nope. I'm not that lucky. If anything, with age, she aggravates me more. After all, she's had damn near ten years to learn the best way to get under my skin. We fall into a somewhat comfortable silence after our little exchange. Thank God.

I'm roughing a towel through her wet hair when she clears her throat to get my attention. "Myla Rose, did you hear about Taylor—"

"NO!" I all but shout. Every damn time she comes in, she tries to update me on her son's life. It's like some sick form of punishment.

She was delighted to tell me when he transferred from our local community college to the big state university—full academic scholarship, at that. And in her very next breath, she told me all about his new girlfriend. A respectable girl, with a good pedigree and the right kinda family. What is she, a dog?

Swear to God, it feels like she plans her color services with me around his life events. "Please spare us both and just don't go there, 'kay?"

Switching on my blow dryer, I let the noise drown out any response she may have had. I finish styling her hair to Southern Blonde Perfection—the higher the hair, the closer to Heaven, y'all—and she is *finally* out the door and on her way.

I'm finishing up my last client of the day when I hear the door to the salon chime, and I'm suddenly hit with the strongest perfume ever. *What fresh floral hell is that?*

Throwing my hands over my mouth, I dash to the restroom. There's that morning sickness again. Yeah, smells trigger it too. Go figure. After washing my hands, popping a mint, and fixing my smudged makeup, I hold my breath and make my way back to my station. I sweep my eyes across the salon and slowly release the breath I was holding. Whoever it was must have left because I don't see anyone other than Azalea.

"Myla Rose! My goodness, are you okay?" she inquires in that sweet Southern drawl of hers.

"I'm fine," I say as I rinse my color bowl in the sink. "Don't you worry about me. Dr. Mills says morning sickness usually only lasts the first trimester. So, it should be on its way out the damn door."

I step back over to my station, gathering my things while simultaneously working up a plan to tell Azalea that I'm flaking out on our plans for the night. "AzzyJo, I'll see you tomorrow." She cuts her eyes at me, and they blaze like emeralds. Such a contrast to her pale hair and tanned skin.

I raise my hands, as if I'm trying to keep her at bay.

"I know, I know. Taco Tuesday, but I am dog tired. I just want a bubble bath and my bed."

"Myla Rose, you will not ditch me next month, tired or not. In fact, you can treat me," Azalea retorts with a false look of exasperation. We walk together to the door, where she engulfs me in the biggest, tightest hug—just what I needed after today.

I'm halfway home when I realize I need groceries. Sure, a drive-thru is an option, but my little bean is making me crave a BLT with Thousand Island dressing on sourdough bread. So, to Piggly Wiggly I go. I figure I'll grab just enough for dinner tonight and some Cliff Bars for breakfast—the rest can wait.

I'm pushing my buggy through the store, humming to myself, mentally checking my shopping list when I walk right into a...wall?

No, not a wall.

A person.

A man.

He towers over my five-foot-three frame by at least a foot, all broad-shouldered and solid. "Oh, my stars—I am so sorr—"

I don't even finish my sentence before he whips around to face me, and I'm met with the most stunning gray-blue eyes, the color of the summer sky right before a thunderstorm. And his hair. He has gorgeous brown ringlets that flop every which way—a bit of boyishness to temper his ruggedness.

His mere presence unsteadies me, causing me to wobble on my feet. I reach an arm out to balance myself, only he beats me to it, dropping his big, warm hands to my shoulders to hold me still.

His touch is like nothing I've ever felt before, and if I never moved from this spot, that'd be fine by me. All this time, while I'm caught up in my own crazy, he just stares down at me with a slight smirk, waiting on me to finish my forgotten apology.

I clear my throat and rush my words out. "I am so sorry. I was caught up in my own head, checking my list and not paying attention at all. I didn't hurtcha with my buggy, did I?"

I chance a look up at him. He chuckles and shakes his head. "No, ma'am, I'm just fine." His voice is nothing more than a deep rumble, and it hits me straight in my belly, sending those butterflies swooping. "You have a nice evening, yeah?" Just like that, he turns and walks away.

"Uhhh. Um, yeah, you too," I holler to his retreating back. Mindlessly, I walk to the checkout and then out to Bertha, my old Land Cruiser. Mint green paint still gleaming, she's a thing of beauty, passed down from my Grams.

I drive home without really being aware of the trip. Highway Hypnotism, they call it. Y'all know what I mean? One second, you're starting the car, and in the blink of an eye, you've reached your destination with no memory of the trip? *I know you do.* I'm too busy thinking about Mr. Good Eyes with that deep voice and luscious curly hair.

Once I get home, I lug my groceries up the porch stairs and into the house, where I get to work making that BLT. The scent of the bacon as it pops and sizzles in my cast iron skillet has my mouth watering. I step away to grab a plate from the cabinet and get sidetracked wondering how the kitchen walls would look painted a deep shade of...*dammit, I'm picturing my walls the color of his eyes.* Absurd...and I overcooked the bacon. I will away those foolish thoughts and finish preparing my dinner, burnt bacon and all.

After rinsing my plate and collecting the bacon grease, I go through the motions to get ready for bed, removing my makeup, changing into my PJs, and making sure my alarm is set for tomorrow. I skip my bubble bath. I'm *that* tired.

As I drift off to sleep, my thoughts turn back to him. I imagine what it would be like to have him here, in my space. With me, with his strong arms wrapped around me. I imagine running my fingers through his loopy curls as he kisses my neck.

And just like that, I'm wide awake, because get real, Myla Rose. What man would be interested in a pregnant woman? I must be exhausted to be having those kinds of thoughts. Maybe I'll take that bubble bath after all.

Chapter Five

Cash

Goddamn, it's been a long day. It'd be one thing if I had been doing actual work, but I spent the day in the workshop office, hunched over my desk, sending invoices and emailing potential clients. My legs and back ache, and all I want to do is head home, shower, and call it a night. That's not in the cards though—it's Family Dinner Night.

"Crap, that was the street," I gripe as I hit the brakes and pull a U-turn. These back roads can be downright tricky at night. I haven't lived in Dogwood since my dad's job brought us here when Jake was thirteen and I was three, so it's for sure been an adjustment.

We were only down here for two years, but Jake always remembered it and loved it. A couple of years ago, he was offered a job in the area, and that was the catalyst for our mom *finally* leaving our piece-of-shit dad. She'd stuck it out for so long because she didn't feel like she had any options. But when Jake announced that he and his wife and their twin boys were moving, she was all about it. She hired a lawyer, packed her shit, and moved with them before the ink on the papers was even dry.

After everything went to shit with Kayla, I asked Jake and my lifelong friend, Drake, to put out some feelers on some work in the area, and the response was fan-fucking-tastic. I packed up and moved down here just shy of four months ago, but already, it's quite possibly the best decision I've ever made. My business is taking off, and Carson's Custom is quickly becoming the first choice for contractors in the area for woodworking.

I'm pulling into the Piggly Wiggly parking lot when my phone vibrates against the cup holder, rattling the loose change lying at the bottom. Grabbing it, I swipe my thumb across the screen to answer my brother's call. "Hey man, what's up?"

"Mom wanted me to make sure you remembered to bring a bag of ice," he tells me in a bored tone. This is a common occurrence. We all have to bring something to Family Dinner Night, and I *always* bring a bag of ice.

With an eye roll, I reply, "Yeah, Jake, tell her I'm at the store now. You might as well ask her if she needs anything else while I'm here." I hear him set the phone down and call out to our mom, but I can't quite make out her muffled reply.

"Hey, Mom says to grab a bag of croutons, too."

"Ten-four, see you soon." I end the call and slide my phone into the pocket of my jeans.

Real talk? I missed Family Dinner Night, and I am so damn glad to be back where my family is. They're amazing, and it saves me from cooking every once in a while—a double win for me.

I'm wandering through the store, looking for the crouton aisle, when someone rams into me with their shopping cart. What the hell?

My cart-rammer starts to apologize, and I turn sharply at the sound of her voice, all soft and southern. She's a tiny thing, at least a foot shorter than me.

I inspect her from head to toe. Long hair, the color of mahogany with lighter streaks swirled through it. Big, brown doe eyes. The kind you can get lost in. Other than a smattering of freckles across the bridge of her nose, her skin is flawless, smooth, and pale. Her petite figure is full of lush curves. I zero in on her slightly flared hips. I can't form words. I just stare.

I can't explain it, but I'm so drawn to her—like a moth to a flame. I'm itching to reach out and touch her, to feel her skin. I fist my hands at my side. Then, mercifully, she teeters, gracing me with the opportunity to give in to my urges. I bring my hands down on her shoulders to steady her, and *goddamn*. It's like electricity is pumping from her and into me.

After what feels like an eternity, she speaks, finishing her forgotten apology, freeing me from the spell she's cast. "No, ma'am." My voice is thick. "I'm just fine. You have a nice evening, yeah?" I drag my eyes down her body once more before turning and walking away. My reaction to this girl is visceral—one look, one touch, and I'm damn near ready to offer her the world. *Fucking insanity.*

I smile to myself as I hear her call out to me once more before I'm out of earshot.

She consumes my thoughts the entire drive to my mom's house, which is about as dumb as the day is long. I don't even know the girl. I probably won't ever know her. A random encounter with a lasting impression... nothing more.

I park behind my brother in the driveway and try to shake Grocery Store Girl from my brain. The last thing I need is for the hounds behind that front door to get a whiff of my *slight* interest in a woman.

They have been relentless about my moving forward, incessant in their *Not all girls are like Kayla* tirade. Logically, I get that. I know not all girls are lying, cheating, heartless bitches. But nothing about love is logical.

I missed the signs with Kayla. I mean, I knew our relationship wasn't perfect, but *damn*. I thought she wanted a deeper commitment, a ring. I *never* thought she'd cheat. We all know how that turned out.

Who cares if Grocery Store Girl is hot? I have eyes, but that doesn't mean I want cards and flowers and all the other romance bullshit. Fuck that. Even if her smile made my heart feel like it was going to beat right out of my chest, I don't make the same mistakes twice.

Do I sound bitter? A bit jaded? Yeah, well, I am. I'm just gonna do me and worry about growing my business and bettering myself.

"MOM!" I call out as I walk through the front door. "Dinner smells amazing!" It really does. And if I'm right, she made my favorite.

"It's chicken-n-dumplings, baby." She greets me with a hug and a kiss on the cheek. Hot damn, I was right. My favorite.

"Thanks, Mom, sounds good after a long day," I call out over my shoulder as I walk into the kitchen with the bag of ice and the croutons.

I'm standing in the doorway between the kitchen and dining room, bracing for my nephews to plow into me, when Jake tells me, "You might as well have a seat. Preston and Lucas are at home with Paige. Both boys have ear infections." I nod my head and take a seat at the table, disappointed.

Dinner is delicious, and I thoroughly enjoy catching up with my family. I miss my nephews, but I get a kick out of hearing about them. Mom asks about my business and tells everyone about this new recipe she wants to try for our next dinner. And throughout all of it, I can't stop smiling.

All in all, it was a great night—good food, good conversation—but I'm beat and ready for bed. "Mom, you need any help with the dishes?" I ask as I stand to carry my plate to the kitchen.

"No, baby, I got it. You call me later this week, okay?" I kiss her cheek and promise I will.

I head to my truck with my brother hot on my heels. "You seem happy," he throws out.

"And that's weird because...?" I challenge as I fish my keys out of my pocket, hitting the *Unlock* button.

"No, not weird. You just seem more...jovial than usual." *Jovial? Who even says that?*

"Nah, man. Nothin' new here," I counter, holding his gaze. "Nothin' at all." He regards me suspiciously, not quite believing me.

"Nothing, huh? All right, bro, if you say so. Have a good night." I start to get in my truck. "And whenever you want to tell me about her, I'm here to listen."

I freeze. Shit, he knows me too well.

"Man, I don't even know her name." It slips out before I can stop it. I think he's almost as surprised as I am by my accidental admission.

"Ha! I knew it! Tell me about her," he demands, pumping his fist in the air. I roll my eyes, crank the engine, and ease out of the driveway, not bothering to answer him.

Chapter Six

Cash

B*EEP–BEEPBEEP–BEEP*. My alarm clock blares, even though it feels like my head just hit the pillow. Another night of shitty sleep. I'm not sure why I've been so restless. Maybe I've been working too hard? *Yeah. That's it.*

Add in that I probably haven't eaten a good meal since those chicken-n-dumplings the other week. Today calls for some real food and some relaxation. I blink the sleep out of my eyes, snatch my phone off the nightstand, and notice a text from Drake.

Drake: Whatcha got going on today?

Me: Not much. Got a few emails to send and a call or 2 to make.

Drake: Perfect. Get that shit done and head over. Ribs on the grill.

Drake: Simon's coming too.

Me: Sounds good. See you soon.

After a scalding shower, I throw on some cargo shorts and a Carson's Custom tee and head into my office to hammer out those emails. I take a seat at my desk, a one-off made from gorgeous quarter-sawn white oak and stained a deep golden brown. It makes a statement against the beige walls and light wood floors. Pulling up my calendar on the computer, I make a short list of who I need to email and who I need to call. After sending a handful of emails, I've had it with office work. Shifting the calls to Monday on my schedule, I power down the computer and head to Drake's.

The winding country roads make the drive feel longer than it is. Surrounded by open fields, it's like Drake lives in the middle of nowhere, which I guess he does. Gotta have a lot of land to peanut farm.

Drake is standing in the yard, talking on his phone, when I pull up. Running a hand over his freshly buzzed head, he laughs silently, his brown eyes crinkling at the corners. I can't tell if the person he is talking to is amusing him or aggravating him. He signals for me to head around to the backyard. Ignoring him, I head inside. It's crazy hot.

A few minutes later, the front door slams—aggravated it is!

"What's up, D? What's got you all pissed off?"

He glares at me. "Not a damn thing. Why aren't you out back?"

"It's only April, and it's already hotter than blue blazes. Fuck that."

He just grins and gestures for me to follow him out to the back deck.

"Damn, dude. This is legit." He has the back porch rigged up with a misting system. Two hoses run along either side of the deck, and two large industrial-looking fans blow the mist toward the center of the deck. Genius. "This is *badass*, Drake. You set this up?"

"Sho 'nuff. Gotta stay cool. These summers get brutal." He looks smug as shit, but I guess he earned it.

"I need something like this for my workshop." I run my hands through my thick mass of curls, tugging on the ends.

Drake laughs. "How do you work in that hot-as-balls workshop with that mop on your head?"

"I know, *I know*. Shit's too long. I've been meaning to get over to the barber shop in town." I shrug my shoulders and once again run my hands through my thick hair. "Just haven't made it."

"Nah, man. Don't go there. Those old dudes will jack your shit up. Ask Simon about his last time there." He's doubled over from his effort to contain his laughter at our friend's expense. "Seriously, Cash. Save yourself the trouble. Go to Southern Roots."

"Southern Roots? That sounds like some chick shit."

"Yeah, it is. But they know how to cut some hair. Seriously. Either girl there will rock that shit. They're sweethearts too. Well, one of them is sweet. The other is full of nothin' but piss and vinegar. The sweet one, she's preg—"

The sound of tires crunching on the gravel drive derails his train of thought. "Fucking finally! Took you long enough," he calls out as Simon walks through the door. "You bring that potato salad you wouldn't shut up about the other day? If not, you can head your ass right back home and get it."

"Quit your bitchin'," Simon counters with a lazy smile as he sets a bowl on the table. "Now, what're we talking about?"

"Yeah, yeah, I was just telling Cash here all about why he shouldn't hit up the barber shop." Drake chuckles, ambling off toward the grill.

The look on Simon's face is priceless, like he's smelled something foul. His thick brows pinch and his mouth sets in a firm line. "No, just no." He pulls off his ball cap, runs a hand through his shaggy blond hair, and readjusts it on his head. "Go see the girls at Southern Roots. Ain't no one else taking scissors to my head except one of them."

"Guess that settles it—Southern Roots it is."

A plate of mouth-watering ribs appears on the table we're seated around. "Y'all gonna sit around and chat all day, or are we gonna eat?" Drake asks, smirking like the asshole he is.

Chapter Seven

Myla Rose

I feel his hand resting on my growing belly and I snuggle into his warmth. He brushes my hair out of my face and places a soft kiss on my neck, just beneath my ear, and murmurs, "Good mornin', darlin'." I roll over and reach out for him, only to find cold sheets.

No one is there. It's that damn dream. Again. Mr. Good Eyes has been the star of my dreams almost every night since I assaulted him with my buggy at the Piggly Wiggly. That was weeks ago. So, for *weeks*, I've been dreaming of some guy I talked to for a total of sixty seconds, tops.

Maybe when I see Dr. Mills for my sixteen-week appointment, I'll ask him if outrageous dreams are a pregnant thing. Because that is the only word to describe these dreams. We don't even know each other, and I can guaran-damn-tee that man wouldn't have a lick of interest in me.

Even though the salon is technically closed today, I'm meeting AzzyJo there to talk about hiring a third stylist. Dogwood may be a small town, but Southern ladies are religious about their hair—every four-to-six weeks, like clockwork.

I'm barely through the door when Azalea is shoving a piece of paper in my face. "Myla Rose, just look at this flier I made for the salon. Gorgeous, huh?" She is literally so close to my face that everything on the page blurs together.

I swat her hand away. "Well, AzzyJo, I would certainly love to offer my opinion, but you have the damn paper so close to me I can't see shit!"

"Sorry, I am just so excited! I worked all night on this." She takes a breath. "So, what do you think? I'm dyin' here, Myla!" Her blonde curls spring and boing all around as she bounces on the balls of her feet. I swear, someone put crack in her coffee this morning.

"Girl. Calm down. I'm too tired for your level of perky this morning. Let's sit down, and I'll take a look, okay?"

"Fine. Just come on. I worked hard, and you know how I am. I thrive on positive praise." I roll my eyes and inspect the flier. It really is beautiful. A background of watercolor flowers, with our salon name in a brushed script front and center. The flier also details our need for a third stylist. Azalea outdid herself with this. It's perfect, and I tell her so.

"Oh. I'm so thrilled you like it. I was worried you'd hate it." Her smile stretches wide from one peridot eye to the other.

"Nope, AzzyJo, it is just what we need. Do whatcha need to and get it posted." I stand and hand the paper back to her. "Now, I have errands that need runnin' and laundry that needs tendin'. So, I'll see you tomorrow, bright and early."

"Yes, ma'am, bright and early. And you wear some yoga pants or something stretchy, because tomorrow is Tuesday, and we ARE going to eat our weight in tacos after work! No excuses, Myla Rose. Tired or not!"

AzzyJo was good on her suggestion for yoga pants. My jeans are all too damn tight thanks to my ever-growing baby bump. I mean, I'm hardly showing, but my clothes sure don't fit right. With a resigned huff, I pull on my most comfy black yogas and pair them with a loose-fitting, sleeveless white trapeze top. I slip my feet into my trusty, well-worn Keds and finish the look with a messy bun—let's call it I'm-too-tired-for-this chic.

I decide to walk the few blocks to the salon today, hoping that the fresh air, along with my travel mug of coffee, will energize me.

By the time I make it to the salon, I am slightly sweaty—or as Azalea would say, glistening. It's only April, but it's already warm as hell this morning. That's life in the South though. The warm weather comes quick and lingers long.

"Whatcha smilin' about?" Seraphine asks as I set my station up for the day. G*uess that fresh air did the trick.*

"I didn't realize I was smiling. Must just be a good morning."

She tucks her waist-length black hair behind her ear, waiting for me to elaborate. After a short pause, she moves on. "Well, I wanted to tell you that I added an appointment to your book this morning. Some guy called—said he was new in town and that his buddies told him this was the only place worth coming to. Hope that's okay?"

"Of course, that's totally fine. New business is always good. What time did you book him?"

"I stuck him in your ten o'clock slot."

"In my ten? I thought Mrs. Sutherland was—"

"Yeah, she was, but she called right before he did and rescheduled to Thursday. Something about her kid swallowing a penny."

"Poor guy." I grin, thinking that will be my life in a few years. "Thanks for letting me know." I head back to the dispensary, where we keep our excess supplies and color, to chat with Azalea before my first client arrives.

She's sitting at our small break table folding towels, so I grab one and start folding to help out. She looks up and greets me with a beaming smile. "Myla Rose! Are you ready for tacos tonight?"

I can't help but laugh at her excitement. "Yes, I'm ready for tacos—yoga pants and all." I wave my arms Vanna White style to showcase my stretchy, loose-fitting ensemble. "And the bean is on our side. All I can think about is some fresh guac!" I rub my bump to emphasize my point, and she reaches out to do the same.

We simultaneously pause the belly rubbing when we hear the bell on the door chime. "You head on out, Myla Rose. That must be yours. My first isn't until eleven." I nod and head toward my station.

I'm organizing my clipper guards at my station when I hear, "Grocery store girl! It's you!" I gasp and look up to see Mr. Good Eyes smiling down at me.

"Oh, my! It's y–you." I know I'm blushing and internally scold myself. *Get it together, Myla Rose. He is a client in your salon. It doesn't matter one bit that he's too handsome for his own good.*

I tighten my messy bun with a tug before attempting to greet him in a more professional manner. "Hello, I'm Myla Rose, and it's a pleasure to meet you." *Oh, come the fuck on. GET. IT. TOGETHER. A pleasure to meet you?* Could my blush get any deeper?

He holds out his hand. "Cash Carson, and the pleasure is mine." His deep voice moves right through me—straight to my core. Pleasure, indeed.

I place my hand in his to shake it. His hand completely engulfs mine. His grip is strong and his hand rough, callused from what has to be some form of manual labor. He lingers, holding my hand just past what's normal for a handshake. His fingers feather mine as he releases my hand, sending a wave of chills over my entire body.

I blink myself out of the fog he has me in. "Okay,

Cash, how are we cuttin' you today?" I offer a small smile and tilt my chin down, hoping it hides my nerves. I don't know what it is about this guy...

Cash clears his throat, causing me to look up, and his stormy gaze captures mine in the reflection of the mirror. "Well, Miss Myla Rose, this hair gets hot when I'm working in my shop. I'm talking unbearable."

I run my fingers through his curls and a soft sigh escapes my lips. They're every bit as soft as I imagined them to be. "How short you thinkin'?"

"You're the pro here, *Myla Rose*. You tell me." He emphasizes my name, and the way his lips form around it makes it sound sinful. I get chills from the sound of it.

He has me rattled. I do my best to ignore the feeling and set to work shearing off the length on the sides and back, cropping it close. I leave the top a bit longer and cut it to comb back out of his face. Once I finish, I turn him toward the mirror so that he can inspect my work. "You want me to wash it? Keep you from itchin' all day?"

He runs a hand through his hair in that way only a guy can and winks. *He fucking winks*. "Lead the way, Myla Rose." I guide him to the shampoo room and direct him to have a seat and lie back. I lean over him to pull the lever to put up his feet, and I catch his scent. Citrus, spice, and pure man. Good Lord, help me.

"Th–That water feel okay?" He just nods, his eyes pinched tightly closed and his knuckles white from gripping the armrests.

I work the shampoo into his scalp, creating a rich

lather, massaging as I go. “Mmm...damn, girl, that feels good. I need this every day after work.” He groans, and the sound is so sensual, my knees almost buckle.

Holy hell. Thankfully, his eyes are closed so he can’t see my embarrassment. I rinse the suds and grab a towel. “All done,” I announce, ignoring his comment. He follows behind me to my chair, where I run some gel through his locks and give his hair a final inspection. “I think you’re good to go, Cash. It looks mighty fine.”

His eyes hold mine. “Yes, ma’am, mighty fine, indeed. I pay up front?” he inquires with a tilt of his head.

“Mmmhmm,” I mumble, no longer sure if we’re talking about his hair.

Or if we ever were...

Chapter Eight

Myla Rose

I'M STILL STANDING HERE, AT MY STATION, STARING after Cash as he checks out at the front desk. I've never been so...affected by anyone. He just, *damn*. He riles me right up, winking and saying my name with that deep, sexy voice of his.

Good Lord. He's a deadly combination of big, tall, and charming. Shaking off the fog he left me in, I grab the broom and begin sweeping up his hair. The bell on the door dings, and I hear his deep voice tell Seraphine, "Have a nice day, ma'am," and I swear she lets out a dreamy sigh. I mean, I can't fault her. Who wouldn't? I release a long breath and head to the back to try and get myself together before my next appointment.

AzzyJo corners me in the dispensary. "Myla Rose! Who on God's green earth was that?"

"No one. I mean, a new customer. That's all." I refuse to meet her eyes. She'll see right through me. "Nothin' special."

"Then why are you acting so strange?" She eyes me, keeping her distance but never taking her gaze off me. She's appraising me, like I'm a feral cat and she is waiting for my claws to come out.

"I'm not. You're imagining things."

"MYLA ROSE!" Seraphine barges through the door, panting like she's just run a damn marathon.

"Good Lord, Seraphine. Everything okay?" AzzyJo asks, startled. Seraphine is young and fit as a fiddle. If she's winded...

"Yes, yes. Sorry. I just, um..." She's fidgeting, which isn't like her. Seraphine's usually cool as a cucumber.

"Come on, Ser, what's up?" I search her deep brown eyes why she's acting crazier than a loon.

"I just wanted to give you your tip from your last client." Seraphine holds out her hand, and a fifty-dollar bill is sitting pretty in her palm.

"No. I think you're confused. All I did was a cut." My eyes are so wide with surprise they feel like they're going to bug out of my head.

"Nope. Not confused. This is your tip." She thrusts the money toward me. "Take it." I tentatively reach out and grab the money, slipping it into the pocket of my apron. "See, wasn't so hard." She smiles triumphantly and heads back to the front desk.

"Just a new customer, huh?" AzzyJo taunts, taking measure of my response. "Must have made quite the impression, Myla Rose." I shrug my shoulders, ignoring her. The more I say, the more Azalea will pester me. Like a dog with a bone, she won't give up.

"I'm sure he was just being overly nice since he got in last-minute and all."

"I don't care what it was. He's a gorgeous, *gorgeous* man. Next time he comes in, you should get his number." Her eyes are shining, like this is the best idea she's ever had. Hate to burst her bubble, but...

"Get real. That man doesn't wanna play house with me. He could have his pick of the ladies here, and I'm just...well, there's more than just me." She looks at me like I have lost my damn mind.

Obviously, though, I'm the only one of us with any sense.

"You know, some men don't mind. My Pops loved me like I was his. Didn't care one bit that my mother had me—took us as a package deal."

"I get that, I do. Your Pops is a good man, and there are a lot of good men out there, I'm sure. I'm just not interested, okay? Right now, I just need to focus on me and my little bean."

She rolls her eyes, her disbelief evident. She opens her mouth to go on some more. "Listen, Myla—"

I hold up a hand to silence her. I know just how to end this conversation. "Did I tell you that I might be able to find out the gender at my appointment next week?"

"NO! You did not tell me!" She throws her arms around me and squeezes. "I am so...AHH! This is amazing! I *cannot* wait to find out. Then I can start planning your shower, and buying things, and we can go look at paint for the nursery, and—"

Somehow, this hug has turned into her bouncing. And she is shaking me right along with her. I gently remove her arms from around me and take a step back. "AzzyJo. Take a breath." She does, followed by a few more. "That's right, in through your nose. Calm down." She just rolls those green eyes. I swear, she'd bring home gold if eye-rolling were an Olympic sport.

"Sorry, I'm just excited. You know how I get."

Yes, I surely do. After a lifetime of friendship with Azalea Josephine Barnes as my personal cheerleader, I know exactly how much energy she puts into everything. The girl practically radiates sunshine.

"I know, and you'll get to do all of those things, promise. Let's just take it slow. We have plenty of time." I offer a smile to reassure her. "In fact, let's talk about it a bit more over tacos tonight."

She squeals at the mention of our dinner plans. "Yes! Let's do that." I nod and start toward the doorway to head back to my station when she calls out, "Oh! I forgot to tell you, I invited Simon too. Is that okay?"

"For sure. You know I love Simon. Is D coming too?"

She scoffs. "Yes, Drake too, and he mentioned bringing a friend. I swear to God, Myles, if he brings some tramp, I'll gut him like a fish."

"Sure, you will. Play nice, 'kay?"

Simon McAllister has been a part of my life for as long as I can remember. He lived with his daddy in the house next door to my Grams. He's a few years older than me, but his daddy was real piece of work, so he was always over at our house.

He was a quiet boy around most people, but he always talked to me. He said I was special, that I was like his sister, and that family stuck together. And to this day, we have stuck together like glue. He quickly adopted AzzyJo as an honorary sister as well, and the rest is history.

Nothing could tear us apart. Not our age difference, not even significant others along the way. We formed our own little wolf pack. Azalea and I were thirteen when Drake moved to town. He grew up here and moved away with his mama for a bit. He came back as soon as a judge said he was old enough to choose.

The running joke then became that one day, we would split off into couples and live happily ever after. No way, no how. I firmly believe you don't mess with friendships like that. Not to mention, I just don't see those guys that way.

Sure, they're both attractive enough—Simon with his dark blond hair and piercing blue eyes, and Drake with his deep tan from working on the farm, eyes the color of whiskey, and that small gap in his front teeth. They made the girls in Dogwood crazy growing up. Probably still do, but ignorance is bliss, y'all.

Now, Drake and Azalea, that is a different story altogether. They are either thick as thieves or oil and water. You can never know what to expect from them.

They are the very definition of sexual tension.

Azalea and I close the salon down and head over to Azteca's, home of the best damn Tex-Mex this side of the Mississippi. It's a funky little place with large round wooden tables, terra cotta tile floors, and walls painted like the sunset.

Seriously, people come from all over the county for this deliciousness. We walk inside and I'm instantly hit with the aroma of sizzling onions and peppers. My mouth waters, and I swear my little bean does a happy flop in my belly.

I squeal and grab AzzyJo's hand, placing it on my belly. "AZ! The bean moved!" We both know I'm not far enough along to feel any real movement, but all the same, her excitement immediately mirrors mine. I can only imagine the picture we paint, bouncing and squealing and talking to my belly. People probably think we're nuts.

The hostess is kind enough to allow us our moment before guiding us back to our usual table. We don't bother with the menus. This is a long-standing tradition for us, and we get the same thing every time—Tacos de Carnitas with a heaping side of guac for me, and steak tacos for Azalea. Miguel, our usual waiter, knows us and arrives at our table, drinks in hand. "*Hola*, ladies! *Cómo estás*? You have your usual?"

AzzyJo grins. "You know us too well, Miguel. Tonight, we'll have some friends joining us though."

"Muy bien. I'll be back to take their orders when they arrive."

Azalea wastes no time getting down to business and pulls a notepad and pen out of her oversized tote bag. "Okay. So, do you have an idea of how many people you'll want to invite to your shower?"

"I'm really not sure."

"Do you know where you want to have it?"

"I don't—" I'm saved from her line of questioning when Simon drops down into the chair on the far side of Azalea.

"Good evenin', ladies. What are we gossiping about?"

"We are not gossiping, Simon McAllister. We are plannin' Myla's baby shower." Azalea cuts her eyes at him.

Unfazed, Simon just smiles. "Oh, yeah? You gonna invite me, Myla Rose?"

"Ooh. Good question—do you want to invite the guys?" she asks.

"Do guys enjoy that sort of thing?" I can't imagine it'd be much fun for them, with all the silly games and whatnot.

"We just want to be there for you, Myles. I know Drake will agree."

"Agree to what?" Drake's deep voice booms from beside me as he lowers himself into the chair between Azalea and me.

"Coming to Myla's baby shower," Simon tells him.

"Hells yeah, girl. Y'all can even have it at my house, if you want. I've got plenty of room." He smiles, clearly pleased with himself. "Speaking of extra room, I invited a buddy of mine to fill that empty chair tonight."

Azalea's features immediately relax at the mention of his 'buddy'. Still, she scoffs. "Like you have any other friends."

"Oh, hey there, Little Bit. Didn't notice you." Drake fires back with a cat-ate-the-canary grin. These two need to figure their shit out.

"A friend? Who?" I ask, trying to distract them from their bickering.

"Actually, you met him today. Name's Cash. I sent him your way for a haircut."

"Oh, okay...yeah. That's great." I choke on my words, sounding like a babbling thirteen-year-old who got caught passing a note in class. *Lord, help me through this dinner.*

"You okay, Myles?" Simon quirks a brow.

"Your buddy, Cash, has had her tied up in knots since he came in this morning," Azalea tells the boys with a snicker.

"Have I now?" Cash's voice asks softly in my ear as he claims the chair on my other side. His warm breath fanning my neck, combined with that slow Matthew McConaughey drawl of his, and I'm damn near a puddle in my chair. My brain is shouting for me to say something—anything—but my mouth won't cooperate.

I'm so beyond mortified, I'm seriously considering abandoning dinner and crawling under the nearest rock.

Paying no attention to my lack of reply, he introduces himself to Azalea. Conversation carries on at the table. Everyone's either oblivious to my embarrassment—or more likely, enjoying it.

Chapter Nine

Cash

I walk into the restaurant where I'm meeting the guys, and my senses are instantly assaulted from all sides. The smell of grilled meat and a hint of fresh lime juice, the sound of laughter from the other patrons, the music of the three-piece band—it's a lot to take in, but it feels *right.* A quick glance around the dining room, and I find Drake and Simon seated at a large round table toward the back. They aren't alone—two girls are at the table as well.

"Hola, sir. Welcome to Azteca's. Just one tonight?"

I nod my head toward the back. "No, ma'am, I'm joining some friends." The hostess offers me a menu before sending me on back toward their table.

I'm just about to call out my arrival to the guys when the blonde at the table says, "Your buddy, Cash, has had her tied up in knots since he came in this morning."

The girls at the table are the stylists from Southern

Roots. The good Lord *must* be smiling on me this evening. I haven't been able to get Miss Myla Rose out of my head all damn day, and it wasn't the haircut she gave me tying up real estate in my mind either—even if it is the best damn haircut I've ever had. No, it was her soft voice with that Southern drawl, her curvy little body, the freckles on her nose, the thought of running my fingers through her long hair—those were the thoughts I couldn't shake. And now, here she is.

I decide not to announce my arrival. Instead, I walk up quietly, bend toward Myla Rose, and whisper in her ear, "Have I now?" My voice is hoarse from our proximity. I find myself taken by the soft scent of her, my lips a breath away from her neck. Coconuts mixed with vanilla—it's intoxicating. Myla Rose doesn't answer my question, and that's all fine and well. I didn't intend for her to.

I smile at the rest of the table and introduce myself to the blonde sitting between Drake and Simon. "Cash Carson. Nice to meet you, ma'am."

"Azalea, but most people call me AzzyJo," she offers, slightly slack-jawed. I shake her hand, just like I did with Myla Rose at the salon, but it's not the same. With Myla Rose, it was exhilarating, the feel of her skin on mine. With Azalea, it's just a handshake, business as usual.

Drake clears his throat. "AzzyJo, you'd better close that mouth unless you wanna catch flies."

He smirks. She scowls.

"Drake Ulysses Collins, you shut your damn mouth."

"You gonna make me, Little Bit?"

"Oh, my God—"

"CHILDREN! Quit bickering. Goodness, some of us want to enjoy our meal," Myla Rose snaps. Girl has fire, and damn if I don't like it. Probably more than I should.

"Ain't no damn child..." Drake mutters under his breath, sounding very much like a child.

In true Simon fashion, he's just been observing everyone, smiling at their antics. I swear that dude sees, hears, and knows so much more than he lets on.

The waiter returns to ask me what I want to drink, as well as get my, Drake's, and Simon's food orders. An ice-cold Coke and some steak nachos will do me real nice. Everyone also orders a round of margaritas, as well. Everyone except for Myla Rose.

"Not drinking tonight?" I ask her, gesturing toward the oversized fishbowl glasses.

"Um, no." She looks up at me with a hesitant smile and places a hand on her abdomen. "Not for a while, Cash."

That small movement—that tiny unconscious gesture—takes me back to the other day at Drake's when he was telling me to go to Southern Roots for a haircut. He started to tell me about one of the girls being pregnant...

Surely, he didn't mean Myla Rose. She's just so tiny. And don't pregnant woman love to talk about their pregnancies? I know Paige did. Every other word out of her mouth for her entire nine months was about her babies, her stretch marks, her swelling—something. I swear, some days, Jake would hide out at my place just to get a break from baby talk.

"I see. Me neither. Never was much for alcohol. My dad was a mean drunk," I tell her, hoping that tidbit will get her to open up to me a bit about why she isn't drinking.

"Oh? I never knew my dad."

"So, how many girls work at the salon?" I ask her, still fishing.

"Well, I believe you've met us all—I own it with AzzyJo, and we have Seraphine, our receptionist."

Damn, that is not the answer I was going for. Maybe it's Seraphine who's pregnant? Even though she looks even younger than Myla Rose. Deciding to roll with that assumption, I ask, "So, when is Seraphine due?"

"Due for what?" she deadpans, brow arched.

"Her baby...?" My hope that Seraphine is the one with child is fading fast. *Why do I even care?*

"What? No." She shakes her head. "Seraphine's not pregnant. What on earth gave you that idea?"

"The other day, Drake was telling me about your salon, and he mentioned that one of y'all was expecting. I guess I just assumed that Seraphine was..." I trail off, noticing the conversation at our table has ceased. Three sets of eyes are trained on us—watching, waiting.

Myla Rose clears her throat. "Pregnant? Well, she isn't. I am."

Damnit, damnit, damnit. Promptly, I shake that shit off. I'm not looking for love anyway. Love? What the hell? Where did that come from? Hell, I'm not even looking to date right now. Her sweet voice and big brown eyes have me thinking all sorts of crazy thoughts.

"Well, damn, girl, congrats." My voice comes out low and scratchy.

"Thank you." Her response is so quiet I have to strain to hear it.

"Yessir, our girl is gonna have a baby!" Drake sounds downright joyful about it. "Gonna have her shower at my house. You're welcome to come too, if you want."

Azalea shoots him a glare so hard, I'm surprised he's still sitting upright. Myla Rose shifts uncomfortably in her seat, not meeting my eyes. Simon just chuckles.

"Drake, *I* am planning this shower. *Not you.* If Myla wants him to come, she will tell *me,* and *I* will send him an invitation." I swear, Azalea has steam coming from her ears. Her temper is on a hair trigger.

"You two need to fuck," Simon states flatly. That shuts Drake and Azalea right up.

Myla Rose turns those mesmerizing brown eyes my way and says, "I–I'm sure you have better things to do, but you're welcome to come."

"I'll be there. Will your boyfriend be there as well?"

She drops her eyes. That non-answer causes my gut to tighten. After a long pause, she looks back up and says, "No. He won't be there. He isn't..." She pauses again, as if she's unsure how to continue. "He decided he wasn't ready to settle down and be a parent. So, it's just me and the bean." She won't meet my eyes, which is probably a good thing. They're filled with anger, and my jaw is clenched so damn tight I'm surprised I haven't cracked my molars. What kind of asshole wouldn't want to see his baby grow up? *Never mind, I know just what kind of asshole—the same kind that raised me.*

"Yeah, he's a total piece of shit," Simon spouts with a hard edge to his voice. "Thinks he can just go on about his life, ignoring the fact that he has a damn kid." Simon seems protective of Myla. I wonder if that's in a friendly way or if it's something more. I know his dad was an abusive SOB, so maybe that's it? All I know is that any man who leaves his woman high and dry while she's carrying his baby isn't a man in my book.

"I hate that boy. I'd string him up by his damn balls if Myla would let me," Azalea says, her face red with anger on her friend's behalf.

"I'd fuckin' be first in line to help," Drake growls. Huh, I guess if it matters enough, those two can play nice. Listening to them talk about her ex, I realize that they're all protective of Myla Rose, which makes me feel a bit better. Not that I have the right to be worried. Myla Rose is a friend. That's all, and hardly even that. If Simon were interested in her, it wouldn't be any of my damn business. Nope, not one lick.

My thoughts are interrupted by our server bringing out our food. I notice every one is sharing, so I offer up some nachos to the table, and they readily accept.

Conversation trails off as everyone digs in—it's that damn good. As we're all finishing up, I take the time to really observe everyone at our table. Simon is doodling on his napkin. Azalea and Drake keep stealing glances at one another, pretending they don't notice when they get caught. Myla Rose is using the bits of pork left from her tacos to scoop up guacamole.

She lets out a small moan of delight after the last bite and pats her stomach. "Mmm, oh my God, that was so good." It was innocent enough, but *goddamn*. That sound.

Friends, Cash. You want to be her friend. Down, boy.

Pregnant or not, Myla Rose is hands down the most gorgeous woman I have ever laid my eyes on, and combine her looks with sounds like the one she just made...I have a feeling that I'm going to be constantly reminding myself that she's just a friend.

After our dishes are cleared, we all pay our tabs and head out to the parking lot. As the guys leave, Azalea pulls Myla Rose aside. I can't make out all of what they're saying, only a few words here and there coupled with a lot of hand gestures. "Myla...Come on. I...candle burning."

I take a few steps closer to hear them better. "We don't even have a damn candle, Azalea," Myla Rose complains.

"Fine, I left my curling iron on. I need to go back, and—" the car next to me roars to life, drowning out the rest of her words.

I stand off to the side, awkwardly, unsure as to

whether I should wait. Just as I'm about to turn and go, I see Myla give a sharp nod, and Azalea smiles in what appears to be victory.

They both start walking my way, and Azalea calls out to me. "Cash, would you mind giving Myla Rose a ride home? I was going to, but I need to run back to the salon, and I just hate to drag her back with me. She's got a full day tomorrow and needs to rest." Her voice is saccharine sweet—too sweet—and I think I know what's happening here. *We're being set up.*

"Sure thing. I wouldn't mind one bit." Azalea beams at my easy cooperation and sends Myla Rose to me with a little nudge.

"Are you sure, Cash?"

"One hundred percent. C'mon." I take her hand, and there's that jolt again. I swear, every time we touch, it's like lightning is running through my veins. I hold her door open for her and help her into the truck despite her insistence that she can do it on her own.

Once she's buckled, I plug her address into my phone and crank the engine. "Thank you so much for doing this. I don't know why AzzyJo is actin' so damn crazy."

"I'm pretty sure your friend is trying to set us up." I use our time at the stop sign to gauge her reaction to my words.

She snorts out a laugh and shakes her head. "You may just be right. In which case, she *is* crazy."

"Why would that make her crazy?"

"Oh, come on." She laughs again, but this time it's

brittle-sounding. "Why would *anyone* want to get set up with me?"

I grip the steering wheel a bit tighter. "Why wouldn't they?"

She gestures toward her slightly rounded belly.

Suddenly, it clicks. Her self-doubt and hesitation. I guess in all fairness, she has a pretty good point. Whoever she did date would have to be okay with a package deal.

"You think because you're pregnant, no one will want to date you?"

"I mean, isn't that obvious?"

"I think the right man will love you and your child. Don't assume you'll be alone, Myla Rose, and don't settle for anything less than you deserve."

"Sure, Cash, okay." I can tell she thinks I'm feeding her a line, but I mean every word I just said.

Changing the subject, I ask her about the full day Azalea mentioned. "Oh, nothing special. I'm just taking the day off to pressure wash the house."

"By yourself?"

She huffs. "Yes, by myself."

"You sure that's safe?" I ask her as I idle behind the old Land Cruiser parked in her driveway.

"Yes, Cash, I'm sure it's safe. I'm not magically rendered incompetent by a baby growing in my belly."

"Never said you were. What time you plan on getting started?"

"Around eight, if I want to beat the heat. Which I really, *really* do."

"Okay, well be safe, yeah?" I tell her as she unbuckles. I smile because she's in for a surprise tomorrow. I just hope it doesn't offend her.

"Will do, Cash. Thanks for driving me home."

"Anytime."

Chapter Ten

Myla Rose

Cash watches me, his stare unwavering, until I'm safely on the other side of the door. I turn the lock and rush up to my bedroom to peek through my curtains, making it just in time to see his taillights fading.

His words are still *so* fresh in my mind, and my God, do those words have my mind creating scenarios I know are too good to be true.

In my mind, I'm bombarded with images of us. There is no us. *Good gravy, get a grip. He was being hypothetical. He never said he was the right man.*

I'm torn between hugging AzzyJo or wringing her neck. What in the hell was she even thinking, trying to set me up? Obviously, she wasn't. It's truly laughable, but I know her heart was in the right place. "A" for effort, and all that.

Cash Carson may not be meant for me, but that

doesn't mean we can't be friends. *A girl can always use more friends, right?*

Friends. Yup, I'll be his friend, even if it kills me. Because so much about that man is deadly...at least to my heart—and my sanity.

I fall into bed, my mind still circling his words like a hamster in a ball. Eventually, my exhaustion overpowers my late-night musings, and sleep comes fast. Thank God, because morning will be here in no time flat.

My alarm goes off at seven, on the dot, and I skip right over the snooze button. Beating the heat and humidity is my top priority. I've put off pressure washing the house for too long. Grams is probably rolling in her grave at the sight of the grime creeping its way up her house.

I throw on some yoga shorts—seriously, the best damn waistbands for pregnant women—and an oversized T-shirt before making a beeline straight for the kitchen. Coffee first—always.

I'm mid-sip when I hear a vehicle pull up at the front of the house. "Who on earth..." I mutter as I peer out the window.

There Cash Carson is, in all his glory, unloading a damn pressure washer from the bed of his truck. It looks like a nice one, too, not like the little rinky-dink secondhand one I planned on using. But still, why is he here? Why is he doing this?

I rush up the stairs, slide on my sneakers, rush back down, and out into the front yard. "Cash Carson!" my voice carries clear across the yard. I'm expecting him to answer me, but he doesn't—he just points that smile of his my way and nods his hello.

I charge down the steps, not stopping until I'm toe-to-toe with him. "What do you think you're doin'?"

"Take a guess, darlin'." Calling me darlin', in that deep, sexy voice sends a pulse straight to my core.

"I don't feel much like playing games at 7:30 in the morning. Why're you here?" My tone is snippy, though I'm not actually upset with him. I'm just thrown by his kindness and the effect he has on me.

"To help you, Myla Rose." I don't know what's more unsettling—the way he says my name, or his calling me *darlin'*. I guess it doesn't much matter—I feel both all the way down to my damn toes.

"I told you last night, but I'll tell you again—I'm not incompetent just because I'm pregnant."

"Never said you were. Doesn't mean I'm not gonna help. Nothing wrong with a little bit of chivalry." He turns back to finish setting up his pressure washer but promptly turns back to me. "You wanna go grab your extension cord, and we'll get started?"

I shake my head yes and set off to grab the cord from the shed. No use arguing with him. His mind seems made up. Plus, the help will be nice.

"Here you go." I toss the bundled cord to him, and

I'm impressed when he catches it.

Taylor would have taken a big ol' step back so that it would've landed at his feet, and then he would have told me I throw like a girl. Asshole. I guess that's just one more tick in the *Pro* column for Cash. Not that I'm keeping tabs or anything. Because you don't do that with friends.

"Thanks. So, this isn't really a two-person job. You wanna use your sprayer and work on the porch?"

"Sure thing, Cash. Just holler if you need anything."

"Will do."

I get my little pressure washer set up and start blasting the porch clean. There's something so damn satisfying about watching all that yuck rinse away. Once I finish, I stand back and admire my hard work. Sure, I missed some spots, but I'm pleased with it—Grams would be too, and that's good enough for me.

"So much for beating the heat," I whine as a bead of sweat trickles down my back. If I'm this hot and this tired from washing my small space, then I can only imagine how Cash must feel. I make my way to the linen closet to grab him a towel and then back out to find him.

"Hey," I yell, looking around for him. Following the cord around to the side of the house, I freeze, my words drying up on the spot.

The sight of Cash, shirtless, has rendered me speechless. There's no six-pack abs or bulging muscles, but Christ on a cracker, the man is rock solid and just oozes power and strength and masculinity.

He catches me, slack-jawed and bug-eyed. Of course he does. "Aren't you a vision, after all this hard work?" he says as he shuts off his machine.

"Huh?" His words don't compute.

"That for me?"

"Is what for you?"

"That towel you're carrying."

I fight to keep my eyes on his. "Yup." However, it's a losing fight. I take stock of him, from head to toe and back up again—he's even better up close. I can see little rivulets of sweat trailing down his chest, and I swear, I ache to follow them with my tongue. I'm pretty sure I let out a little whimper, because next thing I know, he's smirking.

"See something you like, darlin'?"

I start to nod but come to my senses just in the nick of time. Halle-fucking-lujah. "Ab-absolutely not. I was just startled to find you back here damn near naked." I snark, hoping it will drown out the lust he has swirling all around me.

"Half-naked, huh?" He drags a hand up his torso and back down. "I'd venture to say socks, shoes, boxer briefs, and shorts are a far cry from half-naked, Myla Rose."

Great, now I'm picturing him in those briefs. *Can't a girl get a break?* I toss the towel at him, landing it right over his head—apparently, I've regressed to acting like a toddler. "Come talk to me when you're decent," I huff before retreating to the safety of my kitchen.

Chapter Eleven

Cash

With the towel she threw at me draped around my neck, I reload my pressure washer into the bed of my truck and set off to find her. I tap lightly on the front door, taking stock of the area I told her to work on. She did a pretty good job—got a little too close in some places and flaked the paint, but by the looks of it, the porch could use a new coat regardless.

Her house is beautiful. An old farm house, with what looks like original everything on the outside. The property is huge, with two giant oak trees and slightly overgrown grass. I can almost smell the history of this place. I wonder how long she's lived here?

She doesn't answer, so I knock again, this time a little harder. When she still doesn't come to the door, I try the handle. It's unlocked.

Nudging the door open, I'm blown away by the interior of the house. Wide, hand-scraped wood plank flooring, shiplap walls, and thick molding. This house, much like its owner, is breathtaking.

I follow the sound of Myla Rose singing along—albeit slightly off-key—and find her bent over her freezer in those tiny little cotton shorts. Not gonna lie, seeing her reaction to me without my shirt was good, but watching her wiggle and shake her ass to the music she's listening to in those shorts...hands down, the highlight of my day. Maybe even my week.

I'm too enraptured by the show in front of me to tell her she has an audience. She straightens from her crouched position, and I see she was filling two glasses with ice. She pivots around to set them on the island but drops them with a loud squeal when she sees me standing there.

"SHIT!" she screams, frozen where she stands due to the little shards of glass around her feet.

I rush to her. "Are you okay?" The look she shoots me could melt the ice that was just in those glasses.

"Do I *look* okay?" She's all attitude—eyes narrowed, hands on hips, head cocked slightly to the right.

"Fuck, no. I'm sorry. Where's your broom and dust pan?"

"In the laundry room. Just down the hall, first door on the left." I return to the kitchen, broom in hand, only to find her trying to step around the glass littering the floor.

"Stay still," I command her. She freezes, once again, where she stands.

The glass crunches under my boots as I stalk toward her, each step purposeful. When I reach her, she attempts a step back—away from me. Not gonna happen. I reach out with both hands and hoist her up over my shoulder, navigating us away from the mess and enjoying my bird's eye view of her plump ass along the way.

Once I make it to the dining room, I set her down—slowly. The feel of her body sliding down mine, combined with the sensation of her nails as they slightly rake against my chest—*goddamn,* my mouth is just about watering. With her feet firmly on the ground, I grip her chin with my thumb and forefinger. "I told you not to move." Her cheeks are a sweet shade of pink, though I'm unsure whether it's out of anger, embarrassment, or arousal. I'm gonna bet on a combination of all three.

"Yeah? Well, you're not the boss of me." Her sass—outta this world hot.

"Don't wanna boss you, darlin'." Although, that thought has some merit. "I told you not to move to keep you from slicing up your feet. In case it's slipped your mind, you're barefoot."

"Oh. Guess I am. Still, if you wouldn't have been standing around like a creeper, it never woulda been an issue."

"True, and as I said, I'm sorry. Now, listen this time and stay put while I go sweep that mess up."

"Sir, yes sir!" she says, mock salute and all.

Chapter Twelve

Myla Rose

IT TAKES EVERYTHING—EVERY SINGLE BIT OF MY willpower— not to collapse into a spineless heap on the floor after he sets me down. I'm not sure how I missed it, but as my body *slowly* moved down his, I realized he was *still* shirtless. His bare skin, coupled with his citrus-spice-and-everything-nice scent...*fuck me.*

Cash Carson is mighty fine to look at as is, but shirtless and sweaty? The man is a damn dream.

I watch intently as he sweeps up the mess I made, mesmerized by the way his arms flex and release with every swipe of the broom. I find myself fanning my flaming cheeks, wishing like hell I had that glass of ice cold tea right about now. Anything to cool down the inferno blazing inside me.

He bends to collect the glass into the dustpan and the island obscures him from view—and not a moment too soon, because I think I would die of embarrassment if he caught me staring at him. Again.

I take full advantage of his being out of sight for a few seconds to try and compose myself. *Deep breath in, and out. He's just a man, Myla Rose. No need to make a fool of yourself.*

He stands and dumps the dustpan into the trashcan, and I'm about to thank him when he picks up the entire can and walks to the back door. "Gonna take this to your outside can. Don't want the glass splitting the bag."

"Oh, yeah, thanks." Cash Carson doesn't miss a beat. Small, insignificant things seem to be what he's all about, and boy, does it make me giddy inside. Taylor would have left me to clean the mess, bitching about my clumsiness all the while.

Next thing I know, he's opening and closing cabinets, obviously searching for something.

"May I help you?" I ask him.

"Cups?"

"Oh, they're in the cabinet over the dishwasher." He turns and looks at me like I'm plum crazy. "What is it? Why're you looking at me like that?"

"Myla Rose, everyone knows that cups go in the cabinet to the right or left of the sink."

"Who's everyone? I mean, that's just...silly. Why would they go there?"

"You know, I'm honestly not sure. That's just where my mom keeps hers, and I do, too." He says this like it's an admission. Like he's embarrassed. He even has a faint blush to his cheeks.

"I keep mine by the dishwasher. Makes for an easy unload."

"Damn. That's a pretty good idea." For some reason, his tiny compliment has me beaming. Apparently, Azalea isn't the only one who thrives on positive praise.

Grabbing the dishtowel from where it's hung on the side of the island, I drop down and wipe up the moisture left behind from the melted ice. Last thing I need is either one of us slipping.

Just as I move to stand, Cash walks over to fill the cups with ice. He lowers himself to a crouched position, and suddenly, we're eye-to-eye. I suck in a sharp breath. His eyes hold so much power and emotion in them that it steals the air right from my lungs.

He sets a glass down by his boot and reaches out with his free hand to brush a bit of hair out of my face. His fingers trail across my cheek and down my neck, coming to rest on my shoulder. His light-as-air touch scorches my skin like fire. I give a full-body shiver, and he smirks. He knows he affects me, and he likes it.

He gives my shoulder a light squeeze and stands, grabbing his glass along the way. I follow suit and grab the pitcher of tea from the fridge. "Let's try this again? I can't even imagine how thirsty you are."

"Fucking parched." And just like when he came in for his haircut, I'm not sure if we're talking about the tea or something else entirely.

I pour us each a generous serving, yet he downs his in one gulp—guess he was talking about the tea. "Damn, this is good. Perfectly sweetened."

"Thanks, I make it just like my Grams taught me."

"Y'all were close, huh?"

"She raised me."

"Mind if I ask why?"

"No, not at all. Mama felt tied down and didn't want to give up her fast and easy lifestyle to take care of me. When I was seven, she loaded me up, dropped me off, and never looked back."

"Damn darlin', I'm sor—"

I hold up a finger to silence him. "Nothin' to be sorry about, Cash. My Grams loved me enough that mama's exit from my life is barely a blip on my radar. I'm not sorry about it, and you shouldn't be either."

"Ten-four." He refills his glass, and we both soak in the slightly awkward silence. I think we're both waiting for the other to speak, and finally, he does. "So, whatcha got going on this weekend?"

"Oh! The Strawberry Festival. Have you ever been?"

"Nope. Tell me about it?"

"Well, it's mostly arts and crafts, but they have the most amazing strawberry shortcake. I go every year just for that little slice of heaven."

He thinks on my words for a few, and then he asks me where the festival is, and I tell him. "Great," he says, his smile a mile wide. "I'll meet you there around eleven?"

"You'll what?"

"You heard me, darlin'. See you Saturday." That quickly, his glass is in the sink and he's out the door.

What on earth just happened?

Chapter Thirteen

Cash

I make good on my word and show up at the municipal park at a quarter till. I figure it's a nice enough day that I can chill out in the shade while I wait for Myla Rose. Not even five minutes later, I see her Land Cruiser park a few feet away from my truck. If I'm being honest, I'm pretty damn thankful she doesn't make me wait long. A part of me was a little scared she wouldn't show.

"Hello there, darlin'," I drawl as I open her car door.

"Oh!" She exclaims, clutching her chest. "H–hey there, Cash. Wasn't sure if I'd see you today or not."

"Told you I'd be here." Our steps fall into sync, my fingertips occasionally brushing her arm as she steers us through the crowd toward the festival entrance. "So, what do we do first?"

"I usually walk the loop and look at the booths." She ducks her head.

"Sounds like a plan."

"For real? You don't mind looking at all of this?" she asks, gesturing over to the walking path lined with tent after tent.

"Why would I?" My head pulls back in confusion.

"Taylor never...you know what? Doesn't matter. Let's go." She picks up her pace and sets off again for the entrance.

I swear, the more I hear about Taylor, the more I dislike the guy. Seems like he constantly made her feel like shit long before he decided to end things with her.

"Cash, you coming?" Myla Rose calls from a few feet ahead of me. *Huh*. Didn't even notice I'd stopped walking. Guess I got too caught up thinking about her asshole ex.

"Yes, ma'am," I call back, though I make no effort to move. I'm too busy admiring her toned, pale legs. Girl's got a thing for short shorts...but you won't hear me complaining. I drag my eyes upward, pausing at her midsection. She's barely showing, but it's there. A slight swell, and goddamn if I don't think she's even hotter for it. I finish my perusal with a quick stop at her breasts—small and perky, a perfect handful—before landing on her face. Her eyes are narrowed to slits, and her full lips are pursed. *Busted.*

I hustle over to her and grab her hand without thinking twice about it. "Come on, Myla Rose. Lots to see." She glances down at her hand in mine, gasping lightly, but I pay no mind to her. I just tug her along until we fall into step together.

We've made it about halfway around the tent-lined path, and between listening to Myla Rose tell me about the different vendors and the feeling of her hand in mine, her smooth to my rough, I'm having a damn good time.

"You said you used to come with your Grams every year?" I know I'm prying, but I can't help it. This girl has me wanting to know her *in every way*.

"Mmmhmm, every year, like clockwork. She started coming when she was a little girl, and through the years, she got to know a lot of the vendors. So I guess, eventually, it was kinda like she was coming to catch up with old friends."

"I like that. Tell me about her?"

Her eyes light up at my taking an interest. "Yeah, okay. Grams lived here her whole life. Her husband actually built my house with his bare hands. It was his gift to her when he proposed. Worked on it day and night until it was complete. My Papa passed away shortly after Mama was born, but Grams soldiered on. She raised Mama there, and me. And now, I'll raise my little bean there."

"That's incredible," I tell her honestly. "I can't imagine being grounded by roots like that. Sure would like to, though." She looks at me like she's not quite sure what I mean, so I elaborate. "My dad's job kept us on the move every few years. Actually, I lived here in Dogwood when I was a kid."

"Is that how you know Drake?"

"Oddly, no." Her brows crinkle in confusion, and she

looks so damn cute. "When I lived in Arkansas—"

"You met him when he moved away with his mom?"

"It's a small world after all." She cracks up at my line. Her laughter is contagious, and before I know it, we're both doubled over laughing. Honestly, by the time we regain our composure, I don't think either of us remembers why we were laughing in the first place.

"You ready for what's sure to be the best part of your day, Cash Carson?"

"Lead the way, darlin'."

"The best part of my day is standin' in this long ass line?" I goad her.

"No. The best part is at the end of this line. C'mon."

During our wait, we talk about everything and nothing all at once. I feel so damn comfortable in her presence that the long minutes we spend waiting seem to pass in the blink of an eye.

At the halfway point in the line, they have a small table where a woman's selling...tickets? No words are exchanged. Myla Rose just holds up two fingers and passes her a twenty-dollar bill before I can think to grab my wallet. By the time the lady hands back her change, I'm scrambling to not look like an ass.

"Myla, let me—"

She gently pushes my wallet back to me. "This is my treat. You've never experienced this greatness, and I am excited to be the one to give it to you."

Now, I know she doesn't mean anything dirty, but my mind...yeah, he's not on the same page. My thoughts are racing a mile a minute over all the *greatness* she could give me.

"How many?" the lady barks from inside her booth.

"Two, please." Myla Rose hands her our tickets in exchange for two of the most over-the-top strawberry shortcakes I've ever seen. I'm talking huge, fluffy cuts of angel food cake covered with a mixture of fresh strawberries and compote, with a fluffy whipped cream mountain as its crowning glory.

Myla Rose hands one to me, and together, we head to the makeshift pavilion where they've set up folding tables and chairs. Once seated, Myla wastes no time digging into hers.

"Damn, girl. You gonna eat all that?"

"Eating for two, you know." She giggles and pats her belly.

"Something tells me you devour this cake every year, no matter what."

She snaps her forefinger and thumb together. "Aww, you caught me." I can't help but to smile at how carefree and cute she is. For the first time, she finally seems totally at ease in my presence—and that feels like a victory.

She takes the last bite of her shortcake, and we both stand to throw away our plates. It's then I notice she has a little whipped cream on her bottom lip. I reach out to wipe it with my thumb at the same time she goes to lick it away. Her tongue swipes across my skin, and I'm hit with white-hot need. *I need this woman.* To taste that whipped cream straight from her lips.

Our plates long forgotten, we lean toward one another until our lips meet—a soft brush at first, exploratory. Shifting my hand to cup her jaw, I angle her exactly how I want her. She gasps softly, allowing me to deepen our kiss. I lick my tongue against hers, drinking down her sweet strawberry flavor. She runs her hands up and around my neck, her nails digging lightly into my shirt collar...gripping, grasping, wanting. I work my other arm around her waist, my hand resting just above the sweet curve of her ass. She presses her body in closer to mine, so close that I can feel her heartbeat against my ribs. It beats a fast rhythm, full of want and desire. I'm lost in her. Lost in her taste and the sound of her soft moans. Lost until someone loudly clears their throat, reminding us that we're in a public place.

She looks down and runs her fingers through her hair before nervously dragging her eyes back up to mine. I can tell she wants to say something, but she doesn't. She just shakes her head and gives a little smile before scooping up our trash from the table and walking off to dispose of it.

In the three minutes she's gone, my thoughts kick into overdrive. *What business do I have kissing her? I'm not ready for a relationship, or even these kinds of feelings. How do I know she's not like Kayla? How do I*—my racing mind grinds to a halt when she reappears.

"Myla Rose, listen, I—"

"It's okay, Cash."

"No, listen. I shouldn't have kissed you. I–I'm sorry. I don't want to lead you on."

She throws her hands up as she backs away. "I said it's okay. I get it."

She doesn't stick around for me to reply, and I can't say I blame her. And to top it all off, I'm almost sure I saw tears in her eyes. *Fuck.*

Chapter Fourteen

Myla Rose

I haul ass to Bertha, determined not to let him see my tears. *Stupid, traitorous tears.* Serves me right, though, thinking a man like him would want me. Between his sweet words, even sweeter gestures, and what I thought was mutual chemistry, it's no wonder I misread the situation. As much as I want to chalk it up to pregnancy hormones, I can't help but think there's something wrong with me.

On my short drive home, I debate going to see Simon but ultimately decide against it. I don't want my ignorance and assumptions to upset Simon and Cash's friendship. Simon is so fierce when it comes to me, and sometimes, his overprotectiveness makes him a bit irrational. Once I'm home and cozy in lounge clothes, I fish my cell phone out of my bag and call Azalea.

"Azalea!" My whine carries clear through the phone. "I'm such an idiot."

"Not an idiot, Myles."

"We were havin' such a nice time—a really, *really* good day, and stupid me, I had to go and ruin it," I lament, flopping back onto my bed with a dramatic sigh.

"Sister-girl, I'm gonna need you to start from the beginning."

"If we're starting at the beginning, then this is your fault." Irrational? Yes. Do I care? No.

"My fault? Now I'm really not following."

"You–you tried to set us up by asking him to drive me home. That was the damn catalyst. He was spoutin' all these sweet words and making hope bang around in my chest like fucking butterflies on speed. Had me thinking all sorts of silly things. Then he showed up the next day to do the pressure washing for me—that was a mess in its own right. And today, he met me at the Strawberry Festival." I pause mid-rant, too caught up in my memories of the past few days.

"Keep going, hun."

"Cash was so attentive, Az. He asked about Grams and listened to every word I said. I mean, every word—he didn't act bored or nothin'. He walked with me and took the time to look at just about every booth. It was seriously amazing. Except I kept comparing him in my mind to Taylor. Not that they even compare. Cash is leaps, bounds, and miles ahead."

Azalea snorts. "You got that right."

"Yup, and I ruined it."

"Myla, while you've said a lot, you still haven't really

told me anything."

"We...kissed."

"I'm sorry, y'all what?"

"Kissed. And I thought he was just as into it as me. Until he pulled away and apologized. Told me he shouldn't have kissed me. It was mortifying."

"Oh..." I can tell from her tone of voice that she's searching for the right words to comfort me.

"Yeah, oh."

"Well, I don't know what to tell you. Maybe there's more to it?"

"Doubt it. I feel like an idiot. I really thought he was into me, and I went and ran him off."

"Babe, you didn't run him off. Maybe he just got spooked."

"Yeah, spooked at the thought of kissing someone else's baby mama."

"Myla Rose, you hush up right now. You will not be single forever. The right man will love you both." Her words are so similar to Cash's, I can't help but snort. They've obviously been drinking the same Kool-Aid.

"Yeah, heard that recently. Not gonna put much stock in it though. Single's just fine by me. I'll talk to you later, 'kay?"

"'Kay. Love you, Myles. Don't go losin' sleep over this."

I'm honestly not sure I believe what I just told her—that I'm okay being single for the long haul—but I guess I'd better get used to it.

Chapter Fifteen

Cash

THAT KISS AND THE SUBSEQUENT CLUSTERFUCK have been on a constant loop in my mind since yesterday. I reverted to my default and drove around for hours, feeling like the scum of the earth for making Myla Rose cry.

I tossed and turned all night, debating whether I should reach out to her, talk to her and let her know that she's not the problem. I finally decide against it…it would probably only complicate things more.

Distance—I think distance might be the answer. Distance from her banging body. Distance from her sweet voice. Distance from the tears I caused her to spill. Yeah, distance sounds good—if only I could get my heart on the same page as my brain.

I was up with the sun, still agitated at my behavior from yesterday. I figured hitting the wood shop hard would clear my mind. I figured knocking out a new build would set my soul at ease, but if anything, with every measurement, every cut, every swing of my hammer—I thought of her more.

I made up scenario after scenario of how I could've handled myself better. Who apologizes for kissing someone? Me, apparently. *Fucking idiot.* And I can't even talk to my best friend about it because he's like a damn brother to her.

Aggravated with myself, I stow my tools and check the time. I've managed to spend the entire day in the shop—sun up to sun down—and didn't even notice time passing. Not to mention, I didn't get a lick of actual work done. I did get a good scrap pile going with all the cuts I botched, though.

Whipping out my phone, I dial my brother and tell him I'm coming by. I'm desperate for a distraction.

Paige answers the door and ushers me inside with a warm smile. She's one of the nicest people I have ever met—I'm talking sunshine and rainbows. When she and Jake started dating, we all told him that he'd better not let her go. They had a lot of ups and downs, but he finally got his shit together, and they recently celebrated their eighth anniversary.

"Cash! It is so good to see you! The boys sure have been missing their uncle."

"I've been missin' them too. They still awake?"

"They are," she says as we make our way through the house. "They heard you on the phone and refused to go to bed without seeing you."

I kick off my shoes before stepping down into the family room, the shag carpet plush beneath my feet. "BOYS!" I holler, sneaking up on them, their heads just visible over the back of the couch. They squeal at the sound of my voice, and I revel in it. To be the center of that kind of limitless love, there's nothing else like it.

It's the kind of love I thought I'd have once Kayla and I started a family of our own. *Don't go there, Cash. Not now, not when your mind's already a damn mess.*

"Uncle Cashmere!" Preston shouts, climbing over the back of the couch and leaping into my arms. "Daddy saids you were coming over!" As much as I want to hate my brother for teaching his kids to call me by that stupid-ass nickname, I just can't. It's cute when *they* say it.

"Yeah! He did, he did!" Lucas exclaims, jumping on the couch like a damn monkey, impatiently waiting for his turn to hug me.

Shifting Preston to my right arm, I scoop Lucas up with my left and walk us all around to the front of the couch, jiggling and shaking them with every step. They're laughing like hyenas by the time we collapse onto the soft cushions, and I love it.

"Tell Uncle Cash what's good." Preston and Lucas immediately launch into telling me *every single thing* that's happened since they saw me last.

They are so excited that they're talking over each other, and I'm not actually catching more than a word here and there.

"Boys, slow down. One at a time," I tell them as I settle deeper into the couch with them.

Paige and Jake walk into the room just as Preston finishes up telling me about why you don't junk punch people. ". . . and Lucas nailed him right in the peanuts! He fell over, cryin' like a baby! It. Was. Awesome!"

"Was not awesome!" Lucas insists with a snarl. "I got in trouble, and it wasn't even on purposed!"

"Okay, boys, that's enough," their mom interjects. "Let's go—it's bath time."

Her decree is met with a chorus of whines and a few *but Moms*. Paige isn't having it though. "You heard me—bath time. One...two..." And just like that, both boys take off.

"What happens if you get to three?" I call out as she follows behind them.

"Wouldn't know," she calls back. I just smile. That mom voice gets shit done.

"So, wanna tell me what you're doing here?" Jake questions once Paige is out of earshot.

"What? I can't just come visit?" I feign nonchalance.

"Cash. It's almost ten o'clock on a school night." He cocks his head to the side, studying me closely. "So, I'll ask you again—why're you here?"

"Fuck." Dropping my eyes to my feet, I mumble, "Imessedupwithareallynicegirl."

"I'm sorry. One more time?"

"Nah, if you missed it the first time, that's on you. Got no plans to repeat myself, brother." *Evasiveness. That's the answer.*

"Oh, no, I heard you. Just wanted you to say it again." His grin is shit-eating. *God, such an asshole.* "C'mon, little bro, give it up. Who is she?"

"Her name's Myla—"

"Myla Rose. Jesus Christ." He sniggers and shakes his head. "You do know she's pregnant, right?"

"Yes, Jake, well aware." My patience is wearing thin. Why did I think this was a good idea?

"Just making sure." He steeples his fingers under his chin, a roguish smile playing on his lips.

"It started out like nothing. She accidentally bumped her buggy into me at the store. Then Drake and Simon—who are both like brothers to her—sent me to her for a haircut. I ran into her at dinner with the guys, and her sneaky little friend convinced me to give her a ride home. That shoulda been the end of it." I heave myself back into the cushions. "But no, she started talking about working on her house, and capable or not, I can't let her get out there all alone in the heat, up and down ladders."

Jake shoots me a WTF look, but I just plow on, hoping I'll feel better once it's all out. "So, I show up at her house with my pressure washer, and she's in these barely-there shorts, and there was this tension between us...this push and pull. I don't know how to describe it. There's just something about her, brother."

"Not to be an ass, but get to the point."

"The point is, I'm an idiot. I kissed her yesterday...and then told her I was sorry and that I shouldn't have."

Jake's laughter bursts from his lips like a runaway train—unstoppable. "You weren't kidding. You really are an idiot."

"Real helpful. So, now she surely thinks I'm some dipshit jerk like her ex. I didn't mean to lead her on. I'm just not in the right place for a relationship."

"Who said anything about a relationship?"

"I...fuck. I don't know. I'm *so* hung up on her, and I don't wanna be."

"So, don't," Jake says, like it's as simple as breathing.

What he doesn't get is just the *memory* of the sound of her voice takes my breath away, and now that I've tasted her lips, I'm not so sure I can move her back into the 'just friends' box. Not when she consumes my thoughts, both conscious and subconscious.

I'm startled out of my inner ramblings when Jake claps his hands in front of my face.

"Are you even listening?"

"No, sorry, what's up?"

"Dude. You're obsessing over nothing. If you really stop and think, she's the answer to all your problems."

"Problems? What problems?" Seriously, what's he even talking about?

"She's the first girl you've been attracted to since Kayla. You ever think that's all it is? Attraction, pure and simple, brother. I'll admit, she's a good-lookin' girl, and maybe her being knocked up is just what you need."

"Jake, what are you talking about?" I'm starting to question his sanity because he's damn sure sounding a little nuts.

"You need to rebound. Think about it—you haven't been with anyone since..." he trails off, waiting for me to pick up on the breadcrumbs he's trailing.

Surely, he isn't suggesting what I think he is. "Wait, so you're saying—"

"You know what they say. Best way to get over one is to get under another. What's the worst that could happen? Seriously, bro, it's a win-win. You get back in the saddle, and it's not like you can knock her up." He chuckles at his own joke, though the humor is lost on me. If anything, it pisses me off.

"What the fuck, Jake?" I roar, rocketing up from the couch. "Are you kidding? Are you seriously—" I run my hands up my face and through my hair. My blood is boiling from his words. *Wonder what Paige would think if she heard him talking like this*?

"Why're you so mad? You said it yourself—you don't want to be hung up on her. Maybe you just need to get back in the game and get her out of your system." I pace the living room a few times, reminding myself that his intentions are good. He thinks he's helping.

"I get what you're saying. I do. But that's just not gonna happen. She deserves better, and that's just not me," I tell him right as Paige walks back into the room, the front of her outfit sopping wet from giving the boys their bath.

"What's not you, Cash?"

"Nothing!" Jake scrambles up off the chair he's sitting in and rushes to her side.

"You sure are acting strange." Her gaze darts back and forth between us, eyebrows knitting together in question. "Well, Preston and Lucas are putting on their PJs and want you to read them a bedtime story, Cash. Is that okay?"

"Of course, I'd love to. Tell 'em I'll be right there."

"Will do," she says as she pivots around and heads back to their room.

"Cash, I swear to God—if you repeat a word of what I said to Paige, she'll have me by my balls so fast..." He genuinely sounds worried, which is hilarious to me.

"Sure thing, brother. Not a word." I set off toward Preston and Lucas' room, my laughter trailing behind me.

"And they all lived happily ever after." I snort as I close the book before kissing each of their little foreheads. They fell asleep about halfway through the story, but I had to know how it ended.

Too bad life doesn't guarantee a happy ending for everyone. From what I've lived, they're few and far between. I quietly pull their door to and make my way through the house, looking for Jake and Paige.

I find them in the kitchen having just finished a nightcap. Their glasses sit empty on the island, and Jake has his arms wrapped around Paige as they whisper to one another. It's an intimate moment, and I feel like an intruder. Clearing my throat, I announce my presence. "Boys are out cold. Think I'm gonna head home. It's late."

"Thank you so much for reading to them, Cash. They just love you so much," Paige murmurs.

"Not a problem, I love them too." I give her a one-armed hug and ask Jake to walk me out. "Thanks for letting me stop by tonight. This is just what I needed."

"Anytime, brother." We do one of those man-shake-back-slap kinds of hugs before parting ways.

I meant it when I said that tonight was just what I needed. While Myla Rose still lingers in my mind, she's no longer at the forefront, and that's a start.

Chapter Sixteen

Myla Rose

Today's the day—my sixteen-week appointment, and hopefully, I'll get to find out if I'm having a boy or a girl. I should be overflowing with excitement, but my attitude is still a bit sour from how last weekend ended.

I know I need to move on and get over it. The fact that I care, that I've been stewing over it for this damn long, really irks me.

According to the girls, I've been a straight-up bitch. As far as Seraphine goes, I've chalked it up to hormones. No reason to have both of them on my case about my knickers being in a knot over Cash Carson.

I mean, Lord have mercy, who does he think he is, flirting with me and kissing me like that when he's not really interested? Men are nothing but jerks, all of them.

Though, if I'm honest, it's all too easy to get caught up in him. With the way he says all the right things—

you know, aside from apologizing after our kiss—and the feel of his strong arms around me, with his lips hot on mine and his all-male scent swirling around me like a haze. It's a lethal combination, one that had those foolish thoughts of mine flaring right back to life.

Well, no thank you. I'm gonna stick those thoughts right back up on the shelf, where they belong. He made me feel like a damn fool after our kiss, cementing the fact that those feelings were clearly one-sided.

"Myla Rose McGraw." The nurse calls my name.

Gathering up my purse, I head over to where she's waiting. "Yes, ma'am, that's me."

"How are you today, dear?" she inquires as she escorts me to the ultrasound room.

"I'm doin' fine—excited for this appointment!"

"I bet you are. Go ahead and hop up on the table and lift your top. The ultrasound tech should be joining us any minute."

I do as she tells me, and sure enough, by the time I'm comfy, the tech is here and ready to get started.

She has kind blue eyes and introduces herself as Belinda. After squirting some of the warm gel onto my stomach, she begins pushing around the wand, making notes and taking measurements as she goes.

"Are you finding out the gender today?"

"Yes, ma'am." My voice comes out a bit louder than

this small space calls for. "I would love to know."

"All right, let's see what we have here then." She begins to move the wand and press on my abdomen. This goes on for what feels like an eternity, and I'm quickly losing hope that I'll find out today. I'm working on firming up my resolve to wait another month to find out when she blurts out, "It's a boy!"

She shows me on the screen, and goodness gracious, is she right. My little man is showing it all off, proud as a peacock. I'm overcome with emotion, tears of joy streaming down my face. I'm getting my little prince after all. I'm so high on cloud nine, nothing can bring me down.

"Are you okay, sweetheart?" Belinda asks, softly giving my arm a little squeeze.

"Oh! Yes, ma'am, I'm just so-so-so happy."

"Oh, good. I hate seeing mothers disappointed. A healthy baby is the real goal here." She smiles before telling me that I can head back out to the waiting room because Dr. Mills isn't quite ready for me.

Back in my chair, I flip through the ultrasound images Belinda gave me before digging my phone out of my purse to call Azalea with the news. Lord knows, she'll kill me if she isn't the first to know.

"It's a beautiful day at Southern Roots! This is Seraphine, how may I assist you today?" Her creative greetings always amuse me.

"Well, hello there, Seraphine. Is Azalea with a client?"

"Myla Rose! Did you find out? Do you know? Hang

on, I'll go grab her!" I hear her drop the phone to the desk without putting me on hold, and within a few seconds, they are both yelling into the receiver. "Myla, we put you on speaker. Now, did you find out? Do you know?"

"I do." I let my words linger.

"Are you gonna tell us?" AzzyJo barks.

"Yup." I keep on with the short answers just to ruffle her feathers.

"Myla Rose, you tell us right this instant, or I'll—" her threat is cut off by the nurse calling me back to finish the rest of my appointment.

"Sorry, sister-girl, they just called me back. I'll have to tell y'all later!" I end the call and chuck my phone back into my bag before she can start griping at me.

After the dreaded weigh-in at the nurses' station, I'm led to an exam room to wait on Dr. Mills. I'm sitting on the table giggling softly to myself at the flurry of text notifications from Azalea and Seraphine when there's a soft knock. "Come in," I call through the door.

"Good morning, Ms. McGraw. I presume you and baby are well? According to the ultrasound notes, the little tyke is right on track." He always makes a point to ask about the baby, and not necessarily in a doctor way. Sometimes, it's in a more concerned way. He never gets too personal, but I can tell from his tone of voice that he wants to know more about his grandson, so I always try to offer up little tidbits here and there.

"Yes sir, we are. I'm so excited for a little boy."

"Good, good. I–I'm glad to hear that." His voice is soft, almost wistful. I know he cares about this baby, even if his wife and son don't. "Lie back now, please, and I'll take some measurements and then we can listen for the heartbeat." I follow his instructions, and he goes about his work in silence.

"All right, Ms. McGraw, you're measuring right at 16 weeks. Let's take a listen to baby's heartbeat."

More warm gel, and then the small exam room is filled with a swooshing sound, the most beautiful sound I've ever heard—my little man's heartbeat. My eyes once again fill with tears, and with a quick glance at the good doctor, I see his have, too. It's moments like this when I truly want to hate Taylor for not being involved. How he cannot love this baby is beyond me. Dr. Mills may not be the most affectionate man, but his heart is good. It's a damn shame Taylor didn't take more after him.

"Sounds good, 135 beats per minute." He rolls over to his desk and hands me a towel to wipe off the goo, discreetly wiping his eyes before extending a hand to help me sit back up. "Do you have any questions for me today?" he asks as he enters notes on the computer.

"Um, yes sir. I do." He swivels around to face me with an arched brow. "Is it a pregnancy thing to have weird dreams?" I stare at the wall behind him, embarrassed by my silly question.

"Oh, yes. Yes, Ms. McGraw. It's from your increased

hormone levels. Nothing to worry about. Anything else?" I shake my head no. "All right then, please have them schedule four weeks from now, and be sure to call if you have any questions."

He stands and leaves the room, and I follow quickly behind. I'm sure the girls are losing their minds waiting on me.

Deciding to take a page from AzzyJo's book, I want to get creative with telling the girls I'm having a boy, so I make a quick trip to Sprinkles, our local cupcake shop.

On the drive over, I call the store and ask them if they can whip up what I'm wanting on short notice, and they assure me they can. Fifteen minutes later, I'm out the door and on my way to Southern Roots, cupcakes and all.

Walking into the salon, I head straight for the dispensary, gesturing for Seraphine to tag along. She holds up one long, slender finger to let me know she'll be a minute. I place the cupcake box down onto the table in front of Azalea, next to the salad she's picking at.

She arches one perfectly sculpted brow as if to say, *What the hell, Myla?* Huh, guess she didn't appreciate my hanging up on her earlier. Oops. My smile stretches from ear-to-ear, showing every bit of the amusement I'm feeling.

"Having a good day?" I ask her.

"If you don't tell me what that baby is right this cotton pickin' minute, I'll—"

"Hush up and open the box," I tell her, nodding toward where it sits on the table.

Seraphine walks in right as she flips back the lid to reveal a half-dozen cupcakes iced in different shades of blue. Azalea's eyes are as big as dinner plates between the cupcakes and me.

"Does this mean what I think it means?"

Seraphine peeks over my shoulder into the box before turning to look at me, anxious for my reply.

"Yes, it's a boy!" I shout. The next thing I know, they both have their arms wrapped snuggly around me, murmuring their congratulations.

"We have to start plannin' your shower now, Myla Rose!" Azalea insists. "Oh, and we need to get you registered too!" She lets out a loud squeak and gives my shoulders a tight squeeze. "I'm just so excited! I'm getting a nephew! Have you told Drake and Simon?"

Seraphine excuses herself back to the front desk when the salon phone rings. She's young, but a hard worker—and I'm damn sure glad she's a part of my tribe.

"No." I scoff. "Like I'd be dumb enough to tell anyone before you! I value my life, thank you very much. Plus, I think I want to surprise them. I just need to figure out how."

"Ooh! Let me think on that. I know we'll come up with something good. Anyway, Drake said we could have your shower at his house. I won't tell him it's a boy or anything, but I'll go ahead and get with him to start plannin'."

"You sure y'all can handle that?" I ask her, fighting to conceal my grin. Those two are a hot mess.

"What is that supposed to mean? Are you implyin' that I'm incapable of handling Drake-freaking-Collins?"

"Oh, I'm sure you'd love to handle him," I tell her with an impish grin.

"Don't you start, Myla. I swear to high heavens." She rolls her eyes as she tosses her cupcake wrapper into the trash.

"Not startin' a thing, Az. I'm just saying."

"Yeah? Well, don't." She's smiling though, so I know she isn't really mad at me. "Call me tonight, and we can talk about everything for your shower, okay?"

"You know I will," I tell her as we head out to the main area of the salon.

Seraphine is finishing up a call when we hit the reception area. "I'll talk to the girls, 'kay, Mags? I'll let you know in a day or two, I promise," she says before replacing the phone in its cradle.

I shoot Azalea a quizzical look, which she mirrors right back at me. "Well, ladies, I might have some good news," Seraphine tells us, and we both wait for her to elaborate. "That was my cousin, and she's moving to Dogwood soon. Like real soon. Anyway, she was a hairstylist back in South Carolina, and I think she'd be a perfect fit here." She rips a piece of paper from the notepad in front of her and hands it to Azalea. "I wrote down her info for y'all to look over."

"Myla, we *have* to call her!" she exclaims.

"Have to? Why?" I question, her excitement surprising me.

"Magnolia. Her name is Magnolia." And that's all she needs to say. I don't even have to meet her to know she belongs here with us. Nodding my head, I tell Azalea to set up an interview with her before heading out. It's just past lunch time, and the only thing I've eaten today is a cupcake. The bean and I need real food, and some chicken salad from Dream Beans sounds like perfection.

Chapter Seventeen

Cash

I PULL UP TO THE LOCAL COFFEE SHOP AT ELEVEN forty-five on the dot. My meeting with the owner isn't until noon, but I'm a firm believer that fifteen minutes early is on time, and on time is late.

Not to mention, I want to make a good first impression. Word of mouth is the way of life in small towns. If they like me and my work, they'll tell their friends.

Stepping inside, I take a look around. My eyes are instantly drawn to the coffee bar. It's made from what looks to be salvaged barn wood. It's gorgeous. Continuing my inspection of the place, I'm getting more than a little excited for this job. The owner has a good eye and I'm looking forward to leaving my mark behind with the custom display cabinet they want me to build.

I saunter up the bar and introduce myself to the girl working it. I'm just about to ask her if it's okay for me to head on back to speak with the owner when he claps me on the shoulder. "Mr. Carson. Right on time."

"Please, call me Cash," I tell him as we walk back to his office. We both take a seat and immediately start discussing his wish list for the cabinet he wants from me. "Well, Mr. Brooks, I really like the feel of this place, and I think a custom cabinet from me would fit the bill just right. Let me ask you a question real quick though..." He nods and I continue. "That wood on the bar, where's it from?"

"Ah, yes. That's wood from my great-granddaddy's barn. When it came time to re-roof the barn, we decided it wasn't worth the cost with none of us actually usin' it since he passed, so we saved all the wood we could. Got most of it, thankfully. In fact, I should have just enough left for you to build my cabinet."

My face splits into a wide grin. The thought of working with such old lumber has my heart speeding up just a bit. "Well, hot damn, that sounds amazing. You mind if I hang onto this wish list?"

"You go right ahead, son." Mr. Brooks secures his notes into a file folder and slides them across the table to me.

"All right, thank you very much. I'm just gonna take a few measurements and I'll be on my way."

We both stand and shake hands before going on about our business. He heads to his desk, and I make my way out to my truck to grab my tape measure and notepad.

I'm on my knees, bent over my notepad, muttering measurements and calculations to myself when I hear Myla Rose's angelic voice. I swear, I could pick that voice out of a damn crowd, no problem.

She's at the bar, presumably placing her order. Her back is to me, and I take advantage, letting my eyes slowly trail her from head to toe, lingering in all the right places.

Girl is too damn fine. Too bad I probably ruined any shot I had with her—even as a friend. Still, now is the perfect time to tuck tail and apologize.

She pays the barista and spins on her heel, scanning the coffee shop for a free table. Lucky me, the only free table happens to be right next to where I'm set up. I rise from my crouched position as she approaches. "Hello there, Myla Rose. How are you today?"

Her eyes widen, as if she's surprised to see me. "I'm doin' just fine, thanks for asking. How about you?"

"My good day just got even better," I reply as I pull her chair out and gesture for her to have a seat.

"Oh, um..." She's at a loss for words as I lower myself into the chair across from her.

"I wanna apologize for how I acted the other day. I was outta line, and I'm sorry. You think you can forgive me?" I hit her with my most charming smile.

Her cheeks turn that delicious rosy hue, making me

wonder just how far I could make the blush spread, making me wonder if that's how she looks when...

"Of course, Cash." Her words, spoken in such an unsure tone, derail my dirty train of thought, which is probably for the best because this isn't the time or place.

"You sure about that, Myla Rose?"

"Yeah, I'm sure. Everyone is entitled to a mistake or two." Her voice comes out crisp and clear, letting me know she means every word.

Thank God. The thought of this girl being mad at me—yeah, I'll pass.

"Well, good. I wanna make it up to you though." She starts to shake her head to refuse, but I just keep right on. "Please, let me take you out, Myla Rose. What's the worst that could happen?" I plead, hitting her with my best puppy dog eyes.

"Okay, I guess," she relents. *Hell yes!*

"Next weekend, Friday night?" She tells me that's fine with her, and we exchange numbers with the promise of finalizing plans later in the week.

Chapter Eighteen

Myla Rose

"Get up, get in the shower, and dry your hair, Myla Rose. I'm on my way, and if I don't hear the whir of your hair dryer when I get there, I swear I'll knock you into next week, pregnant or not."

I grumble and groan as I disconnect the call and set about following Azalea's instructions. She can be sweet as sugar, but she can also be downright terrifying. Twelve years of friendship have taught me that sometimes, it's best to let her have her way, and this seems to be one of those times. Plus, if she sees that I listened, maybe she'll cut me some slack and let me back out.

I mean, what on earth was I thinking telling him he could take me on a date? *Not a date, Myla Rose.* He said he just wants to make up for his rudeness the other day. And really, that's A-Okay with me, because as much as I hate to admit it, his abrupt change in attitude really hurt. Which is just plum silly. *Silly, silly, silly*. I rinse those thoughts away, along with the suds from my coconut-scented body wash.

After toweling off, I wiggle my way into a pair of cropped jeans and a merlot colored lace top. "No-no-no," I mutter as I stare at my reflection in horror when I hear the creak of the front door. "Myles!" Azalea's voice echoes through the house. "Why don't I hear your blow dryer?"

Maybe if I ignore her, she'll just leave...

"Do you want to wear your hair straight or in waves?" Azalea calls to me through the bathroom door.

"AzzyJo," I whine, "I'm not going, so it doesn't matter. Give me my phone so I can call him and cancel."

"No, ma'am. Not gonna happen." Her voice is firm, unrelenting. This girl is a total force to be reckoned with.

"Okay, then you call him. Tell him I'm sick. Something—anything," I beg.

She drums her nails against the bathroom door. "Come out and talk to me. What's got you all spun up?"

I shove the door open and stalk over to my bed, where Azalea is laid out like a cat sunning at high noon.

"Azalea Josephine Barnes, I cannot go anywhere lookin' like this." I stomp my foot for emphasis. "My jeans don't button, and this top makes me look like ten pounds of shit shoved into a five-pound bag. No, no, no, no!"

Azalea, to her credit, keeps her cool. She slowly assesses my outfit, her lips twitching as she tries not to laugh.

"Oh, Myla. Goodness gracious, you're not lyin'. Take that off and let me pick something out for you."

By the time I shimmy and jiggle out of the offending outfit, AzzyJo has a new one laid out on the bed for me.

"A dress? You want me to wear a dress?"

"Yes, a dress. Put it on and stop acting like I'm torturing you."

I slip the dress over my head and appraise my appearance in the full-length mirror hanging on my closet door. This time, I don't hate what I see. I look... nice.

The dress is a deep navy, almost the color of ink, and made from the softest cotton I've ever felt, and its A-line silhouette is super flattering. "Where did you find this?" I ask, my tone accusing, because I *know* it isn't from my closet.

She ignores me while I continue staring at myself in the mirror, turning every which way to check all my angles. I find no fault—I look *really* good. The dark color of the dress pops against my red hair and pale skin. *Damn her, why is she always right?*

She laughs, knowing she has me beat. "Told you so, and I found it at this cute little boutique across the bay and just had to get it for you. Sit down, I'll dry your damn hair for you, and as I asked earlier, straight or wavy?"

"I know I don't say this enough, but thank you, Az. From the bottom of my heart, thank you."

Chapter Nineteen

Cash

Myla Rose and I settled on six o'clock for our not-date. But damn if it doesn't feel like one. I even washed and waxed my truck. Which is why I'm five minutes past six pulling up to her house. Late. I'm fucking late. I scrub a hand over my face, hoping she doesn't hold my tardiness against me. I sure as hell don't need another tic in the *Con* column.

I take in her house in an entirely new light now. It was beautiful before—but knowing her Grandpa built it by hand...yeah, that blows my mind. As I approach the house, I really take the time to notice the detail, the trim and the intricate wood work on the porch. *Incredible.*

I rap my knuckles on the front door three times and wait. And wait, and wait. Girl's got a thing for not answering the door.

Finally, as I'm about to knock again, the door flies open, and I'm face-to-face with Azalea.

“Good evenin’, Azalea,” I greet her.

“Myla isn’t quite ready yet. You’re welcome to come on in and wait.” She opens the door wide enough for me to pass through.

She guides me to the living room, and just like outside, I take in the interior of the house with fresh eyes. I can almost hear the echoes of Myla Rose running up and down the steps as a little girl.

“Let me just run and check on her,” she tells me as I situate myself on the over-stuffed white loveseat.

I’ve been sitting here, waiting, for what feels like an eternity when I hear hushed voices from just outside the room. “Myla Rose, you get out there right now! That man is waitin’ on you!” I smile to myself, amused at her reluctance.

After a few more minutes, I hear them both approaching. It’s a good thing I’m seated when they come into view, because the sight of Myla Rose would have knocked me clear on my ass.

Her fiery locks are styled in long, cascading waves—it looks so pretty that I can’t help but want to mess it up, to run my hands through it and tug on it.

She may be petite, but in that short, flowy dress, her legs look like they go on for days. But what strikes me the most is that even without a lick of makeup, she glows. She shines so bright that everything around her dulls. It’s like I have tunnel vision, and she’s all I can see.

I stand and walk to her, not by choice, but by force. She’s reeling me toward her, and I’m helpless to stop it. I stop directly in front of her. "You look...absolutely radiant." She tilts her head down to hide the pink creeping up her neck and into her cheeks.

"Okay, you kids have a nice night now," Azalea says, ushering us out the door.

"So, where are we going?" Myla Rose asks as I steer us down her long driveway. I'm not gonna lie. I was looking forward to helping her up into the truck, but she had herself seated and buckled before I even had a chance. As hot as Myla Rose is, her independence is hotter.

"Well, I thought we'd head on over to Cotton?"

"The farm-to-table place?"

"That's the one." I sneak a glance in her direction, only to find her eyes lit up like Christmas lights. Guess she likes that idea.

"Oh, my stars! I have just been dyin' to try that place! I've heard they have the *best* steaks!" Her excitement is so damn cute that I don't even try to conceal the grin spreading across my face.

We fall into a comfortable silence, the tires spinning on the asphalt and the low hum of the radio the only sounds in the cab of the truck.

As I navigate the truck into a parking spot, I clear my throat to get her attention. "Now, Myla Rose, you wait for me to come around and open your door, yeah?"

"I'm more than capable—" she starts to protest.

"Never said you weren't, darlin'. Now, sit tight." I jog around to her side of the truck and open her door, extending my hand to her.

She hesitates but then takes it, her skin warm against mine. She hops down, her body sliding against mine as she does. *God, yes. More, please.*

"Oh! Look how pretty," she squeals as we approach Cotton.

She isn't wrong either. It's got some definite curb appeal. The restaurant is housed in an old white-washed brick building, the entrance framed by a pergola covered in jasmine.

Myla Rose stops just outside the pergola, an awestruck look on her face. "Cash, this is just...perfect."

She's right about that, too, except I'm not looking at the restaurant. I'm looking at her. Looking at the way she appreciates everything around her. I'm taken with the way the setting sun silhouettes her curves.

"Yeah, darlin', it sure is."

Missing the feel of her, I press a hand to the small of her back and guide her inside. We both stop to take it all in—marbled bamboo flooring, sage green walls, and wrought iron chandeliers.

Yeah, this is a place I'd love to do some work for. Maybe I'll try to snag a meeting with the owner.

The hostess leads us to a small two-seater in the back, which I requested when I called to make our reservation. Just like the other day at Dream Beans, I pull out her chair for her before taking the seat across from her. My hand feels empty and cool, instantly missing the heat from her body.

The hostess rattles off the specials and leaves us to look over our menus. I'm leaning toward the filet mignon served over broccolini, topped with truffle butter and a poached egg, when Myla Rose announces she wants the same thing. Girl's got good taste.

"I plan on having the filet as well. Must be fate." I waggle my brows at her, and she giggles at my joke, and goddamn, I'm intoxicated by the sound.

We place our orders and munch on some of the housemade rosemary bread while we wait. During this time, she asks me about the work I'm doing for Dream Beans, and I ask her about the salon. I'm impressed as hell that she owns a business at only twenty, and I tell her so. Her eyes shine with pride at my compliment, which only serves to make me want to compliment her more.

It's moments like these that really hit home for me what a rarity she is. Most women expect to be doted on, but Myla Rose takes nothing for granted—she's appreciative of even the smallest of things.

Our server places our meals before us and we waste no time digging in. The food is phenomenal. Even better? The little noises of delight she makes while eating it.

"So." I clear my throat before asking her, "How far along are you?"

I know most men would be put off by the fact that she's pregnant—and I'm not gonna lie, it threw me for a loop at first—but at the end of the day, the way she's making the best of being a young, single mom and her steadfast dedication to doing what's right for her baby only add to her appeal.

"Seventeen weeks, so almost halfway." She sounds less sure of herself now, like she isn't used to talking about her pregnancy—but with friends like Azalea, Simon, and Drake, I know that isn't the case. They may be more excited about the baby than she is.

"Have you always wanted kids?" I regret the words the second I speak them, and the pained look on her face only firms up my regret.

"Don't you go thinkin' I'm not excited for this baby because of what I'm about to say. Because I'm over the damn moon excited." Her expression is fierce.

"I'd never, darlin'."

"Things just aren't going as I always imagined they would, you know? Back in my skinned knees and pigtail days, I wanted the fairytale. I wanted to wear white and say, 'I do' with my very own Prince Charming. We were going to have it all...a picket fence and a porch swing. We were going to sip sweet tea and watch the sun set while our little ones played in the yard. In fairness, I'll still have most of that. My Prince Charming will just happen to call me ⊠Mama'."

"So, it's a boy?" The thought of a boy growing in her belly makes my heart beat a little faster. I'm instantly hit with visions of teaching him how to ride a bike and how to shave. *The fuck?*

"Yeah, a boy." Her eyes go all soft and dreamy—her love for this baby is palpable. I can feel it clear across the table.

"Got any names picked out?"

"Honestly? No. I didn't want to get too attached to a certain name and then meet my baby and have it not fit." She snorts out a laugh. "Wow, I sound a little crazy, huh?"

"Not at all, Myla Rose. Not one bit."

Our server comes back with the dessert menu, and we decide to share a slice of strawberry cheesecake.

I cut into the desert with my spoon, but before I can eat it, Myla Rose plucks a whole berry from the slice. I stare, transfixed, as she wraps her lips around it, a little juice dribbling down her chin.

"Mmmm," she moans, causing the spoon to drop from my hand and clatter to the table. The noises this girl makes are seriously lethal, and I don't even think she knows it.

I'm so enraptured with that little trickle of juice that it's literally like a bucket of ice water when she asks me, "So, what exactly was your deal the other day?"

I drop my head to my hands. I should have seen this coming a mile away. I was an idiot, thinking I could just sweep my behavior under the rug with no explanation.

"Ugh. This is harder than I thought." Massaging my temples, I try to relieve some of the tension that's accumulating. This is the first time I've really talked to anyone other than Jake about it. "My ex, Kayla, cheated on me. For almost half of our relationship. You're the first…*anything* since her."

Her eyes are wide with shock, and there may even be a little sympathy in there too.

"Cash, I am so, so sorry. I thought it was because of my being pregnant. But I think that'd make just about anyone gun shy."

"I hate that you thought it was you. You're so far from a problem, darlin'—baby and all."

The heaviness of the air around us dissipates a little when our server drops our check. After settling up, I help Myla from her seat, and once again pressing a hand to the small of her back, I guide her to the truck.

I help her in this time, and even though she protests, I know she likes my chivalry. Her lopsided smile is a dead giveaway.

I decide to push my luck and secure her seat belt for her as well. Her breath hitches when my shoulder brushes her chest, and I swear I even felt her nipples harden. All of these little sounds and touches have me wound tight—so tight that I fear I might explode.

"Dinner was amazing, Cash," she tells me as I turn down her driveway. "Thank you so much for taking me."

Why the fuck is she thanking me?

"No need to thank me, darlin'. I had a good time too," I tell her, throwing my truck into park.

"Okay, then. I guess...um...I'll see you around then?" She makes for the door handle, and I reach across the console to stop her.

"Hey! What did I tell you earlier?" I scold before heading around to open her door. "C'mon, I'll walk you."

She grasps my hand, and like an instant replay from dinner, her body slides down mine. The contact is somehow more intimate than it was earlier, making her cheeks turn a pretty shade of pink, only noticeable due to the moonlight peeking through the branches of the oak tree in her yard.

"Okay, Cash." Her voice is nothing more than a rasp.

We make it to the porch, and the inner battle begins. Is she expecting a kiss, or will she slap me for trying, what with how our last kiss ended? I war with myself a little longer before settling on a hug. A nice, safe hug.

"Well, goodnight then," she whispers, looking down as I start to pull away.

Is that disappointment I hear in her voice? *Well, hell.* I can't have that.

Keeping my right arm around her waist, I bring my left hand to her cheek, placing my thumb just below her jaw. Using that position, I pull her closer to me.

"It was a good night indeed, Myla Rose," I murmur just before I press my lips to hers.

Her lips are soft, *so damn soft*, even more so than I remember. I nip at her bottom lip, causing her lips to part. I use that small opening to deepen the kiss, and Myla Rose digs her nails into the base of my neck.

Slipping my hand from her waist and down over the curve of her hip, I hike her dress up and settle it on the smooth bare skin just under her ass, pulling her closer—closer—closer. Trailing my fingertips across her cheek and through her hair, I tug on it just a little, just like I'd imagined doing at the start of our night.

Damn, she likes that. It's like I flipped a switch. She's no longer kissing me—she's devouring me.

I hoist her up, and she wraps her legs around my waist. The front door is the only thing keeping us upright. I press my hips into hers, showing her just how much I want her before pulling her hair again. She throws her head back, hitting it on the door with a loud thump.

That breaks the spell. She lowers her legs and untangles herself from me, and I step back, unsure of what comes next. Is she going to ask me in or send me on my way?

"Do...do you want to come in?" She looks up at me expectantly.

"Lead the way, darlin'," I rasp out—because really, is there any other response?

She slides her key into the lock, and I follow her inside. "Do you want some coffee or tea?"

"No, I just want you." I settle myself into the same over-stuffed loveseat as before.

"Well, I need a drink of water—be right back."

While she's gone, I check my phone. A text from Jake and a few work emails, nothing that can't wait until later. I set my phone, keys, and wallet on the coffee table and wait for Myla Rose to return.

She approaches me hesitantly, as if she's now the one who's unsure of what comes next. I reach out and take her hands into mine and pull her closer so that she's standing between my legs.

"Don't be nervous, darlin'. I just wanna spend time with you, and I'm damn sure okay with it being on your terms." Just like that, she's relaxed and at ease.

I pull her closer still, causing her to tumble down onto my lap. I take full advantage of our new position and kiss my way up her neck before whispering in her ear, "This okay, darlin'?"

She squirms around on my lap a bit but nods. I know she can feel just how much I want her, so I press my hips up into hers. She gasps, and I shift her around so that she's straddling me before kissing my way back down her neck, peppering little open-mouth kisses along her collarbone.

Her breaths are shallow as she guides me back up to her lips. She traces my lips with her tongue, and I drag my hands up from her hips, caressing the outer swell of her breasts. Before long, our hands are exploring, and she's rocking against me as we're once again lost in each other.

Slowly, I break our kiss. I need to take things slow with Myla Rose. She deserves nothing less than the best. I run my hands through her hair and she drops her forehead to mine.

"You are so damn beautiful," I tell her as she stands

from my lap, looking dazed and content.

"Th–thank you, Cash." her cheeks are that sweet rosy hue, and I'm struck hard by the fact that even though she's pregnant, she's so damn innocent. That just solidifies my decision to slow us down—to take my time.

"Anytime, darlin'. You mind if I use your restroom?"

"Not at all. Down the hall, first door on the right."

I stand, adjusting myself as I go, which causes her blush to shift from rosy to red hot.

A splash of cold water to my face, and I'm good to go. Making my way back out to where Myla Rose is waiting for me, I stop dead in my tracks when I see her pacing the room...with *my* phone in her hands.

"Everything okay?"

"I don't know. Is it?" Her voice is like ice.

I rack my brain, desperately trying to figure out why she's upset with me. "You tell me, darlin'."

"I'm not your damn darlin', so cut the shit. I've gotta admit, you've got a hell of a good game going, Cash Carson. Long game too, huh?"

Another text rolls in and she drops my phone to the coffee table like it burned her. "I'm honestly not following. You've gotta help me out here."

"Why'd you take me out, Cash?" I walk over to her, slowly, not wanting to upset her even more.

"A few reasons..." I trail off when I see why she's so

angry. Goddamn it.

Jake: You take my advice, brother?

Jake: The best way to get over someone is to get under someone new.

Jake: Seriously, you hit that yet?

"Myla, it's not what you think—"

"Just save it. I'm not an idiot."

I slip my phone back into my pocket, panic and guilt rioting inside me.

"If you—if you'd just let me explain..."

"Let you explain what? That you're only with me to get laid? No, you can get out." She tosses my wallet and my keys at me and points to the door.

"Okay, I'll go...but this isn't finished." I roll my head from side to side, trying to release the mounting pressure. "Far from it. You be sure to lock up," I tell her before trudging back out to my truck.

Slamming the shifter into gear, I haul ass out of there, ready to tear my brother a new one. What the fuck was he thinking?

Chapter Twenty

Myla Rose

I stand there, staring out my front window, long after his tail lights disappear. After what feels like an eternity, I turn and head upstairs, making sure to lock up behind myself.

"Stupid-stupid-stupid-stupid," I mutter as I strip out of my dress.

"Stupid-stupid-stupid-stupid," I lament as I braid my hair and again as I brush my teeth.

Stupid-stupid-stupid-stupid, loops through my mind like a broken record until sleep finally finds me.

I wake the next morning, still feeling dejected. If I thought the Strawberry Festival was bad, it doesn't hold a candle to this. He was literally only interested in sleeping with me to get over his ex. All those sweet words...nothing more than lies. Here's history, repeating itself. *When will I ever learn?*

Fuck Cash Carson and his bullshit. I'm done.

Thankfully, Grams taught me a thing or two about making lemonade out of life's lemons.

"Lemonade, Myla Rose, lemonade." With my new mantra in mind, I decide to take the rest of the day to pamper myself, starting with a relaxing soak in the tub—lemon-scented bubbles and all. *Take that, universe.*

After doing a face mask and a deep conditioner, I call Azalea to see if she feels like getting in on all this goodness.

She doesn't answer, which is unlike her. Especially after my 'not-date' last night. Honestly, I half expected her to be beating my door down before the birds chirped.

So, I redial.

It rings and rings and rings. She answers just before her voicemail picks up.

"Hello? Myla?" She sounds winded, completely out of breath.

"What on earth are you doin'?"

"Nothing! Not a single thing!"

"Okay..." I know she's lying, but decide not to call her on it.

"Jesus. Can't a girl just be out of breath? Maybe I was exercising—did that ever cross your mind?" She's being downright defensive now.

"Nope." I snort. "It sure didn't."

"Yeah, you're right." She relents, sending us both into a fit of laughter. "Oh! So, how was last night with Cash?" she blurts, like she's just remembered that I had a...whatever last night was.

"Long story. Want to meet me at the nail salon, and I'll get you all caught up?"

"Well, duh." I can just picture her sarcastic smile. "When have I ever said no to a mani/pedi?"

I'm just about to agree with her when I hear a scuffle in the background. A scuffle—and a man's voice?

"Who are you with?" I ask, keeping my voice calm to keep her calm. She doesn't do so well with corners.

"What?" she shrieks, her voice several octaves higher than normal. "I'm not with anyone."

"You sure? I swear I heard a guy's voi—"

"Nope! No guy. See you in ten!" And just like that, she hangs up on me.

Well. Okay, then.

I'm soaking my feet, enjoying the magic of the massaging pedicure chair when Azalea flies through the door, looking rode hard and put up wet. She blindly grabs a polish and throws herself down into the chair next to mine.

Neither one of us speaks. She's looking at everything but me—literally everything. I ignore her, knowing eventually, she'll break.

After damn near ten minutes of awkward silence, I give up on waiting her out. "Azalea Josephine, what gives?"

"Whatever do you mean?" she inquires with all the

charm of a debutante. She even bats her lashes at me.

"Puh-lease, sister-girl. Take that shit somewhere else."

"Okay, fine." She inhales deeply, and with all her words running right together, she blurts, "ImighthavesleptwithDrake!"

"Huh?" I must have misheard her. Because there is no way she did what I think she said.

Another deep breath. "I slept with Drake. And it was amazing. And I loved it, every second. It was a one-time thing, and it'll *never* happen again. So, how was your night?" Her smile is tremulous, at best, and her tone brokers no room for negotiation.

"Last night was a shit-show," I deadpan. She raises a brow at me, silently saying *please continue, Myla.*

So I do. "It started out really, really good. He was such a gentleman, opening doors for me and walking with his hand at my back. He took me to Cotton, and the food was *delicious.* Like, oh-my-God good. We even ordered the same thing, and we shared a dessert. We talked about the baby, and Az, he seemed so interested and not at all put off by it. And he told me about his ex, and it just seemed like this could maybe lead to more one day." I sigh, thinking back on how amazing dinner was.

"I'm missing the bad part..." Her words cause my smile to drop, an ugly scowl taking its place.

"The bad part is what came after dinner."

I lean back harder into my pedicure chair and use the remote to ramp up the massage before releasing a long, drawn-out sigh.

"Okay, so we left Cotton and the drive back was fine. And by fine, I mean I was a hot damn mess on the inside. He not only helped me into the truck—he also buckled me in. I know, it sounds absurd, but when his shoulder brushed across me—hell, every time he touched me—my heart rate skyrocketed. When we got back to my house, he even insisted on walking me to the door! Taylor sure never did that."

"Yeah, well, Taylor is a douche-canoe." We both smile at that.

"That's when it got a bit weird. He leaned in, and I thought he was gonna kiss me. Again."

"You have this real knack for talking without ever saying anything, Myles."

I roll my eyes, even though she's right. I'm a bit long-winded, just like Grams. "Anyway, he didn't kiss me."

"So, what did he do?" God bless her, she's waiting for my next words like a dog waiting for a Milk Bone.

"He hugged me. So, yeah, I was a little disappointed—I guess I got my hopes up." AzzyJo's looking at me like I've spontaneously sprouted antlers.

"Cash must've felt bad or something, because *then* he did kiss me. And, girl, it went from zero to sixty, quick, fast, and in a hurry."

"How fast? More, Myla, I need more!" Seriously, you'd think the girl was watching Lifetime she's so entertained.

"I'm glad my humiliation is bringing you such joy," I

quip just as the nail technicians roll their stools over to our chairs. I hand her my polish, appropriately named *A Good Man-darin is Hard to Find.* Thank you, OPI.

AzzyJo hands over a dark mauve colored polish, a far cry from her usual. "No *Strawberry Margarita* today? What gives?"

"Just trying new things, Myla. Now, finish your story."

I eye her suspiciously before continuing, "Yeah, okay. So, super fast. From a peck to up against my front door in the blink of an eye fast." My voice is wistful, which just grinds my gears. *Get over it, Myla Rose. Remember that lemonade.*

"Nope, still not seeing the issue." She's smirking, like she knows how this ends.

"Well, once our kiss cooled down, I invited him in."

"You little hussy!"

"And things heated right back up." Tears are welling up in my eyes at just the memory of the texts on his phone. "The issue is that he went to the bathroom, and a few texts came through on his phone. I didn't even mean to look, Az. But they were awful, and they were about me."

"What do you mean, about you?" Her eyes are narrowed to slits and her tone is like steel.

"They were from his brother, asking if he had fucked me yet. Reminding him that the best way to get over his ex is to sleep with someone new."

"Are you kidding me? Please tell me you're kidding."

I try my hardest to blink back my tears, but a few spill

over, letting her know that I'm absolutely not kidding. Not at all.

"That dirty, rat-bastard motherfucker. Swear to God, Myles..."

"I've never felt so little, or so stupid, in my entire life. When Taylor broke up with me? Sure, it hurt, but I knew it was because he was an immature little asshole with no sense of responsibility. And when Mama left me? That hurt too, but I had my Grams to help me wade through the mud. This time, though...this time, it was all me. He thought I was gonna be his rebound. He figured he'd lead me on long enough to get in my pants and then hightail it out of there. Am I just too dense to read the signs? Because I was dumb enough to think a man like that would want someone like me?" My voice breaks and the floodgates open. I'm right back to where I was last night—*stupid, stupid, stupid.*

Azalea reaches over the arm of her pedicure chair and grabs my hand, squeezing it tightly. "What do you mean, someone like you?"

The outrage in her voice brings me a small slice of satisfaction. Whether she knows it or not, she's quite the Mama Bear.

"I mean a woman carrying another man's baby," I admit, feeling lower than the damn floor.

"I'm sorry, Myla. I'm sorry he hurt you. I really, really am." All I have for her is a watery smile. "But it's on him, not you. You didn't do a damn thing wrong. You know that deep down, right?"

Do I? Do I know that? I shake my head. "If you say so, Az."

My nail tech hands me a tissue to dry my eyes and cheeks with and tells us we can head over to the manicure stations. *Goodness gracious—because last night wasn't bad enough, now I'm crying in the nail salon.*

"You know what?" Azalea asks me as we get our nails polished to match our toes.

"What?" Now it's me, hanging on her every word, like I'm convinced that whatever she says next will be the answer to everything.

"Fuck him. That's what. Fuck him, and put him out of your mind, because it's his loss."

"Easier said, sister-girl."

"Don't you worry. I have a plan." I'm not sure what she has up her sleeve that will cure this heartache, but I'm willing to try anything. "We're gonna go shop for that sweet baby boy of yours. A little retail therapy will do the soul good."

"That sounds...perfect."

Chapter Twenty-One

Cash

Talk about a colossal screw-up. I was lucky to earn her forgiveness the first time—I'm not sure there's any coming back from this.

I was ready to charge straight over to Jake's last night, but I quickly realized Paige and the boys didn't deserve my busting down their door in the middle of the night.

This morning is a different story though—before a shower, before coffee, before anything, I'm hitting *Send* on a call to him.

"Have a good night, brother? That why you were too busy to text me back?"

"You sorry-ass motherfucker!"

"Say that again?"

"You heard me. Wanna guess who was holding my phone when your childish, bullshit messages came through?"

"Oh, shit."

"Yeah."

"Is it bad?"

"She kicked me out. Can't say I blame her."

"I really am sorry, Cash. I was only messing with you."

"Yeah, you sure messed something."

The sound of Jake tapping his fingers against his phone trickles through, along with his words. "How can I make this up to you?"

"Doubt you can, Jake. This was already my second chance."

"Well, let's hope she plays by the three-strike rule?" I end our call, already over this conversation. I know he didn't mean anything by his messages. I just wish *she* did too.

What I need to do is man up, call her, and apologize. But I'm scared. A fucking coward. Yellow-bellied. And I have no clue how to make this right.

Now, she's off thinking God knows what. Probably telling Azalea what a damn dog I am, surely glad things didn't go too far. Yeah, she's probably thanking her lucky stars and stripes that things didn't go further.

Who am I kidding? I saw the look of hurt and humiliation in her eyes. She may not be ready to listen to me, but I'm not willing to let her go without a fight.

Goddammit, I have to fix this.

I'm going to fix this. Now. Right fucking now. I fly through getting ready, jump into my truck, and head straight to Myla Rose's house. Face-to-face is better than a phone call.

I'm halfway to her house when I see the farmer's market has fresh flowers. Making a quick detour, I grab a bouquet, hoping it'll sweeten the pot.

Myla Rose's Land Cruiser is nowhere to be seen when I pull my truck to a stop under the shade of her oak tree. Getting out, I make my way to her front door anyway. I give the door two short taps. Nothing. I try again—four taps. Still nothing. With a dejected sigh, I turn to head back to my truck.

I'm just about to climb into the cab when I hear, "Cash? That you?" I stand, with one foot on the running board, allowing me to see over the roof. Simon is standing a few yards away, in a small clearing on the periphery of Myla Rose's yard.

"Yeah. Um, yeah," I tell him as I walk over to where he's...pulling weeds? "What are you up to?" I ask as I approach.

"Just clearing out these weeds." *Such a smartass.*

"Yeah. I see that. Why?"

"Why wouldn't I? It is my property."

"You live here? Like *here?*" Wonder why Myla Rose never mentioned it.

Simon grins and knocks his head back over his shoulder toward a log cabin-style house. "No, there. Moving on, why are you here? And what's up with the flowers?"

Well, shit. This is awkward. "I'm...well, Jesus...it's a long story. How much time you got?"

"Plenty. I got all my grading finished up last night.

Bring your truck on around to my place and I'll see you in a few."

I nod my agreement, but before driving over, I grab some scrap paper from my glove box and pen a quick note to Myla Rose, leaving it along with the flowers on her porch.

Here's hoping...

Right after I pull into Simon's equally long driveway, another truck pulls in behind me. *Great*. In the short time it took me to write my note and drive over, Simon had managed to call Drake and get him there as well. This oughta be fun...*not*.

"Cash-Man." Drake claps me on my shoulder. "Simon said he found you over at Myla's house?"

"Sure did."

He presses his lips together and makes a humming sound before opening the door to the house. "Okay. Let's head inside. You can tell us what's up. And don't try feeding us any bullshit. I've known you too damn long."

Following the scent of freshly brewed coffee, we find Simon in the kitchen pouring himself a mug. "So, you want to tell me why you were at Myla's place? On a Saturday morning, with flowers?" Simon keeps his eyes trained on me.

"I, uh. Well, I guess I need to start at the beginning."

They both nod, waiting for me to continue. "So, the other night at Azteca's, Azalea asked me to give Myla Rose a ride home..." I fill them in on bringing her home and helping her pressure wash the following day.

When I get to the part about our kiss at the Strawberry Festival, I'm prepared for chaos, but it never comes. Other than Simon cracking his knuckles, I'm met with silence. Like, you could hear a pin drop silence. That silence makes me nervous.

Clearing the cobwebs from my throat, I continue. "So, when I ran into her at Dream Beans last week, I asked her to let me take her out to make up for it. She agreed, and last night I took her to Cotton. Dinner was delicious. I mean, outta this world good. And Myla Rose, *damn*."

"Myla Rose, what?" Simon questions, his voice deeper than before.

"There's just somethin' about that girl. She gets under my skin."

Simon's fists clench. He repeats the motion, this time holding—with enough force to turn his knuckles white.

"After dinner, I drove us back to her place and walked her to the door. Being all gentlemanly and shit. We got to the door, and I was trying to read her, figure out what she wanted."

"The fuck you mean, 'What she wanted'?" Simon's voice has taken on a hard edge.

"Uh, I was trying to figure out if she wanted a goodnight kiss. I settled for a hug, but she seemed disappointed, so I went for it."

Simon is pacing the kitchen, the muscles in his jaw popping.

"You went for it? Just like that?" Drake asks, calm as ever. It's like *Body Snatchers* or some shit. Simon is acting a fool, and Drake is all but inscrutable.

"Yeeeaaah..." I draw out the word. "I did. But, the moment my lips touched hers, I was gone. Out of this world, out of my mind. All I could think was *mine* and *more.* Full-on caveman brain."

Simon stops his pacing and whips around to face me, his glare pinning me in place.

"So, yeah. It got...intense. Skipping to the end of the story—she asked me inside and saw a few texts on my phone from my brother asking me if I had fucked her yet—"

Before I can even finish my sentence, Simon is right there—right in front of me. He yanks me up from the barstool by the collar of my shirt and shoves me back into the wall.

"You even think about touching her, I'll put you down like a goddamn coyote. You hear me? Friend or not, my loyalty is to her."

Drake tries to pull him back from me, but it's no use, and I know he needs to say his piece.

"I mean it, Cash, I'll mess you up. She's had enough hurt to last a lifetime, and she doesn't need some jackass lookin' for an easy lay to mess with her head." He emphasizes that last little bit by tightening his grip on my shirt.

Looking Simon dead in the eye, I tell him what I never got the chance to tell Myla Rose. "I am *not* looking for an easy fuck. And if I were, it wouldn't be Myla Rose. You're right—that girl deserves the damn world, and I intend to be the one to give it to her."

My words must shock them as much as they do me because Simon all but drops me from where he had me pinned, and Drake is doubled over laughing so hard that he sounds like he's howling.

"What makes you think you're good enough?" Simon says, pushing me back into the wall.

"Honestly? I'm not. But I can't explain it...they say when you know, you know. I swear to y'all, I wasn't trying to hurt her. My brother's an asshole and thought he was being funny."

"Well, as entertaining as that was, let's all settle down, yeah?" Drake says once he's composed himself.

Shit's twisted when he's the voice of reason. Simon, however, doesn't budge.

"Gotta make sure he knows," Simon clips out. I can tell he isn't sure whether he should believe me or not.

"Listen, I know she's like a sister to you. I get that shit, and I respect it. But I also respect her. Hence, the flowers. I know those texts hurt her, and I want to apologize. I'm just not sure how." I let my words settle. His grip on my collar slowly loosens before his hand falls away completely, releasing me.

"I, for one, think y'all are perfect for each other,"

Drake says.

"How you figure?" Simon spits back.

"Cash has always wanted a family. He's good with kids. I know he'll treat her right. Steady income..." I tune them out as they discuss me like I'm not standing *right fucking here*. It's like I'm in the Twilight Zone.

"I'd say I'm sorry, but I'm not." Simon shrugs his shoulders.

"Yeah, no problem, man," I tell him, because honestly? I get it. If I had a sister, I'd go to bat for her too. Not to mention, that's more emotion than I've ever seen from Simon. Dude can go from Bruce Banner to Hulk in 5.2 seconds. "I need to find a way to say sorry for this shit. Got any ideas?"

They bend their heads together, whispering back and forth, once again like I'm not even there. After what feels like an eternity, Drake pops his head up and says, "Sure do. You're gonna build that baby of hers a crib."

"Y'all really think that'll work?" I question, my skepticism heavy.

"Know it will," Drake replies. Simon nods his agreement.

Chapter Twenty-Two

Myla Rose

"Azalea," I whine as I hobble behind her, my arms so loaded down with shopping bags that I'm not sure I can walk the five feet to the car.

"Oh, hush up and quit your fussin'. We're heading home now."

Azalea stops abruptly to check her phone, causing me to almost walk into her. *Again*. It feels like she's been on that damn phone the last hour or so non-stop. I'm about to ask her who's blowing up her phone when she bursts my peace and relaxation bubble.

"Oh, wait. We have one more place—"

"Are you kidding me? One more place?" I say, dropping the bags I'm lugging to the ground beside my car.

"No, ma'am, not even a little." She opens the car door and scoops up my shopping bags, tossing them into the backseat with hers. "Now, hand over your keys. I'll drive."

I do as she says, cranking the AC to high. "Wanna tell

me where we're going?"

"Sure, we're going to this sweet little furniture boutique."

"What? Why?"

"To look at cribs, Myla," she says like I'm as dense as a brick.

"Right, because why wouldn't we?" The sarcasm seeping from my pores goes unnoticed by Azalea as she haphazardly steers us out of the parking lot.

She drives for about thirty minutes, weaving in and out of traffic at breakneck speeds before we reach out destination. The sign reads *STORK: An Upscale Baby Boutique*. It's cute as can be but way out of my price range, I'm guessing.

I mean, I live nice and easy with what Grams left behind—the house and car were paid for and passed down as well. And yeah, the salon is profitable, but I can just feel it. This place is going to be outrageous. Plus, I'm officially building a nest egg for little man—college isn't cheap.

Everything inside STORK is luxurious. From the oh-so-soft new baby scent tickling my nose to the feel of the velvety soft blankets, this place is mom-to-be heaven.

The back of the boutique is divided into five small rooms, each one set up like a nursery. There are two girl rooms, two boy rooms, and one gender-neutral.

The third room is practically shouting *Myla Rose, come in, come see*. The walls in that room are an ivory color, *Swiss Coffee*, according to the plaque on the wall. But what really draws my eye is the crib. It's a farmhouse crib, if there ever was one, and I absolutely love it.

Walking further into the room, I trail my fingertips along the edge of the crib. I can just see myself laying my little man down to sleep in this bed. I can see myself watching over him in it as he snoozes—until I see the price tag.

Good gravy, it's almost $2500. They've lost their ever-loving minds. I can find something that'll do just fine at the big box store for way, *way* less. Even if I don't like it as much. *It's just a crib, Myla Rose.*

I turn to go and search for Azalea, only to find her standing in the entryway to the room I'm in snapping pictures. "Why're you taking pictures?"

"Memories, Myla. Memories."

"Sure, okay. You ready to go *now*?" I ask her. My earlier tiredness is hitting me hard all of a sudden.

"Yeah, let me check out really quick. You go on out to the car." She tosses me my keys, and that's that.

My head's resting against my seat with the air conditioner on high. I'm thumbing through notifications on my phone when a text from Simon pops up.

Simon: You okay, Myles?

Me: Yeah, I am. Why?

Simon: Just checking on you. Saw Cash outside your house this morning.

Me: What? Why was he there?

Simon: We'll talk later.

Why would Cash have been at my house? That's just the strangest thing. Before I can stew on it too much, Azalea throws herself into the passenger seat. Maybe she can make heads or tails of it.

"Simon just texted me and said Cash was outside my house earlier. That's weird, right?"

She's on her phone again, so she doesn't respond, her fingers flying across the screen faster than a hot knife through butter. I guess I'll just have to wait for Simon to tell me.

"Huh? What'd you say?" she asks me several minutes later.

"Nothin', AzzyJo. It's not important." I figure it's better not to get into with her. She'll have me thinking it means more than it does.

While she may not be much for romance in her personal life, she loves to set others up. Dogwood's very own Cupid.

After dropping Azalea at her car, I head home. I need to get the stuff from our shopping trip sorted, and then I plan on having a little chat with Simon McAllister.

I pull up to my house, beyond exhausted. A nap sounds like heaven. Then, I'll head over to Simon's house. Maybe I can talk Drake into coming over—two birds and whatnot.

I'm just about to slide my key into the lock when I notice flowers propped up against the door. What on earth?

Reaching down, I grab them and feel paper brush against my knuckles. I snatch the folded sheet of paper up from the porch as well and head inside. After lugging my shopping bags up to what will be the nursery, I plop myself, and the bags, down onto the floor.

The paper I'm holding looks like some sort of scrap paper. It's smudged and there's an assortment of numbers scrawled in the margin.

As I slowly unfold the note, I'm hit with the delicious, familiar smell of Cash Carson. Did he leave these flowers? The handwriting is masculine and messy. It looks slightly rushed, like he was in a hurry to leave—though I'm surprised he was even here.

> Myla Rose-
> Sorry for...everything. Again.
> Please know those messages weren't what you think.
> I'm just...sorry. I'm sorry.
> -Cash

The gesture's sweet, though I'm not sure I believe him. Those texts had surely meant something...right?

I snip the ends of the flowers before arranging them in an antique brass vase. I have always loved fresh flowers.

They just brighten up a room—that's what Grams always said, and it stuck.

Ever since she passed, I've made sure to have them in at least one room of the house. Though I haven't bought any since being pregnant. Turns out that my little bean didn't share my fondness for fresh flowers for the first bit of my pregnancy.

Thankfully, my sensitivity to fragrance hit the road, along with my morning sickness, a while ago. *Lord, yes*. And now, I can start back up with my flower habit.

Carrying the vase out to the dining room, I place the arrangement in the center of the table. As much as I hate to admit it, he picked some really pretty flowers. An assortment of wildflowers, and you guessed it—roses.

It's like the man has insider information on the things I love or he's an incredibly lucky guesser. Whatever. I'll send him a thank you note and call it a day. I have no desire to play with the fire that is Cash Carson. None whatsoever, at least that's what I'm telling myself.

Chapter Twenty-Three

Myla Rose

I wake from my nap, not necessarily tired, but cranky as all get out. What should've been a peaceful and relaxing sleep ended up being filled with restless dreams of Cash.

Yes, dreams. Plural.

One about how our night could have ended if I hadn't seen those vile texts. Another about him being my little bean's daddy instead of Taylor. And oddly enough, a dream about him taking me to...a drag race? Beats me. All I know is that he needs to vacate my damn mind before I lose it.

Tapping out Simon's number, I hit *Send*, waiting impatiently for him to pick up.

"Myles! What's up?" He sounds really...excited. Wonder what that's about. One more thing on the list of shit he and I need to talk about, I guess.

"Hey, Sim, can I come by?"

"You know my door's always open for you. Come on, girl. D's here too."

"Oh? Perfect, that's perfect. I have somethin' for y'all. Be over in a few."

Disconnecting the call, I fly back up the stairs to fish out Drake's and Simon's gifts. I've been thinking of a good way to tell the boys that they're getting a nephew, and I know I've struck gold with this plan.

"Eww-eww-eww!" A shiver of revulsion runs through my entire body as I hop my way through the field between our yards. I need to talk to Simon about cutting this clearing down a bit.

The cool evening breeze only intensifies the feeling of the dewy grass licking at my ankles, and there is nothing I hate more than wet grass. Except for maybe my ex. Yeah, he's high on the list.

I'm just about to walk into Simon's house when the door flies open...

Bringing me face-to-face with Cash. Neither of us speaks. He stares down at me, and I stare up at him, my thoughts going a thousand miles a minute. *Why is he here? Why was he at my house? Why is he looking at me like that?*

After a few moments, the Southern manners my Grams taught me kick in. "H–hello, Cash. Thank you very much for my flowers. They're beautiful. Have a nice night." I slip between him and the opening in the door.

"Sure thing, darlin'. You do the same," he says over his shoulder before pulling the door shut behind him.

There's something about that man calling me darlin' in that deep, rough voice of his. *Gracious*, it almost makes me come undone. Which is *bad, bad, bad*. Cash Carson is a no-good dog, sexy voice or not.

I linger in the entryway, trying to get my bearings and calm my thoughts. Two deep breaths, in and out, and I'm feeling a bit more put together.

"Boys," I shout, way louder than necessary.

"In the livin' room, Myles," Simon shouts back, equally loud.

I'm met with the sight of Simon and Drake bickering quietly over something—probably some SEC football nonsense. Ignoring both of them, I set my tote bag on the coffee table and retrieve their gifts from it.

"What are y'all talking about?" I ask, dropping the packages into their laps, causing them both to stop and look at me.

"Nothin' of any importance. Now, what're these?" Drake asks, gesturing to the tissue paper-wrapped bundles.

"Well, why would I tell you when you can just open it and see?"

That's all the encouragement they need, because the next thing I know, tissue paper is flying.

"Myles, why did you buy us—"

"Drake, shut your trap and look closer," Simon interrupts, his voice thick with emotion.

Drake does as he's told, taking in the words embroidered across the onesie: *UNCLE DRAKE'S*

WINGMAN.

"It's a boy? You're havin' a boy?" I nod, my smile out of control.

"Well, hot damn!" Drake exclaims as he grabs hold of my wrist, pulling me down onto the couch between him and Simon, where they swallow me up in a bear hug.

I wiggle out of their arms and settle in for the long haul. I'm sure they have questions. I know I do, and I'm gonna get some damn answers.

"Kid got a name yet?" Simon asks, trying to discreetly wipe the moisture gathering in his lashes on his shirt sleeve.

"Nope," I say popping the 'P'. "Figure I need to meet him first."

"Drake! Name him Drake." I laugh and shake my head no, causing Drake to pout. Which only makes me laugh harder.

"Drake Collins, you're enough trouble on your own. The world don't need two of you," I tell him once I catch my breath.

"Now, boys, let's get down to business." I school my features, trying to look stern and serious.

As much as I want to question Drake about Azalea, I don't. She'd kill me if I told him I knew they hooked up, and obviously, he doesn't want me to know. So, I swallow those questions down and focus on getting some answers about this morning.

"Why was Cash Carson at my house?"

"He said he was coming to apologize, but you weren't

home. Said y'all went on a date." Drake trails off.

"We may have," I hedge. "Well, not really. He was only taking me out to say sorry for the other time he was an ass. See a pattern emerging?"

"I'm not sure two times makes a pattern, Myles."

"I dunno, Simon. Two times seems legit. Is there a formula for that shit or something?" At least Drake has my back.

"Yeah, actually. They say it takes three to make a pattern."

"Who is *they*?" Drake questions him, doubt evident in his tone. Simon just shrugs his shoulders before kicking his feet up onto the coffee table.

"Not the point, D." Simon scoffs before turning to look at me. "Myles, you know we have your back, right? Cash is cool and all, but if he hurts you, we'll—"

I cut him off with a snort-laugh. "Y'all know y'all are idiots, right?"

"Sure enough," Drake agrees.

"Totally," Simon adds.

"Plus, I can handle Cash just fine on my own."

"Handle him how?" Simon asks, sitting up board straight.

"Chill out, Sim." I can't help but smirk at his over-the-top big brother act.

He's always been fiercely protective of me. Honestly, I'm surprised he didn't manage to scare Taylor off—not for lack of trying.

"Y'all wanna order pizza and watch a movie?" I ask,

trying to change the subject.

Drake and Simon agree, and I snatch up the remote before either of them can put on some dumb sports movie.

I must've fallen asleep during the movie at some point. One second, I was laughing at the antics on screen and the next, Drake is nudging me with his elbow, whispering for me to wake up.

I glance around the room, trying to find my phone, but I come up empty.

"D, what time is it?" I ask through a yawn.

"It's two thirty. Simon went to bed. Want me to drive you home?"

"Yeah, sounds good. Help me find my phone?"

"It's in your bag. I gathered everything up when I woke up a few minutes ago. I guess we all fell asleep."

"Thanks, Drake," I tell him as I try to haul myself up off the couch.

This baby bump, I swear it gets bigger every day. After watching me struggle for a few moments, Drake extends his hand to help me up, chuckling all the while.

"Thanks, asshole," I snap, even though we both know I'm not mad. I'd laugh too if I were him.

We walk out to his truck, and he holds my bag for me as I climb up into the cab. There's something to be said for Southern men.

We're silent on the quick drive to my house, both too tired to make small talk, but when I go to get out the truck, Drake stops me. "Hey, Myla?"

"Yeah?" I ask him as I hop down from the truck.

"Cash is a good guy. Give him a chance."

Chapter Twenty-Four

Cash

Don't forget to stop and pick up a bag—"

"Of ice. I know, Mom. I'm almost to the store." Love my mom, but damn. Every Family Dinner Night, it's the same routine.

"Oh, good. You know how I worry. Okay, sweetie, see you soon."

"Hey, Mom!" I call out, hoping I catch her before she disconnects the call.

"Yeah?"

"Will Preston and Lucas be there tonight?" I'm feeling like ice cream, and if the twins will be there, I'll need to pick up some magic shell topping as well.

"As far as I know."

"Great, thanks, Mom. See y'all in a few." I hang up and toss the phone into the cup holder.

Even though I only need to hit the ice cream topping aisle, I find myself strolling through Piggly Wiggly, just praying for a certain redhead to crash into me again. It's been almost two weeks since I left the note on her porch, and aside from a very to-the-point *Thank you* text and our stilted passing at Simon's, I haven't heard a peep from her and it's killing me.

Unfortunately, luck's not on my side today. Grabbing the shell topping from the shelf, I toss some sprinkles into my basket for good measure before making my way to the checkout area.

I'm waiting in line as the cashier bags up the order from the woman in front of me, listening as the she chats on her phone all the while. I'm not even trying to listen, but she's talking so loudly I don't really have a choice.

"Ma'am," I say, inserting myself into her conversation. "I wasn't trying to eavesdrop, but I heard you mention you were lookin' for a new buffet?"

She tells the person on the phone to hold on before turning to face me. She has this pinched lemon look to her, but I keep on. "I only ask because I have a custom carpentry business—Carson's Custom. I'd love to give you a card. You can visit my website and give me a call if you like what you see."

"Well, I suppose that would be okay, young man. Your name?" she asks, looking down her beak-like nose at me.

"Cash Carson. Nice to meet you, Mrs....?" I fish out a business card while I wait.

"Mills, Kathy Mills." She takes the card I offer but doesn't shake my hand. *Okay, then.*

She turns back to the cashier and snatches her receipt

with a rushed *Thank you* before returning to her call. "Sorry, Phil, this young man..." the automatic doors close behind her, preventing me from hearing the rest of her sentence.

"Okay, sir, your total comes to five dollars and—"

"Oh, hey! I need to add a bag of ice, please," I say, cutting her off. I'm on a daggum roll interrupting people today.

"Yes sir, that brings your total to seven dollars and fifty-five cents. Cash or card?"

After I finish checking out, I grab my bag of ice and head on to Mom's house. I'm sure that after walking the aisles like some hopeful, love-struck teenaged idiot hoping to run into the girl he likes, everyone's well past waiting on me.

As predicted, everyone's sitting around the table waiting on me when I walk in.

"Sorry to keep y'all—had to grab a few things from the store," I say, taking my seat in between the twins.

"Sumfin good for us, Uncle Cash?" Preston asks.

"Yeah, is it?" Lucas echoes.

"Might be. Now, settle down." I ruffle their already messy hair. "You boys need haircuts. Y'all are lookin' like ragamuffins."

"I've been telling Jake to take them to the barber for weeks, Cash. But, does he listen?" Paige says, her exasperation backed by an eye roll and a huff.

"Gotcha. Why don't you just take them to the salon in town?" I ask her.

"Oh, I don't want to bother them with my wild boys."

"Wild? They're perfect angels," my mom interjects.

God bless her, she sees the good in absolutely everyone. Not to say my nephews aren't good—they're just boys, and all boy at that. Paige isn't too far off calling them wild, but what six-year-old boys aren't?

"Nah, the girls at the salon wouldn't mind," I say confidently. I'm one hundred and ten percent sure they'd be great with Preston and Lucas.

"Yeah?" Jake asks, looking too smug for his own good. "You'd know, wouldn't you, Cash?"

I'm not sure what his game here is, but he needs to stop. There's no sense in bringing Myla Rose up to Mom. Especially now.

"What are you blabbing on about, Jacob?" Mom asks.

"Oh, nothing, just...y'all know Cash is seeing the owner of Southern Roots?"

Mom's fork clatters against her plate. Paige stops with hers halfway to her mouth. Thankfully, the twins are too busy flicking peas at one another to be bothered with this conversation.

"Cash Michael Carson." *Oh, shit, she full-named me.* "You have a girlfriend?"

"Mom, no—"

"A girlfriend you haven't ever mentioned? One I haven't even met? A girlfri—"

This insanity has to stop. "MOM! I don't have a girlfriend. I promise."

"You want her to be your girlfriend," Jake tosses out. Apparently, he's feeling real helpful tonight. I'm *this* close to throwing him under the bus with Paige.

"You know what? You're right. I'd love nothing more than to date her. But thanks to you, she won't even speak to me. Wanna get into why?" I can feel my blood pressure rising. Damnit.

"You're getting awfully upset over this, Cash. That's not like you," Mom says in that soft, soothing way only a mom is capable of. "There's obviously something. Tell me about her."

"Fuuuu..." I clear my throat. "All right. Her name is Myla Rose. She owns the salon in town with her best friend. She's really good friends with Drake. We've spent some time together, and like I keep saying, your *other* son ruined any chance I had with her." I'm trying my hardest to keep my anger at bay. It's a battle to not be mad at Jake over this to start with, and with the smarmy way he's acting? I'd say it's a losing battle.

"Jacob Paul, what did you do?"

"Mom, it's really nothing—a misunderstanding."

I snort my disbelief. "Of epic fucking proportions."

"Cash Michael, you watch your mouth!" Mom smacks the back of my head.

Twenty-four years on this earth, and my mother still scolds me like a child, God love her. "Yes, ma'am. Sorry."

Jake chuckles, which causes Paige to smack the back of

his head. "I swear, Jake, y'all act like children sometimes. I mean, the twins are behaving better right now."

"What did you do to cause a rift between Cash and his girlfriend, Jake?"

I'm looking down at my lap, just waiting to see what story he spins. Though, I guess I shoulda been looking at him. Then, maybe, I'd have known this was coming.

"Did I mention she's pregnant?" He casually throws it out there, almost like he's trying to deflect from the shitstorm he caused with her. Because he fucking is...*asshole*.

I'm not ashamed that she's pregnant. *Hell, no*. I think she's strong as shit—willing to go it alone and raise that baby. It's actually a bit of a turn-on...like everything else about her. *Jesus, I gotta get a grip on this shit.*

"Oh, she's...expecting?" Now, most people would be waiting for some judgey remark to fall from my Mom's lips, but I swear, the woman's a damn saint. "Well, isn't that wonderful? Babies are a gift from God." Her eyes are all watery, like she's just been told she's getting another grandbaby.

Oh, shit. That train needs to pull right back into the station.

"Yeah, Mom, it is. For her. Not us. Not you. Myla Rose is my...well, my nothing now. She's my nothing." I cut my eyes at Jake.

"Sure, sure. Of course," she says.

"But you want her to be more?" Mom's tone is feathery soft. It's also a front. She's trying to lull me into a false sense of security so I'll open up and spill my heart to her.

Like I said, these people are hounds, and now they have a scent to suss out.

"All right, let's leave Cash be," Paige scolds, though by her smile, I can tell she's enjoying this just as much as they are.

"Yeah, let's leave Cash alone. Lord knows he's too sensitive—"

Paige cuts her eyes to Jake. "Oh, you hush up, Mister. Don't think you're off the hook. Because you're not. We'll be talking later about your part in all of this." Jake sinks into his chair with his mouth and eyes turned down, looking very much like a scolded puppy.

Over this conversation, I stand to start clearing the table. As I'm walking into the kitchen, I hear my mom ask, "Now what salon does she work at again?" Paige tells her the name before glancing up at me and lowering her voice before continuing. Mom's reply to whatever Paige said is just as hushed.

"Cash, baby," Mom yells. "Why don't you load the dishes tonight?" Because that's not at all obvious.

"Sure thing."

I load the dishwasher the exact way I know she likes it, dry my hands, and make my way back out to the dining room—only to be met with a roomful of shit-eating grins. *I'm in trouble.*

"Cash," Paige starts, puppy-dog eyes in full effect, "I totally forgot that we have to go out of town this weekend. Is there any way you could watch the boys?"

"I would, but I have work all weekend," Mom throws

out.

I scrub a hand over my face. I know a setup when I see one. "Sure, Paige, I'll keep the boys."

"Great!" she exclaims. "Oh, and one more thing... think you could take them for a haircut?" Her smirk is now every bit as devilish as her husband's.

"Mmm. Sure thing."

"Uncle Cash, we gets to meet your girlfriend?" Preston asks. The twins were so quiet throughout dinner, so focused on their food. I figured they weren't listening. They're like little sponges.

"Not my girlfriend, bud, but yeah, you'll get to meet her."

He turns to Lucas, and they start doing that weird twin thing where they communicate with blinks and nods—Lord only knows what they're saying.

"Yes, ma'am, Mrs. Mills, I'm so glad you reached out," I say into my phone.

"When would you be available to take measurements, Mr. Carson?" she asks, proper as can be.

I toggle over to my calendar app before replying. "Well, I'm about to pick up my nephews to keep for the weekend, so how about..." I scan my schedule, just to double-check. She doesn't seem like the type of woman to forgive mistakes. "Tuesday afternoon around three thirty?"

"I suppose that will work. Do you have a pen and paper on hand to take down my address?"

"Yes, ma'am, I'm ready when you are." I jot down the street number and name before ending the call with the promise to confirm her appointment at least twenty-four hours in advance. I'm already regretting giving this lady a card, but work is work, and work leads to money.

Not to mention, she seems like the kind of lady who knows people, and that could be very beneficial for Carson's Custom. So I'll grin and bear it.

Once Mrs. Mills is added to my schedule, I check the time and gather up my stuff to head home. It's just after lunch, but Jake and Paige will be by around two with the boys, so I'd better make sure the house is kid-ready.

Sure enough, at two o'clock on the dot, my doorbell starts buzzing. And buzzing. And buzzing. There's just something about kids and doorbells.

I unlatch the door, and before anyone can say a word, the twins are wrapped around me, trying to wrestle me to the floor. "Uncle Cashmere, we stronger, we gonna beat you!" Preston shouts, warrior-voice in full effect.

"Yeah, prepare to be defeasted!" Lucas growls, backing his brother.

I wrap an arm around each of their waists, hoisting them over my shoulders. "Bud, I think you meant defeated."

"That's what I saids!" Lucas protests.

"Boys, let your uncle breathe. Y'all have all weekend. Now head on inside," Paige admonishes as she walks up from the car, a blanket and stuffed animal bundled in each arm. A few seconds later, I hear the trunk slam, and Jake walks around from the back of their SUV, wheeling two small suitcases behind him.

"You can just leave those by the front door. I'll get them settled in a bit," I say, gesturing toward the pint-sized luggage.

"Will do. Y'all got big plans? You know, other than their haircuts?"

"I swear, I oughta knock that smirk right off your face."

"Yeah, okay. All talk, baby brother. For real, though, y'all have fun."

"But not too much fun," Paige says. "And don't forget bedtime is at eight. Please make sure they brush their teeth—"

"Mom!" Preston whines, "Uncle Cash knows dis stuff."

"Yeah, just go!" Lucas chimes in. These boys always have each other's back. I love it.

"I'm just trying to spare Uncle Cash from y'all's dragon breath—it ain't no joke," she retorts before flapping her arms like wings, roaring like a dragon. "Come give me hugs. Dad too, and be good. We love y'all." She and Jake both kneel, wrapping the boys in a big group hug.

"Be back Sunday. Don't call unless someone is dying," Jake shouts as they walk out the door, earning him a smack from Paige. I just smile and tell them we'll be fine before closing the door.

"All right, boys. What's first?" I ask the twins once we hear their parents drive away.

"Nerf guns!" they shout in unison.

"Nerf guns," I echo, heading to the hall closet where I keep the toys for when they visit. "Got a few new ones too." Preston and Lucas come running behind me so fast, they skid into each other when they try to stop. They're jumping up and down like they have springs in their shoes, grabby-hand-mode activated. "Now, y'all know the rules. No shooting them inside, and no face or junk shots. Got it?" They nod. "Good, let's go!"

Forty-five minutes later, we're all worn slap out. Those two go hard, that's for damn sure. "Okay, what's next?" I ask them between sips of ice water.

"Haircuts?" Preston asks, his sly grin so much like Jake's.

"Yeah, so we can meets your girlfriend?" Lucas chimes in.

"Guys, she's not my...never mind. Let me see if they have time, okay? Because y'all for sure need haircuts."

Heading inside, I dial Southern Roots, refilling my ice water while I wait for someone to pick up.

"It's a glorious Friday here at Southern Roots. This is Seraphine." Her greeting causes me to chuckle. Girl's got spunk.

"Hello there, Seraphine. This is Cash Carson."

"Well, well, well. How may I help you, Mr. Carson?" she drawls into the phone.

"I was hoping to set up haircuts for me and my two

nephews. Any time available this weekend?"

"Hang on, let me check..." I hear her clacking away on her keyboard. "You're in luck—I can squeeze two of y'all onto Myla Rose's book, and one onto Azalea's if y'all can do 10:45 tomorrow mornin'?"

"Yes, please, put us down. Do you need their names or anything?"

"Yep, sure do." I rattle off their names, and then she hits me with, "Now, I have *you* and Preston down with Myla and Lucas down with Azalea. We'll see y'all tomorrow." Something about the way she emphasized my name has my gears turning.

I rinse my glass in the sink and grab the boys each a popsicle before rejoining them in the backyard. "Okay, we're all set to get haircuts tomorrow mornin'."

"We gots to wait all the way to tomorrow?"

"Yep, all the way until tomorrow, bud." And damn, tomorrow can't come fast enough. To say I'm anxious to see Myla Rose is an understatement. Other than our stilted exchange at Simon's and a quick 'thanks for the flowers' text, I haven't heard from her at all.

So, tomorrow, I find out if my olive branch was enough to at least earn me an attempt to get back in her good graces.

Chapter Twenty-Five

Myla Rose

"Myla, don't kill me, but..."

"But what, Seraphine?"

"I booked you two more haircuts tomorrow."

"Okay, that's no biggie. I only have Mrs. Cumberland, so I have room."

When Azalea and I opened Southern Roots, we decided to only do half a day on Saturdays—and with how busy I've been lately, combined with how tired this little bean keeps me, I'm glad for it. "Are they new or repeat?"

"Both?" Seraphine replies, wringing her hands together.

"Okay...you're acting ten kinds of crazy. What gives?"

"I booked you Cash and his nephew," she confesses.

"Oh." My nightmare of a date with Cash is common knowledge at the salon, so I can see why she's hesitant. *Lemonade, Myla, lemonade.*

"All right, still no big deal. Thanks for letting me know." Cool, calm, and collected may as well be my middle name—never mind that my left eye keeps twitching.

"Uh, yeah, no problem." She doesn't look convinced that I'm okay with her booking him.

But, I am. *I totally am.* Oh, bless it, I can't even convince myself, much less someone else. There is just something about him that I can't shake. And I need to shake it, pronto.

Like, by tomorrow. I can't pinpoint what exactly it is about him. I mean, he just does it for me. Which is ab-fucking-surd, especially since he only wanted to get some.

Yet, I constantly find myself thinking about the lazy way he drawls out my name, as if he's savoring every letter. At night, I dream about the feel of his strong hands and his heart-stopping smile. *Snap out of it, Myla Rose*

"Hey, I'm sure you already know, but AzzyJo—"

"I did what, now?" Azalea sasses, inserting herself into the conversation.

"Well, I was trying to tell Seraphine that you called her cousin to set up an interview."

"Yes! Mags mentioned it when we talked the other day." Seraphine's smile is so wide her cheeks look like they might split.

"I bet you'll be glad to have her here, huh?" Azalea asks.

"I really am. It'll be nice to have a little help taking care of Daddy, that's for sure."

"Heard that. When Grams got sick, I wouldn't have made it without the help of Az and the boys, that's for damn sure. You know we're here if you need help, right?"

God bless Seraphine, she's tough as damn nails. Her mama, much like mine, ran off, which is what brought us together. Her daddy, on the other hand...the man's got a heart of gold.

Unfortunately, that heart's failing him, and Seraphine's doing her best to take care of him. She graduated high school last summer and has been working for us at the salon because the hours match up to when his nurse can be there. But I know she wants to do more than be a receptionist for us. She's just biding her time. One day, I know that girl will spread her wings and fly. I mean, fucking fly—she'll do great things.

"I know, but y'all have your own things going on." We both dead-eye her, causing her to add, "Seriously, with the nurse and Mags arriving next week, I've got a good handle on things. But if it ever feels like too much, I promise to call y'all first, okay?"

Azalea and I both nod, finding her answer up to par.

"So, what were y'all discussing before all of these emotions got involved?" Azalea asks.

"Well, I was tellin' Myla that I added two haircuts to her book tomorrow. Speaking of, I added one to yours as well. Lucas Carson at 10:45."

"Lucas Carson? Never heard of him." AzzyJo tilts her

head to the side as if she's trying to reach deep for a face to put with the name.

"You wouldn't have. He's a kid. You know his uncle though."

"His uncle?" She tilts her head the other way. Seraphine and I stay silent, knowing she's only seconds from connecting the dots. "Oh! No way!"

"Yes, ma'am, and he's on Myla's book along with his other nephew."

"You good with that, Myles?"

"Mmm, sure thing. Can't friggin' wait."

"You ready for today?" Azalea asks as we go about setting the salon up for the day.

"Why wouldn't I be?"

"Hey, I'm just asking—"

"Good mornin', ladies," Seraphine sing-songs as she walks into the salon.

I twirl around at the sound of her voice. "Hi. You're off today—what gives?"

"Oh, like I'd miss today," she replies, and I roll my eyes and Azalea snorts. "And I brought coffee. You're welcome."

She sets a to-go cup on each of our stations before marching back to the dispensary. Azalea shoots me a look full of amusement before picking up her coffee and following Seraphine.

I reluctantly follow suit. "Are y'all ever going to stop giving me shit about him? I mean, my stars alive."

They exchange a knowing look, and Azalea asks, "Did you ever let him explain himself?"

"She's right, you know?" Seraphine quips. "You should hear him out and then decide if you wanna be mad."

"No, no, no. I'm not mad. Not one bit. We hung out a few times and went on one date. Turns out we weren't on the same page." *Minimize and hide those feelings, girl.* "Sure, I hate that he led me on, but we're both adults and capable of acting like it. He left a note saying sorry, and I just wanna let the past be, got it? I mean, it's not like I'm pining away for him." I slap a hand to my forehead—*why did I say that*?

"Aren't you?" AzzyJo fires back.

"Ugh, forget this." I check the time on my phone. "This conversation is finished. It's time to open." I snatch up my coffee and stomp out to my station.

I know I'm overreacting, but still. My grand exit has me feeling a bit better, and I know chatting with Mrs. Cumberland will finish the job. That woman is a ball of energy and so full of life, it's impossible to be anything but happy in her presence.

Just what I need before *his* haircut.

Azalea and Seraphine file out behind me, and Seraphine drops her gaze to the floor as she walks past me on her way to the front desk.

Great, now I feel bad.

"You know we were only messing with you, right?"

Azalea asks. "No need to pitch a fit."

She walks away and joins Seraphine at the front desk before I can even form a reply. Looks like I'll need to add groveling to my to-do list today.

"Oh, Myla Rose, this color is just a little slice of heaven. Exactly what I was goin' for!" Mrs. Cumberland exclaims when I spin her to face the mirror after blowing her out.

I lightened her hair up a bit to blend out those *pesky silver strands*, as she calls them. But God bless her, you'd think I'd performed a miracle with how excited she is over it.

"I'm glad you like it. And you should definitely be able to go a week or two longer between touch-ups."

"You know, with this new color, maybe I'd like a new cut as well? What do you think?"

"I think you'd look amazing with some soft layers around your face and maybe a side-swept bang."

"Well, that sounds like a whole lotta gibberish to me, but I trust you."

I section her hair for how I'd like to cut it while she tells me about this new recipe she found on Pinterest. Except, she calls it Pin-Interest every time she mentions it. I'm fighting hard to hold back my smile—she's just too cute.

The door chimes as I'm about to snip the last section

of her bangs, and Mrs. Cumberland pulls her head back from me.

"Myla Rose, would you take a look?" Her eyes are laser-focused on the front desk. "That man is a cool drink of water on a hot day. I mean, gracious, if I were single and maybe twenty years younger..."

I chance a peek over my shoulder and see Cash standing there, nephews in tow.

"Yes, ma'am, he sure is something, all right." I run my flat iron through her bangs to smooth out the marks my clips left behind and once again swivel her to face the mirror. "Here you go. What do you think?"

"Oh, Myla Rose, this is perfection personified. I just love it!"

My smile is beaming. This is why I do hair. There is nothing better than making someone love what they see in the mirror.

"I'm glad you like it, Mrs. Cumberland. When you set up your appointment with Seraphine, remember to have her book it out two weeks later."

"I sure will," she says before wrapping me into a tight hug. The kind of hug a mom gives—the kind I'll give my little man.

Chapter Twenty-Six

Cash

PRESTON, LUCAS—SHOES ON AND TO THE TRUCK. We don't wanna be late for our appointment."

"We's waiting on you, Uncle Cash," Preston informs me as I walk into the living room, and sure enough, both boys are on the couch, ready to go.

"Okay then, let's go," I tell them, grabbing my keys from the hook by the door. They hop off the couch and race out the door, neck in neck the whole way.

"SHOTGUN!" Preston yells loud enough for the whole damn neighborhood to hear.

"Try again, little man. It's the backseat for both of y'all."

"But Dad lets—"

"Your dad isn't here, dude, and your mom left strict instructions. What Mom says, goes." I open the back door and make sure they're both properly buckled before getting us on the road toward Southern Roots.

It's only about a fifteen-minute drive, but in those fifteen minutes, they've asked every question known to man. From *Why is the sky blue?* to *Where do babies come from?* I swear, I've never been so glad to see a hair salon.

"Now listen," I tell them as we approach the door, "Use your manners, sit still, and for the love of God, don't call Myla Rose my girlfriend. Got it?"

"Got it," they reply in unison.

"Good mornin', Cash and company. Y'all can take a seat. It'll be just a few," Seraphine says, directing us to the waiting area. I'm about to tell her that sounds fine when I feel someone staring at me.

Surveying the salon, I immediately find the culprit—a blonde middle-aged woman sitting in...Myla Rose's chair. *Interesting.*

Azalea shuts off her blow dryer, allowing me to hear a snippet of their conversation. "Myla Rose, would you take a look? That man is a cool drink of water on a hot, hot day. I mean, gracious, if I were single and maybe twenty years younger..." Myla freezes and then slowly looks over her shoulder at me. I attempt to catch her eye, but she whips her head back around so fast I'm surprised it doesn't spin.

That doesn't stop me from hearing her words though. "Yes, ma'am, he sure is something, all right." *Even more interesting.*

"We don't mind waitin', Seraphine. Just call us when you're ready." I take a seat by the twins on the couch that's positioned across from the reception desk and thumb through some chick magazine while we wait.

Not even five minutes later, our names are being called. "Come on, boys, Myla Rose is ready for Preston. Azalea will be ready for Lucas in just a bit. That okay?"

"Sure thing." We all stand and follow Seraphine back to Myla's station. She attempts to introduce the twins to Myla Rose, but they just stand there and stare at her—and damn if I don't get it. I get awestruck by her too. After a few seconds, Seraphine shrugs her shoulders and retreats to the front desk.

"Well, boys, looks like the cat's got your tongues. Which one of you cuties is Preston?"

Preston ever so slowly raises his hand. "Me. I'm Preston."

"Nice to meet you. You wanna hop up into my chair?"

"You're so pretty—like a princess!" he blurts, his cheeks taking on a pink tinge from embarrassment. "I–I mean...yes, ma'am, I can do that."

The booster seat she has in the chair makes it a little difficult, so it takes him two tries to get up into her chair, but when he does, she smiles at him like he's just crossed the finish line in first place.

"Good job, P. Can I call you P?" she asks him as she mists the water bottle over his hair.

"Like a nickname?"

"Just like a nickname."

He beams at her. "I like that."

Not one to be left out, Lucas pipes up, "I wants a nickname too!"

"You do, huh?" Myla asks him. He gives her three sharp nods. "Well, how about...Lou?"

"Lou. Lou. Lou," he says, testing it out. After rolling it around a few more times, he gives his approval.

"You needs one too, Miss Myla Rose," Preston declares.

"Hmm, I guess you're right. I do."

"Could it be Princess Myla?" he asks.

"I think I'd like that very much. So, P, how are we cutting your hair today?"

I like how she directs her questions to him and not to me, and I know he likes it too.

"Uncle Cash saids I look like a raggle-muffin. So, um. Just make me look like a normal boy."

"One normal boy haircut, coming up."

Lucas and I watch as she combs and cuts his hair, and while Lucas is much more interested in the hair on the ground, I'm interested in her.

The way she's so damn confident. The way each and every cut is precise. The way she holds a conversation with Preston while maintaining her focus. Watching her work is something else.

Just as I'm about to attempt to insert myself into their conversation, Azalea comes over to let us know that she's ready for Lucas. "Hey there, Lucas. You ready to get your haircut?"

"Yes, ma'am. I'm ready. I want a normal boy haircut, just like my brother, please."

"Bud, we can do that for sure." She pauses to examine

the way Myla is cutting Preston's hair before taking a hold of his hand and leading him to her chair.

"We are just about finished, P. Let me trim up your neck and you can tell me whatcha think. But you have to sit real, real still—like a statue. Can you do that?" She expertly trims up his little neckline and runs her hands through his hair before rotating him to face the mirror.

"It's perfect, Princess Myla. My mommy will love it."

"Hey, what do you know? That's exactly what I was hoping you'd say." She removes his cape and lowers the chair before telling him, "Okay, dude. If you wanna go back up front, Miss Seraphine will give you a page to color and a small snack." He thanks her and hurries along, anxious for that snack. I swear those boys have holes in their legs with the amount of food they consume.

"Looks like it's just you and me now, darlin'." The words fall from my lips before I even have a chance to think about them.

"Guess so," she says, her cheeks that pretty shade of pink I love so much. I'm not sure why, but it sure does make me feel good knowing that I have some kind of effect on her. "We cutting like we did the last time?"

"Yeah, I liked that. Just trim it back down." She runs her hands through my hair, trailing her nails across my scalp. It takes every ounce of self-control I possess to hold in my groan.

When she makes it to my neck, though, all bets are off.

"*Goddamn.*" My voice is gruff and low. Gritty, like

sandpaper. She jerks her hand away from me like she's been burned, so I know she heard me. And that's okay.

Instead of acknowledging my remark, she jumps right into her work. She's buzzing down the sides when I finally speak up. "Listen, I know we haven't really talked about anything, but I–I'd really like a chance to explain."

"Let's just let sleeping dogs lie, okay?"

"Not gonna happen. I *need* to talk to you. Please hear me out?"

"Cash, please. It's okay. I just—I wish you'd have been upfront with me. Instead, you filled my head with all kinda thoughts. Really, though, let's just move on."

I hate the sadness I hear in her voice. It guts me. I have to find a way to get her to listen to me.

"*Shit.*" I run a hand through my hair, knocking her hands away. "Listen to me and listen closely. Those texts were from my brother. He's usually a good guy, but sometimes he's an immature asshole. He wasn't being serious—he was giving me a hard time. Doesn't make it right, but that's the long and short of it. I'm so goddamn sorry. Truly."

"Oh, okay. If you say so, Cash." She still sounds unsure, and that's not working for me.

"I swear it. I was lucky you even gave me the chance to take you out again, and I promise you with all that I am—that isn't the kind of guy I am. I don't sleep around, and I sure as hell don't treat women like they're disposable. I've only been in one serious relationship, and you know how that ended. Jake thought he was being funny. He knows, now, that he wasn't."

I rotate the chair around so that I'm facing her. She needs to *see* me. I plant my feet firmly on the floor and reach out and pull her closer, my hand to her hip. I'm operating on pure instinct. The need to feel her is almost overwhelming.

"Please, darlin'. I'm sorry, so fucking sorry."

I hold her stare—I want to be sure she *sees* my apology in addition to hearing it. "And know this, Myla Rose. If you ever give me the privilege of taking you out again, I won't mess it up. Not even a little."

With my last words, I give her hip a light squeeze, just for emphasis. Startled, she tips toward me. Her hands fly to my shoulders to brace herself. For a few seconds, we stay just like that, and all feels right in the world.

Chapter Twenty-Seven

Myla Rose

His eyes have me rooted. I don't think I could move even if the building were on fire. His mouth's moving, but his words are silent—I can't hear them over the ringing in my ears.

The very second his fingers wrapped around my hip, I'm pretty sure the earth stopped spinning.

I know we've been standing like this for longer than we should. I'm all but on top of him. But from this position, I can see his truth swirling about in his thunderstorm eyes. I can see that he didn't mean to hurt me and that he wasn't just trying to sleep with me. I can see it all, laid bare.

But I can't seem to speak.

"Myla Rose, you okay?"

"Yeah. Yup. Sure am." I push myself into an upright position, using his broad shoulders for leverage. The feel of him under my hands is almost too much. My brain is screaming for me to move away, but the rest of me is begging to move closer.

"You sure, darlin'?"

"Absolutely. Let's finish up this haircut, 'kay?" He gives a gruff nod and unplants his feet, allowing me to position the chair how I want it.

Which would be facing away from the mirror. I'm trying with all my might to pretend he doesn't melt me, and seeing his face every time I check his reflection won't do a damn thing to help.

"All done. We gonna wash it?"

"Not today." He shakes his hair out and finger combs it out of his face. "I'm thinking of taking the boys to the beach."

"It's a gorgeous day for sure. Perfect beach weather." I twirl the ends of my hair around my fingers, hating this awkward small talk were making.

"You like the beach, Princess Myla?" Preston asks.

"I sure do, P. I haven't been in forever, though."

"You can come with us. Uncle Cash won't mind."

I'm racking my brain, trying to come up with a way to let Preston down easy when Azalea and Lucas walk over to where we're all gathered.

"Go where with whom?" Azalea asks.

"To the beach. With us. She saids she loves the beach."

I can see it all over her face—how badly she wants to laugh at my predicament. Instead of coming to my rescue, she decides to play Devil's advocate.

"Oh, yes. Ms. Myla *loooves* the beach! And she's all

finished at work for the day!"

"YES!" the twins shout together with a high five.

"Darlin', you don't have to go..." Cash offers, though his tone betrays his words. He wants me there just as much as they do.

"No, Cash, it's fine. I'll meet y'all down at The Pass in about an hour—sound good?"

"Fucking amazing," he whispers, loud enough for only me to hear.

"I can't believe you, Az. You hung me out to dry!"

"Oh, hush up. You were gonna say yes. I could see it in your eyes, sister-girl."

I scowl at her from where I'm sitting on my bed as she flits around my room, packing my beach bag.

"I might not have. You don't know that I was gonna—"

"I do, and you were. No way in hell were you gonna crush those boys' hearts."

Every word she speaks is truth. I guess when you're friends this long, you can't hide much.

"I just...the thought of parading myself around in a swimsuit with this big ol' belly is bad enough. Doing it in front of Cash is downright mortifying."

"You are b-e-a-u-tiful, Myles. What gives?"

"Have you seen my stretch marks?"

"No, idiot, and you haven't either. You look adorable, like you swallowed a soccer ball. You give other mamas bump envy."

I work my way up off the bed and lift my top. "Look! See!" I point to the small white lines marring my lower abdomen.

"Once again, you're beautiful. If something as insignificant as stretch marks is a deal breaker, then he really is an asshole."

"You really think so?"

"I know so, babe, so go get changed. You don't wanna be late."

I immediately spot Cash and the boys playing in the sand near the lagoon. From the looks of it, they're constructing an incredible and intricate sandcastle.

"Hey, boys! What're y'all building?"

Preston rushes over to me, kicking sand up with his little feet the entire way. "We're building a castle for you, Princess!"

Be still my heart..."For me?" I ask, stooping down to his level.

"Yes, ma'am. Uncle Cash saids all princesses need castles."

"Your uncle's a wise man, P. Any chance y'all wanna let me help?"

"Yes-yes-yes-yes!" We walk hand-in-hand to where Cash and Lucas are diligently working on my castle. "Uncle Cashmere, Myla is gonna help us!"

I linger just a moment before plopping down in the sand next to where Preston is digging a moat around the castle.

"What can I do to help?"

Lucas hands me a plastic sand mold. "We needs some starfish, Princess Myla. You like starfish?"

"Love em, Lou. Did you know they can regenerate?"

"Agenerate? What's that?"

"Re-gen-er-ate. It means if they lose a limb, they can grow it back!"

"Like a lizard!" Preston pipes up.

"Yeah, bud, just like a lizard."

After about ten more minutes of construction, Preston sighs loudly, announcing his boredom. "Can we swim now?"

"Sure thing, little man. Y'all just stay in the lagoon," Cash tells them before turning to me. "You wanna swim too?"

"Sure, it's some kinda hot out here today."

He stands and whips the shirt he's wearing over his head and extends a hand down to me. My mouth's so dry it feels like it's been stuffed with cotton balls.

Have mercy, he is *all* man.

"Come on, darlin'. Up you go," he says, hauling me to my feet. "And ditch that cover-up."

Chapter Twenty-Eight

Cash

I walk to the edge of the water, right where the twins are playing, but my eyes never move from her body. No, I stare unabashedly as she removes the breezy cover-up she's hiding under.

She toys with the hem, running the gauzy fabric between her fingers before ever so slowly lifting it. When she reveals her string bikini-clad bottom, I almost tell her to pull the cover-up back down.

She's too damn beautiful, and I know for a fact that every man on this beach is imagining untying those strings.

She continues, revealing her rounded belly and then her perky, high breasts. I make a break for deeper water to hide my body's reaction to her. I have no desire for the entire beach to witness the tent in my swim trunks, especially the twins.

Myla Rose neatly folds her cover-up and heads toward

where the boys are playing. "Y'all know how to swim?"

I watch her as she stands there with the twins, her pale skin glowing in the sunlight. I don't remember where I heard it, but someone once told me a woman is her most beautiful when she's with child, and looking at Myla Rose, all belly in her two-piece, I have to agree.

"We do!" Preston tells her proudly, adjusting his life jacket.

"Well, come on then, boys!"

I meet them about halfway out, where the water is waist deep on the boys, and immediately, they start splashing up a storm. I freeze, worried Myla is going to be pissed, but before I can even scold the boys, she's splashing them right back.

I swear, this woman might just be perfect.

"I'm hungry!" Preston whines as we walk back to our towels.

"I'm tired and hungry and my fingers feel like...what's the word?" Lucas wriggles his fingers in front of his face.

"Prunes, Lou. Your fingers feel like prunes," Myla tells him as she begins unpacking her giant tote bag.

She pulls out a small cooler, and I shoot her a questioning look—no lie, the girl could give Mary Poppins a run for her money.

"What's all that?"

"Just some sandwiches, fruit, and water—nothing

big."

"Damn, girl. You didn't have to go to all this trouble."

"No trouble at all. Now, eat up."

We dig into the chicken salad sandwiches she brought, and much to my surprise, the twins don't complain—not even once. Must be the hunks of bacon she put in it.

I'm draining the last of my water bottle when Myla Rose nudges me with her elbow, gesturing over to Preston and Lucas. They're both curled up on their towels, sleeping soundly.

"Isn't that the sweetest?" Her voice is wistful and dreamy, a straight shot to my heart.

"Sure is, darlin'." I look back over to her, and she's rummaging around in her bag again for something. "Whatcha looking for now in that big-ass thing?"

She riffles around for a few more seconds before triumphantly holding up a bottle of sun block. "Aha!"

"Need some help with that?" I waggle my eyebrows and shoot her a lascivious smile.

"Sure, why not?"

She tosses me the bottle, and I have to chuckle. "SPF 80, Myla?"

"Do you see my skin? I'd rather not be burnt to a crisp, thank you very much," she says as I situate myself behind her.

I squirt a dollop of the cold lotion into my palm before working it into her soft, freckle-kissed skin. I massage it into her shoulders, working her tense muscles long after the lotion has absorbed. I trail my fingers down toward her chest, slipping them under the straps of her swim top, running my fingertips in small, feather-light circles.

"Feels so good," she moans as she leans back into me. Burying my face in her neck, I press a small, open-mouthed kiss right below her ear.

"Well, aren't you two cozy?" My eyes pop open, and Myla Rose shoots away from me as if she's been scalded.

"T–Taylor. I thought you were off at school?"

"M–Myla," he mocks. "It's called summer break. Surely, you aren't that dense? Then again, you are a high school dropout." His words hang heavy in the air, and when Myla Rose dips her head in shame, my blood boils.

This beautiful, strong, stunning woman has nothing be ashamed of, high school diploma or not. And fuck this ass-clown for trying to make her feel like less.

"Taylor, just go. I mean, good Lord. Don't you have better things to do?"

He gestures to a few yards away where a buxom brunette is standing, watching us like a hawk. "Sure do, Myla." He turns to head back over to her, but calls out over his shoulder, "By the way, you're a little...big to show that much skin, don't you think?"

Myla Rose fumbles around for her cover-up, trying several times before finally getting it over her head.

I'm so done with this idiot. "Now, you wait one fucking second. I don't like the way you're talking to her."

"And I don't recall ever asking your thoughts on the subject. I'll talk to her however I damn well please." He puffs out his chest and squares his shoulders to intimidate me.

Please. The only person this douche is capable of intimidating is his own shadow.

I stand, rising to my full height, making sure he has to look up to see me. "You need to go."

He bristles at my tone and takes a step back. "Yeah, whatever. Have fun with my leftovers, dude."

I rear back, but the little fuck turned and tucked tail before I could swing.

Chapter Twenty-Nine

Myla Rose

With all of my heart, soul, and body, I hate Southern stereotypes. Mostly, I guess because I am one. I'm a young, single, pregnant dropout. Just the kind of girl you *don't* bring home to mother. Maybe Taylor was right when he told me I wasn't a forever kind of girl.

I start stuffing my belongings back into my beach bag, desperately trying to keep my tears at bay. I'm not usually some weepy, shrinking violet, but these stupid hormones have sure turned me into one.

I cry at the drop of a damn pin, and I get mad even faster. And don't even get me started on the angry tears. Those might be the worst, because then I'm mad that I'm crying—because I'm mad. It's a mess...I'm a mess.

I can hear Cash and Taylor exchanging words, but I have no plans to stick around to see the disappointment on Cash's face. It's fight or flight, and I'm ready to hightail it outta here.

"Myla Rose." Cash grabs my wrist. "What're you doing? Where are you going?"

"Home." I slide my sandy feet into my flip flops before hefting my bag up and onto my shoulder.

"Why?" He looks so genuinely perplexed, like he truly doesn't get why I'm leaving.

"Cash, be real."

"What, because your ex is a jackass?"

Oh, how I wish it were that simple. Because yes, while Taylor is a jackass, his words have a certain truth to them.

"Or are you running away because you think it matters to me that you didn't finish high school?"

"I'm not running away, I'm just going—"

Cash stops my words with a finger to my lips. "Shh, you're not going anywhere."

He slides the straps of my bag back down my arm, dropping it at our feet before pulling me to him.

"Why'd you drop out, Myla?" Even though his tone is soft, the question sets me on edge.

"My Grams. She got really sick when I was in high school and needed more care than what her insurance covered." I suck in a deep breath through my teeth. "So, I dropped out just before I turned seventeen to help take care of her."

Cash steps closer to me, so close that I can almost feel him. "Darlin', I want you to listen to me. Not too many people would do what you did, and I don't care what that entitled little prick says. You're something special, and if he was too dumb to see it, that's his problem."

I shake my head, causing my nose to brush his chest. "You're wrong. I'm not worth it, Cash. I have nothing to offer you except another man's baby and a metric ton of baggage."

"That's not true." He tilts my face up to his. "You have your heart, darlin', and that's more than enough."

His voice is adamant, and his eyes are firm. He means what he says. This man...this man thinks my heart is enough. He thinks my heart is worth my baggage.

He leans down, pressing his lips to mine, and I can taste the salt on his skin from the water. He nips at my bottom lip, and I love it.

"Uncle Cash, why're you kissing Princess Myla if she's not your girlfriend?"

Pulling back from him, I smile. "Guess the twins are up?"

"Sounds like it." He smiles right back. I could get lost in those eyes and that smile. One look, and this man melts me without even trying.

"Uncle Caaaaash..." Preston and Lucas whine simultaneously. I almost wonder if they sit around and plan this stuff.

"Ah. Well, boys. Sometimes, when two grown—"

I smack my hand over his mouth, "Hush. P, Lou, your Uncle Cash kissed me because he likes me and because he wanted to. Grown-up perks. Simple as that."

"Perks? What you mean, perks?" Preston squinches

up his little nose while his brother leans in a little closer, like he's about to learn the secrets to the universe.

"Perks. Like, it's the upside. The good parts."

Lucas makes a gagging sound. "If kissing girls is a perk, then I don't wanna grow up."

"Yeah, girls have cooties."

Cash and I are both doubled over, gasping out our laughter. These boys are too much. I wonder if my little man will be as funny as Preston and Lucas?

"What else do you have planned for this weekend?" I ask Cash as we all make the trek through the sand toward the parking lot.

"Not really sure. What I do know is you should join us for dinner."

His invitation to have dinner with them has my heart swooping low into my belly. I guess he isn't ready for our time together to end, and that makes two of us.

"That sounds amazing, as long as P and Lou don't mind." I turn to face the twins. "Is that okay with y'all?"

"Can we have pizza?" Preston asks with all the seriousness a six-year-old boy can muster.

"Well, of course. Pizza is my favorite." Preston and Lucas slap their hands together in a double high-five.

"You wanna follow me back to my place?" Cash asks as he hefts my beach bag into the backseat of the Land Cruiser.

"I really wanna take a shower, and I'm sure y'all want to rinse off as well."

Cash's rain cloud eyes are shining with mischief, and

I already know what he's going to say. "Could shower togeth—"

I quiet him with a finger to his lips. "Text me your address, and I'll head over in a little bit."

He makes this adorable *aww, shucks* gesture but agrees all the same as he stalks toward me. He backs me right into Bertha and wraps the ends of my salt-dried locks around his fingers, pinning me with a heated look. He lowers his head to mine, his lips hovering.

"Gross! Are you gonna kiss her again?" Preston cries out in disgust.

Cash pulls away begrudgingly. "Guess not, little dude." He ghosts his fingers over my collarbone, sending a shiver through my entire body. "See you soon, darlin'."

I stop by the house for a quick shower and a change of clothes before heading to Cash's. He lives clear across town, but it's still a short drive. Not even ten minutes later, I'm pulling into his driveway. Perks of small-town living.

His house is a bungalow-style cottage, picket fence and all. Definitely not what I was expecting from someone so...masculine. The yard is immaculate, and the exterior of the house is pristine. Even his hydrangea bushes are trimmed perfectly even.

I can't help but smile as I imagine the chipping paint and overgrown grass at my place. We couldn't be any more opposite. But we all know what they say about opposites.

I ring the bell and wait. After a few minutes, I try again. I guess with all the times I've kept him waiting at my door, turnabout is fair play. I push the bell once more before trying the knob.

Unlocked.

"Hello? Cash?" I walk further into the house, and through the dining room picture window, I can see the twins playing in the backyard.

I'm just about to head out through the back door when I hear footsteps padding my way. I twirl around toward the sound, only to be met with the drool-worthy sight of Cash, freshly showered, still dripping wet, with only a towel around his waist.

He glances in my direction and widens his stance. "Hey there, darlin'."

The smile he aims my way, combined with the knowledge that he's naked under that towel, is panty-melting. My mind plummets straight to the gutter, picturing him naked with that towel on the floor. *Yes, please.*

"H–hey, the door, it was open. I mean, I rang the bell, but—"

"No worries. You come right on in, *anytime*. Consider it our very own open-door policy."

The way he says *open-door policy* sounds so illicit and dirty. Like he's talking about much more than his actual door. His words are thick and warm like maple syrup, and they send a shiver down my damn spine.

Well, little does he know, two can play that game. I take two steps forward, getting close enough that I can feel the warmth of his bare chest. "Anytime, Cash?"

"God. Yes." He pulls me into him, closing the gap between us. With my head against his chest, it's a perfect fit, like two pieces of a puzzle. I brazenly press my lips to his skin, just above his heart. "I mean it, darlin'. Anytime."

He steps back from me, angling his body away from mine, and I instantly miss his heat. I see him trying to adjust himself. "You good there, Cash?"

With his hands still on his junk, he turns to face me and slowly moves them away, giving me quite the eyeful of his terry cloth tent. "Not even a little bit. So, Imma go and throw some clothes on before things get out of hand."

My bravery has seemingly run dry, unlike other parts of me that are dripping, and damn it, I can feel the blush I'm rocking. "Yeah, probably for the best."

"Trust me, darlin'—if my nephews weren't out playing in the yard, this story would have a different ending. A happy one, you feel me?" He winks. "Now, go on out back. I'll be there soon."

Chapter Thirty

Cash

DAMN HER. DAMN HER AND HER SWEET VOICE, gorgeous face, and killer body. Damn her for the way she lights me up without even trying. That girl's something else, and if I have any say in the matter, she'll be mine by the end of this weekend.

I'm done letting my past chain me, and so what if she's pregnant? I've always wanted kids, and this here—it's nothing more than a jump start. I'll love that little boy with my whole heart. Now, I just have to convince her that I'm in this for the long haul.

I know she believed me when I told her she was more than a hookup. I'm just not sure she realizes how true my words were when I told her I wanted her heart.

She's had me on edge all day, from seeing her in that skimpy swimsuit to watching her play with the twins. Shit, even the way she handled herself with grace in front of her douche-canoe ex.

And then she shows up here, looking good enough to eat in a pair of loose linen shorts and a tank top that accentuates her perky tits and growing belly. I didn't stand a chance.

But she didn't stop there. Oh, no. She waltzed right up to me, bold as fuck, and pressed those bee-stung lips into my skin, searing me, branding me. It took all of my willpower—and then some—to walk away. But believe you me, next time, I'm not walking away. Next time, *it's on*.

In the time it takes me to shower—a cold one, this time—and throw on some clothes, Myla has not only managed to wrangle the twins inside, but she's also miraculously gotten them to wash up and has them setting the table. Girl's gonna make a damn good mother.

I'm hovering just outside the kitchen, so preoccupied with watching her that it takes me a minute to realize the doorbell's ringing. I course-correct and make my way to grab our pizzas, but she beats me to the door.

"How much do I owe you?" she asks the delivery boy. Poor kid. I can see him fighting his desire to talk to her boobs instead of looking her in the eye. I feel his pain.

"It's pa–paid for, ma'am," he stammers, holding the pizza boxes off to the side. "Just need a signature."

His eyes drop to her cleavage as she ponders whether she should sign for me or not. He looks up just in time to see her reach for his pen. "Does this price include the gratuity?"

"Yes, ma'am, your husband tipped when he ordered."

"Oh, he's not my—"

I silence her with my arms around her waist and my lips to her neck. "Thanks, darlin', you go on and take that back to the boys—they're starving."

She huffs at me but plays along. *Good girl.*

"You h–have a nice night, sir, and congratulations on your baby." I know the kid is just trying to be polite, but his words are like an arrow to my heart. I fucking wish that *were* my baby. Even still, I'll love him like he is...if she'll let me.

After dinner, the twins beg to stay up and watch a movie. We all snuggle up on the couch to watch Pixar's latest creation, and wouldn't you know, Preston, Lucas, and Myla Rose all fall asleep before the opening credits even finish. My arm is numb and my back is aching, but they all look so peaceful I'm hesitant to move.

Eventually, my discomfort wins out, and I gently extricate myself from the couch and carry the twins one-by-one to the spare bedroom. Once they're tucked in, I'm facing an entirely new dilemma.

Do I wake Myla Rose and send her home? Do I drape a blanket over her and call it a night? I want her in my bed, but just up and taking her there would make me the ultimate creeper. I'm talking next-level creeper, and that's a no-go. Especially if I want her to be mine. Which I do, *I really fucking do.*

I don't know when or how, but this girl has woven herself into the very fabric of my existence. One look from her—one smile—and it's like the air has been sucked from the room, but that's okay, because somehow, she's all the air I need.

I'm still debating my options when Myla Rose begins to stir on the couch, slowly blinking herself awake. "Whaa...where..." She looks around, panicking slightly, until her eyes land on me. "Sorry, didn't realize I was so tired."

"Not a problem. If it makes you feel better, Preston and Lucas fell asleep too."

She smiles through a big yawn. "Yeah, not so much. I guess I'd better get going."

"You, uh, don't have to. You can stay. I'll sleep on the couch," I offer, though I'm secretly hoping she suggests we share the bed. Not even in a sexual way. I'm just desperate to have her in my space. Desperate to wake up next to her. Desperate for her scent to linger on my sheets.

She glances from me, then to the couch. "Oh, Cash." She stands and walks toward me. "There's no way you'll fit on that couch, and if I'm being honest, I'm way too tired to drive home. So c'mon, big boy, let's go to bed."

It takes a minute or two before her words register, and as fast as I can, I'm scrambling down the hall after her.

I direct her into my room before heading to the closet to grab her something to sleep in. "Here, these should get you through the night," I tell her, handing her a pair of my boxers and a T-shirt. "The bathroom is just through there if you wanna get changed." Myla Rose smiles and thanks me as she accepts the clothes and heads into the bathroom.

I'm pulling back the covers when she steps out of the bathroom. My eyes move slowly up her body, taking in her toned, bare legs. The sight of her in my boxer shorts with the waistband rolled gives me pause...because *holy shit*.

I'm damn near drowning in lust as I continue my perusal. I'm pretty sure I'm drooling a little when I realize she passed over my shirt and is still in her tank top, and judging by her pert nipples, she's braless. I know I'm staring like a perv, but I can't help myself. She's everything I've ever wanted, all wrapped in one delicious package, and here she is, standing in front of me nearly naked and about to get into bed with me. It'll be a goddamn miracle if I make it through the night.

She finishes pulling back the covers and slides under them, completely oblivious to my dilemma. After tossing and turning for a few seconds, she finds her sweet spot, but I'm still standing at the side of the bed, staring.

"Cash?" Her sleepy voice breaks my trance, and I climb into the bed next to her. She's close enough that I can feel her heat, even though we're not touching, and I swear on all that's holy, this girl is *it* for me. If just lying here like this has me feeling like the king of the goddamn universe, I can only imagine what being inside her will be like.

My thoughts are put on hold when she rolls away from me and snuggles her ass right into me, murmuring, "G'night, Cash."

I reach over to switch off the lamp before pressing a soft kiss to her shoulder. "Sweet dreams, darlin'."

Though I doubt I'll be getting much sleep.

By some miracle, I manage to fall asleep—and yes, I mean it when I say miracle. Myla Rose kept her body pressed firmly into mine all night, which is why this morning is a little painful. I mean, waking up to her in my bed...yes, please. Every day.

As much as I'd like to stay in bed, wrapped in with her, this morning wood I'm sporting needs to go if I have any hope of surviving the day. This girl has me wound so tightly, I'd probably blow if she shifted in the slightest.

I check the time and groan at the numbers on the clock. Five thirty. But I'm too wired to fall back asleep. Slipping out from my spot behind her, I take care not to jostle her and make my way to the shower.

The hot water pours over me as I do my best to will away thoughts of her out there in my bed. It's no use, though. The image is branded into my brain, and I'm helpless to fight it.

Even here, in my shower, her scent surrounds me. Inhaling deeply, I'm hit with a barrage of images and memories—the way her body feels pressed into mine, the feel of her soft skin, the sounds of her breathy moans...

I close my eyes and give in to the fantasy. I'm so caught up in it, in her, that it only takes four strokes before I'm chanting her name like a prayer, my release circling the drain.

Chapter Thirty-One

Myla Rose

I ROLL OVER, AND JUST LIKE IN THAT STUPID DREAM I had right after meeting him, I'm met with empty, cool sheets. However, I can hear the water running behind the bathroom door, so I know I'm not alone.

I turn my head to glance at the clock. It's not even six yet. I toss and turn before settling myself on his side of the bed, burrowing myself under his citrus-scented sheets. I'm on the brink of falling back asleep when I swear I hear him groan my name.

Sweet baby Jesus. His voice is heaven in everyday conversation, but that sound was *pure sin.* It was feral, and it has me wanton and needy. Too bad I'm too chicken shit to do anything about it.

The water stops, and I hear the clink of the shower curtain being pulled back. I do my best to pretend I'm still sleeping. The last thing I want is for him to know I heard him.

The door opens, and the mouth-watering shower steam seeps out into the bedroom. It's a heady combination of citrus, soap, and deodorant—I swear, it's like I'm cocooned in all things Cash, and I'm pretty damn sure this is what Nirvana is like.

I peek my eyes open as he walks past the bed, and the sight I'm met with elicits a loud gasp from me.

He isn't wrapped in a towel...no, he's as naked as the day he was born. Now, mind you, my view is of his backside, but it is mighty fine all the same. His shoulders are broad and his back is strong. And his ass, *Jesus*, don't even get me started.

"'Morning, darlin'," he says with a devilish smile before making his way into his closet, presumably to get dressed. *What a shame.*

A few moments later, he emerges, much to my dismay, fully clothed. "You a breakfast person?"

"Best meal of the day," I tell him sincerely.

"I could think of one I'd like better." He winks and extends a hand to me. "C'mon, you can help me get food ready for the twins. They'll be up shortly." I take his hand and quickly shimmy into my bra and shorts before trailing behind him to the kitchen, where he starts gathering ingredients. "You like French toast?" I nod, and he starts cracking the eggs into a bowl.

Sure enough, by the time the food is ready, two bed-headed, sleepy-eyed little boys shuffle into the dining room. Neither of them speak. They just plop themselves down into their chairs and wait for their plates.

After a few forkfuls of French toast, though? A different story. It's like they mainlined the sugar because they are wired now.

"Princess, did you sleep over too?" Preston asks.

I freeze, unsure of what to tell them. Thankfully, Cash saves the day. "Yup, she sure did."

"Cool. Can we go play outside?" Cash nods, and they tear out of the room like rockets.

"Boys!" he hollers, and they freeze. "Y'all need to get dressed first. C'mon." As Cash leads them from the room, I start cleaning up our mess.

I'm standing at the kitchen sink, up to my elbows in suds, scrubbing our dishes when I feel Cash come up behind me. He reaches around me, bringing his strong hands to rest on my bump. He drops an open-mouthed kiss to that sweet spot where my neck and shoulder meet. "Mmm," I moan at the contact.

"Shh," he warns as he peppers kisses up and down my neck while lightly caressing my belly.

"Can't help it, Cash. When you lay your hands on me, I'm helpless to fight it."

"Good," he grunts, pressing his body closer to mine. I can feel the evidence of his desire for me, and I lean fully into him, tilting my head back against his chest.

He captures my lips in an aggressive kiss. "Need you, darlin', so bad."

Good God, his words have my heart soaring. This man...he makes me more than want it all—he makes me believe I can have it.

"Need you too." I drag my wet, soapy hands from the water and place them over his on my belly.

Just as he moves to turn me in his arms, a male voice rings out from somewhere in the house. "Cashmere... OH, SHIT!"

We break apart, both of us panting. "Awesome timing, Jake."

Ah, so this is his d-bag brother. Lovely. I can only imagine how this looks. I keep my eyes focused on the floor at his feet.

"This her?" his brother asks.

"Jesus Christ," an unfamiliar female voice scolds, "Have some manners."

"Yes, this is Myla Rose." Cash wraps an arm around me. "Darlin', this is my idiot brother, Jake, and his *much* better half, Paige."

I finally look up, steeling myself for whatever may come. However, nothing could have prepared me for what came next. Instead of judgey looks and nasty glares, Paige draws me into a tight hug. "It is *so* nice to meet you, Myla Rose. We've heard only good things."

"Sure enough, Cash never shuts up about you," Jake adds, and I can hear the smile in his voice. "Also, guess I need to apologize for the texts you saw. That wasn't me at my best."

"Nowhere near your best," Paige adds.

It would be so easy to stay mad, but if Cash is gonna be in my life the way I hope he is, then I need to be able to forgive and forget. Deep down, I know he meant no harm.

Stepping back from Paige's embrace, I address him. "It's already forgotten, and I'm really glad to meet y'all both. And your boys—they're absolutely precious."

Paige beams and asks me if I know what I'm having. She and I fall into easy conversation while Cash and Jake head out back to get the twins.

I'm not sure how long Paige and I have been in the living room chatting, but I adore her. She's everything right and good in this world, and despite our gaping age difference, I can easily see us grabbing lunch and whatnot.

"Honey, you ready?" Jake calls as he, Cash, and the twins file into the room.

"MOM!" Preston and Lucas yell as they both rush over to Paige, wrapping their tiny arms around her.

"Hey, sweet peas, I missed y'all." I can hear her love for them, and it really hits it home the fact that this'll soon be me, telling my boy sweet things.

"We missed you too, Mom, but Princess Myla is AWESOME! She cutted our hair, and played with us at the beach, and she spended the night too!"

Oh, Jesus. They're going to think I'm some kind of two-bit whore, having spend-the-nights when their children are here.

"Oh, yeah?" Jake asks through a snort. "Getcha a little brown chicken—" Paige smacks a hand over his mouth just as Preston says, "No, Dad, we had pizza!" At that, we all laugh. From the mouths of babes.

"Okay, boys, time to go. Y'all head on out to the car. I'll grab their stuff." She stands and sets off toward the spare bedroom, still chuckling.

When she returns, Cash swoops in and grabs the boys' stuff from her and carries it out. My belly dips—such a damn gentleman.

"Paige, it was so nice to meet y'all, and please know that nothing inappropriate happened last night. I fell asleep on the—"

She cuts me off. "Even if something did happen, y'all are grown. No harm, no foul. Now, give me your number, and I'll text you about setting up a girls' day." I fire off my number and in turn save hers before hugging her bye.

I swear, Cash's family is almost as amazing as he is. I smile to myself, thinking that Grams would approve for sure.

"What else you got going on today?" Cash asks as he drops down beside me on the couch.

"Hmm, not really sure. Probably laundry."

"Living the life, huh, darlin'?"

"You know it." I can't help the smile that stretches wide across my face. Being here with him, discussing mundane, everyday things...it just feels right. Like it's where I'm supposed to be. He gives me this sense of belonging I've never felt with anyone else.

"Well, my day isn't gonna be any more exciting than yours. Gotta clean up from Preston and Lucas. Then, I'll probably head down to my shop and get prepped for the week."

"Need help cleaning up?"

"I mean, shit, darlin', if you're offering..." His smirk leads me to believe cleaning is the last thing on his mind.

"Yeah, Cash, I am." And maybe it's the last thing on mine too.

The moment the words pass my lips, it's as if time stops. Cash is like a statue—totally unmoving. His eyes are molten, pinning me in place as they search mine, making sure we're on the same page. Lifetimes pass, or maybe it's seconds. He must find the answer he's looking for, because all at once, he lunges toward me, plunging his hands into my hair as he lays me back onto the couch.

His lips meet mine, and I swear—*I swear*—this man was made for me, to be mine. Our kiss is frenzied, more teeth than tongue, but it's perfect. It's passionate. It's us.

"You sure?" he pants, pushing his hips into mine.

"A hundred and ten percent," I whisper-moan.

"We do this, you're mine, darlin'."

"I'm already yours, Cash."

Just like that, we're a flurry of limbs, pulling at one another's clothes until there's nothing between us. The feel of him, of his skin, has me drunk—floating, flying... falling.

Cash stops, wrapping an arm around my shoulders and one under my legs, and he lifts me from the couch like it's nothing. "Where're we going?" I pant.

"Want you here, darlin'," he tells me as he gently sets me on his bed. He stands at the end of the bed, staring at me like I'm the most precious thing. Like I'm delicate and fragile, but I'm not. I want his rough side. I need it.

"I'm not gonna break, Cash," I tell him as he gently runs his strong hands up and down my calves.

"I know that, Myla." He places a soft kiss to my right calf and then another to my left thigh. He pauses, level with my belly button, and holds my eyes before placing a soft kiss on my rounded belly. "That's mine too." I swear, *this man*, he is so much more than I could've ever hoped for.

He drops small kisses all along my chest and neck before finally making it back to my lips. He groans as he pushes into me, and oh, my stars...I know that I'm ruined for any other man. Cash is using his body to take mine to places I've never been. With every shift and every thrust, this man is moving heaven and earth, all for my pleasure.

"Never felt this good, darlin'."

"No. Never," I whine as I fall apart beneath him, all shuddered breaths and soft moans.

"*Goddamn*, Myla, so good," he growls, following after me.

Chapter Thirty-Two

Cash

Between Myla Rose's hormones and the way we were burning up the sheets, she was fast asleep by the time I rolled over to settle myself next to her in the bed. As I pull the sheets up over us, I can't help but chuckle at the small smile she's sporting in her sleep, knowing that it mirrors my own. We're both sated and spent, and I know soul-deep that I'll never get enough of this girl. Wrapping an arm around Myla, I pull her close, her back to my front, and drift off to sleep with her.

Afternoon sunlight filters through the cracks in the blinds, rousing me. Myla Rose is still snoozing, wrapped in my arms. "Darlin', time to get up." I gently draw my fingertips across her belly, barely touching her. "C'mon, rise and shine." I press my lips to that spot below her ear that I know makes her crazy.

She shifts and turns her head to look at me, all sleepy-eyed and hazy. "Hey there, handsome. This is a wakeup call I could get used to."

"Is it, now?" I ask, pulling her back into me.

Her cheeks pinken, like she's embarrassed. "That's the sleep talking. Feel free to ignore me."

With my thumb and forefinger, I grasp her chin, tilting her head to look fully at me. "I won't ignore anything you say, darlin', not ever. If you talk, I'm gonna listen. Your words are important, Myla."

"Um...oh–okay, Cash."

"I mean it, and forget anyone who's ever made you feel differently," I tell her, making my way from the bed to the closet. I throw on some sweats and a Carson's Custom tee and return to her. "And for that matter, don't censor your words around me. If it falls from your lips, I wanna hear it. Now get dressed, babe. I'm gonna make us lunch."

Sensing she needs a few moments to herself, I don't wait around for her reply. Instead, I head out to the kitchen and set about making us lunch.

I hear Myla's bare feet padding across the tile floor and turn to find her once again dressed in her clothes from yesterday. "Hope you like sandwiches, darlin'. My cupboards are bare. Just shopped, too, but those boys ate me outta house and home."

She smiles and shakes her head. "Sandwiches sound great, Cash. You think you've got it bad? Just think about their mama."

"Think about you, darlin'. Soon enough, that little

rascal you're carrying will eat up all the food in your pantry, too."

"Don't I know it. He's already making me eat damn near everything in sight."

"Well, you look good for it, so keep at it." She blushes as she finishes off her sandwich before collecting both of our plates and depositing them in the sink.

"Thanks, Cash. I wish I could stay and actually help clean. I mean, not that I'd change what happened, because it was..." she trails off.

"It was what? Magical? Phenomenal? Damn near religious?"

"Perfect. It was perfect," she tells me with a soft push to my shoulder. "Now hush up and walk me to my car."

"Yes, ma'am, and as the saying goes, 'I hate to see you leave, but I love to watch you go.'" Myla Rose turns her head to look at me, amusement swimming in her deep chocolate eyes, but a snort is all she offers in return.

Much to Myla's dismay, I not only open the door to Bertha, but I also buckle her in before sealing my lips to hers in a scorching kiss. "I'll talk to you soon, darlin'. Let me know when you make it home, 'kay?"

"You know I will, Cash." I close the door and give the hood two taps before watching her reverse down my short driveway.

I head back inside and clean until I can no longer take the silence screaming at me. Myla Rose spent less than twenty-four hours in my house, but damn, it doesn't feel like home without her.

I already miss her voice—that sweet Southern drawl. I try to watch some TV, mindlessly flipping through the channels, but nothing holds my interest. My thoughts are too eaten up with remembering the feel of her. The way her long hair fanned out on my sheets like a fiery halo. The way she moaned my name as she shattered beneath me.

I fire up the computer in the office, trying to immerse myself in the business side of my work. Nothing like numbers to quiet your soul. Except it isn't helping. Not one lick. I pull up my Spotify to drown out the lack of her presence, but it's no use. Every goddamned song makes me think of her.

The fact that I'm missing her even though she's barely gone has me feeling a little crazy. In my head, I know I'm being irrational, but I've said it once and I'll say it again...nothing about love is rational.

Fuck. *Love*?

I...love her?

I love her—I love Myla Rose McGraw. The realization smacks me square in the chest, stealing the air from my lungs.

With that revelation fresh in my mind, I tear ass out of the house and head straight for my workshop. I want to channel this feeling into every part of the crib I'm building, and what better time than when it's fresh in my mind?

While I'm well aware she's more than forgiven me, I have every intention of following through on the plan

Simon, Drake, and I came up with. Only now, this crib will be built not as an apology, but as a way to show Myla Rose my love for her—every part, package deal and all.

With the plans I drew up the other week laid out before me, I set to work marking, measuring, and cutting the lumber. I went with a stunning pine for the build and plan to varnish it. I know it's gonna be amazing, and I know it will measure up to the one she saw in that boutique.

About half an hour into the actual build, my phone finally chirps with an incoming text. I all but throw my speed-square and pencil to the ground in hopes that it's Myla Rose.

Myla Rose: Home! Sorry I kept you waiting. My phone was dead.

Me: Just glad you made it safe, darlin'.

Myla Rose: Thank you for this weekend, Cash.

Me: Nothing to thank me for. I enjoyed it just as much, if not more.

Me: You work Monday?

Myla Rose: Kind of. We're interviewing a stylist.

Me: Gotcha. You have lunch plans Tuesday?

Myla Rose: Just work. A whole lotta work. Call me later? XOXO

I smirk at her little 'XOXO', because hell yeah, I'd sure love a bit of that from her. A bit of that, and then some. And I'm not just talking about sex either. I'm talking about everything that is Myla Rose.

It's the little things. Like the way she looks at me when she thinks I'm not looking. A shift of her eyes, a lilting smile. It heats my blood, causing it to run faster in my veins. I know this feeling. Need—it's need. Indescribable and insatiable need.

I mean, yeah, it's her touch, especially now that I truly know it, but it's still more.

So much more.

It's her laugh. Her thoughts. It's the glint in her dark chocolate eyes. It's the way her freckles dance across her skin. It's the swell of her belly. Fuck, just knowing she's growing life inside her. It's the soft, quiet way she sighs my name. It's all-consuming. She's all-consuming, and I wouldn't change a goddamn thing. I just hope she's feeling it too.

I'm so focused on the task at hand that everything else falls to the wayside. Time, food, hydration, comfort... all of it. This crib needs to be perfect, and I'll settle for nothing less. Hours and hours of marking, cutting, and sanding, and I think I'm just about ready for assembly.

It's not until a bead of sweat drips from the tip of my nose that I realize just how hot it is in here. With a quick check of the time, I see that I've been here far longer than I thought. Hours upon hours have passed. It's damn near nine o'clock and well past dinner time.

Calling it quits, I clean my work station and cover the crib with a tarp for safekeeping. It's time for food and sleep. Keeping Preston and Lucas all weekend drained me. But I loved every second of it, and I sure as shit hope that one day, it'll be Myla's little man wearing me out, and if I'm really lucky, calling me 'Dad'.

Ain't no sense in working when I'm tired and risking being sloppy. First thing tomorrow, though? This bad boy is getting nailed and varnished.

Chapter Thirty-Three

Myla Rose

I'm lying in bed wide awake, knowing—dreading—the fact that my alarm clock is about to buzz. I'm so far beyond exhausted, and this time, it's not pregnancy related.

No, this is all due to Cash Carson. He called me last night around ten...said he wanted to hear my voice before his head hit his pillow. *Talk about butterflies.*

However, what was meant to be a quick good-night turned into hours. We talked about everything under the sun, and eventually, I fell asleep to the sound of his voice. Which is better than any damn sound machine.

My eyes drift shut as I replay events from the past week in my mind. While the direction I'm heading in surprises me, I wouldn't change a thing. Cash is the very embodiment of everything I've ever wanted. Where Taylor belittled me and made me feel small, Cash is constantly building me up. I swear, the man is one part easygoing, one part good looks, and two parts Southern charm. More importantly, though, he's mine. All mine.

With a long stretch and a groan, I force myself out of bed. Today is a big day at the salon. We're meeting Seraphine's cousin, Magnolia, and I want to make a good first impression.

A quick shower, a dollop of tinted moisturizer, and a swipe of lip gloss and I'm out the door. I also detour to Dream Beans for an extra-large vanilla latte, because caffeine. I savor that first piping hot sip, relishing the way it warms me from the inside out.

Azalea's voice comes from behind me. "Myla Rose, how did I know I'd find you here?"

"Great minds think alike?"

"That they do, sister-girl, that they do." She pops the lid off her coffee and adds three packets of raw sugar. "So, you ready to meet Ms. Magnolia?"

"I really am. I hope she's what we've been looking for," I tell her as we make our way across the street.

"I have a good feeling about her, Myles, I really do."

Azalea and I are sitting in the waiting area when there's a light knock at the front door. "Come on in, it's open," AzzyJo calls out, and ever so slowly, the door opens.

I'm pretty sure we're both struck dumb when Magnolia steps through the threshold. With her sun-kissed skin, dirty blonde hair, and dazzling baby blues, she's out of this world beautiful. Like, I'm talking highest-paid, Fashion Week runway model pretty.

"H–hi, I'm M–Magnolia," she says with her eyes glued to her feet.

Azalea and I exchange glances, not knowing quite what to make of her. I think we were both expecting Magnolia to be a mirror of Seraphine when it turns out they couldn't possibly be more opposite.

"Nice to meet you. I'm Azalea," she says as she extends her hand toward Magnolia, causing her to jump back. Her cheeks pinken and her eyes dart around the room, seemingly embarrassed by her reaction.

"And I'm Myla Rose. Have a seat. We're so glad you're here." I gesture to the waiting area, trying my damndest to make her feel welcome and at ease. My gut, coupled with her mannerisms, tells me she's as skittish as a foal and that we need to go slow with her.

Magnolia lingers on the welcome mat for just a moment before lowering herself into the nearest chair. "S–sorry, I'm not normally such a mess." She lets out a humorless laugh. "At least not this much of a mess."

"Hey, no problem. Nerves get the better of us all from time to time. Just ask Azalea over there about the time she almost peed her pants because Drake Collins laughed at one of her jokes."

With an eye roll, Azalea scoffs. "Shut up, Myles! Jesus, I was like fifteen. Move on already."

"No way, no how. Never gonna happen." I turn my back on a sulking Azalea and focus my attention on the dark blonde beauty. "So, Magnolia, what brought you to Dogwood?"

She fidgets in her seat, ruminating on her answer. "Um…I needed a change. Badly. And with Seraphine and Uncle Dave being here, it just seemed right."

"Well, it's a great place, that's for sure. We're both lifers," Azalea tells her with a saucy grin. "So, how long have you been doing hair?"

"Six years. But I took the last two off, so I guess four."

"Two years off? Wow, how come?" Azalea asks.

I swear, that girl is clueless sometimes. "Ignore her, Mags. Can I call you Mags?"

"Oh, um, I mean…if you want?"

"No way, girl, *if you want*. Think on it." The more we chat, the more relaxed Magnolia becomes. Eventually, her posture loosens, and while she's not cracking any jokes, she's certainly laughing at ours.

"So, let's take a look at the salon, and we'll show you your station," I tell her as Azalea helps me to stand.

"Oh, I'm h–hired?"

We both look at her blankly and in unison say, "Well, duh."

After a quick tour, she thanks us profusely and tells us she'll get moved in this week. We wait until we see her drive away before squealing like lunatics, because even though she's shy, she's a perfect fit. The calm to our crazy.

Chapter Thirty-Four

Myla Rose

I swear, since Sunday, I've been walking around on a Cash Carson high. But now that I haven't seen him since, I'm crashing and heading into withdrawals.

That man is so far under my skin that he's my first thought every morning and my last every night. I literally fall asleep to his voice and wake up to a sweet text.

A girl could get used to this, that's for damn sure. With that said, insanely busy or not, I need to see him. Need to feel him. Touch him. Taste him.

It's eleven o'clock in the morning, and I've already done three colors and two cuts. I'm dead standing and nowhere near finished, thanks to the fact that I've had to sprinkle my Friday clients throughout the rest of the week to accommodate my twenty-week appointment. I'm way overbooked.

Once the last of the hair on the floor is swept up, I take refuge in the dispensary. I have twenty minutes before my next client, and as hungry as I am, my exhaustion is winning. I plan to sit here until I absolutely have to move.

I swear, no one ever talks about the downsides of pregnancy...bloating, fatigue, swelling, and I'm only halfway!

I quickly tap out a text to Cash, just to say *Hi*, before laying my head on the table. My body is slowly relaxing, and I'm on the verge of a really great nap when that oh-so-yummy citrus scent invades my senses.

Yeah, this is exactly the kind of dream I like. One where my man is the star. And I swear, I hear his voice calling my name.

It's not until I feel a warm, rough hand shaking my shoulder that I realize I'm not dreaming. Cash is here.

Cash is here! I whip my head up, almost knocking it on his. "Easy there, darlin'. Don't want you getting hurt."

"What are you doing here?" My eyes widen as I hear how incredibly rude I sounded. "I mean, not that I don't want you here. I'm just surprised. Very pleasantly, though."

"You told me how busy you were today, and I wanted to make sure you ate, so I stopped and grabbed a few slices of pizza from Rocco's. That suit you, darlin'?" My belly grumbles loudly in response. "Guess that's a yes, then."

Cash pulls up a chair right next to mine, so close that I can feel the heat of his body. That man seems to run hot, but you won't ever hear me complain.

I dig into the pizza, taking one huge bite after another, and like he can read my mind, Cash is there, holding out a bottle of water right when I need it. "Seriously, Cash, thank you so much. I wouldn't have eaten until dinner—"

He cuts me off. "No. That's not okay, Myla Rose." His stern tone takes me by surprise.

"No? Excuse me, but what?"

I know he can see the fire in my eyes. After Taylor, I'm done with men telling me what to do. "Take a breath, darlin'. All I'm saying is you need to look out for yourself. You need to eat three meals and then some. Keep you and that baby fed. I'll bring you lunch every damn day if that's what it takes."

I look down to hide my smile. *This man*. "You're too good to me," I tell him honestly.

"I'm nowhere near good enough, but I'm sure as shit gonna try, darlin'. I know it's fast, but you mean everything to me. I'm falling—know that."

Instead of responding, I push my chair back from the table. Cash's stormy eyes are clouded with confusion, but they quickly clear when I close and lock the door. "You can't say things like that if you don't mean them," I tell him as I straddle his lap.

"I mean every word I say to you...ever."

With my arms looped around his neck, I roll my hips and whisper in his ear, "I'm falling too." He brings my lips to his, and his hands fall to my hips, gripping them to guide my movements, rocking me against him until I'm shaking—gasping—panting.

"You are so goddamn beautiful when you fall apart," he tells me as he brushes my hair out of my face. "So beautiful."

"What...what about you?" I ask, gesturing to the bulge in his jeans.

"Don't worry about me, darlin'. That was all about you."

"Well, hell. This was the best lunch break I've ever had." Lunch break? Lunch break! Oh, Lord have mercy. I just got off at work. I'm going straight to hell. But damn, was it worth it.

"Glad to be of service." He winks and gathers up our trash. "Call me when you get home, 'kay?"

"You know I will, b–babe."

His eyes widen at the endearment but quickly soften. "I like that, darlin'." With a quick press of his lips to my forehead, he's out the door and on his way.

Once I make sure my hair is not a bird's nest, I cautiously open the dispensary door, only to come face-to-face with an incredibly curious Azalea. "Okay, sister-girl, wanna explain that glow you're rocking?" She steps forward, urging us both back into the dispensary.

"Well, you know what they say—pregnant women glow."

"Hmm. Wanna tell me why your man just walked outta here, looking like the king of the world while humming a little tune?"

I can't help the smile that takes over my face at the picture she's painting. I can just see him—a spring in his step and a smug grin. "Couldn't tell you."

"Oh, you most certainly can, and you will. Because if you leave me to piece this together on my own, I can only assume you just had some mid-morning delight... AT WORK!"

With wide eyes, I slap a hand over her mouth just as Seraphine steps into the room. "Azalea Josephine, you hush up."

"Hush up about what?" Seraphine asks.

"Oh, Myles here just hooked up at work. Oh, Jesus! Did you Lysol?"

Seraphine, bless her, is trying her best to maintain her composure, but I can see it's slipping.

"Oh, good gravy! There is nothing to sanitize. We made out, all hot and heavy, but no clothing was removed."

"Oh." Azalea sounds disappointed, and rightfully so. She'd love nothing more than to have something like this to tease me over. "Well, that sounds anticlimactic."

"Not for me," I mumble, causing the cord that is Seraphine's composure to snap. She's doubled over, clutching her stomach laughing.

"Y'all are some kinda mess. I seriously never know what to expect. Anyway, Myles, your client is here."

"Thanks, hun," I tell her with a smile as I head toward the reception area.

"Well, I'm still gonna Lysol!" Azalea hollers at my retreating back.

Chapter Thirty-Five

Cash

I WALK OUT OF SOUTHERN ROOTS ON CLOUD NINE. A little stiff in my stance, but cloud-fucking-nine nonetheless.

Every time I see Myla Rose, I feel a little bit lighter. She just has this constant glow, this joy, and damn if she doesn't pour that light into others. Spending a little time with her before heading out to Mrs. Mills' consultation was just what the doctor ordered.

Plugging the address Kathy gave me into my GPS, I shift my truck into gear, smiling all the while. Legit, after the last few days, there's not a thing on this earth or otherwise that could knock this goofy-ass love-drunk grin from my lips.

As long as I've got Myla Rose, I've got everything I need and then some. She's everything I thought I had with Kayla and so much more. And even though we haven't really discussed it, I'm pretty positive we're on the same page.

"You have arrived at your destination," my GPS alerts me with her crisp British accent, all proper and shit.

I take in my surroundings and double-check the address. What I thought was a narrow road is, in fact, the Mills' driveway. It's long and winding, and about halfway down it is a massive iron gate with a family crest on each side of the opening. The landscaping, which runs the length of the drive and surrounds the house, is impeccable, and they even have a fountain in the middle of the circle drive.

The house itself is towering and slightly formidable with its deep red brick rising three stories high.

Who needs this much? I think to myself as I check to make sure I have everything I need for this consult, which I do. My notebook is nestled in my back pocket, my tape measure is secured at my side, and my pencil's tucked behind my ear.

It's show time.

I lift the ornate brass knocker, tapping it against the glossy black door, and not even two seconds later, the door opens, bringing me face-to-face with a butler. *A butler.* In a little butler suit and everything.

"Please, sir, do come in. Mrs. Mills will see you in the formal living room."

"Uh, sure. Lead the way," I tell him, trying my hardest

not to laugh. He's only doing his job, but *come the fuck on*.

I follow him through the house, taking several turns along the way. The floors are a white marble and the walls are papered in shades of gold. This shit's like something out of a movie.

"Here we are, sir," The butler informs me as we come to a set of French doors.

"Mr. Carson, how nice of you to join us. I was starting to think you weren't going to show." Her words instantly have my hackles up because I know I'm nowhere near late, and for her to imply it—yeah, that pisses me off. But, like they say, *The customer is always right*, so clenching my jaw, I grin and bear it.

"Yes, ma'am, traffic was a real beast today." We both know I'm talking out of my ass, because in a town like this, the only thing that causes traffic is a tractor, and even then..."So, let's talk a little more about the look you're going for."

"Yes, well, as we discussed, I'm in need of a new buffet. It's meant for my son, as a pre-engagement gift. He'll be here shortly, but until then, this is what I am imagining for him." Mrs. Mills gestures to the huge scrapbook on the coffee table, and together, we begin flipping through it, looking at different designs.

Five minutes later, there's a crackle of static before a voice floats through the room. "Your son has arrived, ma'am. Shall I send him back?"

"Yes, please do," Kathy says as she presses a button on the wall next to her chair.

A few moments later, a voice I prayed I'd never—ever—hear again trickles into the room. "Mother, I'm here..."

I hope and pray the body doesn't match the voice. *Please, God.*

But no, they match. Taylor is Mrs. Mills' son and Myla's ex, and he's just as douchey as ever. He's decked out in the official Bro-Douche uniform of the South, a pastel seersucker and plaid patchwork button-down, way too short khaki shorts, and Sperry topsiders.

He stalks into the room, coming to rest at his mother's side before his eyes land on me. "What. Are. You. Doing. Here?" he seethes. "Mother, why is *he* here?"

Kathy looks utterly perplexed. "Taylor, darling, whatever do you mean? Mr. Carson is here to build your buffet."

"That miscreant isn't building shit for us."

"Taylor Augustus Mills, you watch your—"

"I will not. This loser is playing house with Myla Rose. Jesus, he's probably her bastard's dad."

Silently, I sit on the antique couch, listening as he spouts off one line of bullshit after another. This kid is talking straight out of his ass, and my top is about to blow. He's messing with the wrong man and talking about the wrong girl.

"I mean, Jesus, Mother, for all we know, she planned this. When her attempt to trap me with a baby didn't work, she probably concocted some scheme with *Mr. Carson* here to rob us blind under the guise of working."

Does this jerk-off even hear himself? Yeah, no. That's it. I'm done. Quietly, I stand and begin gathering up the things I brought. Without a word, I make my way to the double-doors. Taylor has stopped talking. Kathy has stopped talking. The room is blanketed in silence. The calm before the storm.

I pause in the entryway and turn to face the mother and son, and I know they see the lightning flashing in my eyes, and I'll make damn sure they hear the thunder in my voice. "You keep Myla's name outta your mouth, you hear me? Better yet, don't even think it. She's not your concern. She's mine. But you keep on spreading shit like this around about her? You'll become my problem, and let me assure you...that's not something you want."

"Now you listen here—" I turn and walk away in the middle of whatever garbage Taylor Mills was planning to spew, because I've heard more than enough. He's the goddamn epitome of an entitled, over-privileged prick, and I sure don't know what Myla ever saw in him.

Running on adrenaline and instinct alone, I don't even realize I've driven to Myla's house until I'm parked under the shade of her oak tree. I know she's not home from the salon yet, but the need to be near her is overwhelming.

The way Taylor talked about her made me want to snap his neck, and I know that her presence will calm me. So, I'll kick my feet up and wait. God knows, she's worth it.

I also know she keeps a key under her potted plant, so I shoot her a quick text to let her know I'm here and waiting on her. I'm so fucking anxious to have her near me. I know she didn't hear the things he said, but my gut tells me she's probably heard him say much, much worse.

Gotta be real, too. It's eating at me, wondering why she was with him—what she saw in him—because all I see is a Grade-A loser. He's the kind of guy who peaks in high school and tries desperately to hang onto those 'golden years' for far too long. Guys like Taylor Mills have expiration dates, and goddamn if he isn't way past his sell-by date.

I leave my boots at the door and make myself right at home, settling down into that same loveseat where I first got my hands on Myla Rose.

I smile, remembering how on fire she was for me, how her entire body lit up with my touch, so responsive. Before I know it, my eyes slip shut and I drift off with a goofy-ass grin curled on my lips.

I startle at the sound of the front door opening, straightening up just in time to see Myla walk in. Even after standing all day with back-to-back clients, she's fucking radiant. "Hey there, darlin'," I rasp out as I stand to hug her, drawing her into my arms and holding her there.

"I was glad to get your text—surprised, but glad. What's going on, babe?" She tilts her head up to look at me but stays wrapped in my arms as if she knows I need her touch.

"Let's sit down, yeah?" I realize my mistake the moment it happens. She's staring back at me with fear blanketing her every feature. "Nothing bad, darlin', just got a lot to say, and maybe a few questions." Dropping a quick kiss to her forehead, I pull her down beside me onto the loveseat.

"Okay...talk."

"Well, lemme start from the beginning. The other day, I met a lady at The Pig while I was waiting to check out. She was looking to have a piece of furniture built, so I gave her my card. She called a few days later, and we set up a consultation for today."

"Cash! That's awesome. You're so talented—"

"Hang on, I'm not finished." I reach down and clasp her hands in mine. "So, I get to her house today and we're chatting, going over plans, and her son walks in."

"Right, I'm following. Keep going."

"Her son is Taylor. Your ex." She pales and attempts to pull her hands back from mine.

"O–okay. Th–that's fine. Just because he and I have a history doesn't mean you can't do work for them." She nods her head a few times, as if to convince herself that her words aren't utter bullshit.

"Darlin'. If you think I'd do any work for them, you're sorely mistaken. He recognized me from the beach, and shit got ugly and I stormed outta there. But before leaving, I told him to keep your name outta his mouth."

"Oh, Cash..." She brings her head to rest on my shoulder. "You didn't have to do that. I don't want to harm your business."

"Look at me, darlin'. Don't you know you're worth more than any sum of money? With the shit he was popping off at the mouth with, he's lucky I didn't knock his teeth down his throat. What did you *ever* see in him?"

I'm not trying to be funny, but she cracks up at my question. "Oh, babe. I wish I knew. I've known him my whole life, and I'd crushed on him since we were kids. He used to be so sweet, and I guess over the years, I'd put him on a pedestal, and when he finally gave me the time of day, I was so excited. I thought he was ready to admit he felt the same way when he just wanted to drag me along and brag to his friends. I was nothing more than a game to him...and our game ended with me getting one hell of a prize, huh?"

"That baby in your belly is for sure a prize—the only good thing that deadbeat will ever make. Too bad for him, he'll never know him. Not if I have anything to say about it."

"Wh–what do you mean, Cash?"

"What I mean..." I take a deep breath, praying with all my might that this doesn't send her running for the hills. "Is that, if you'll allow me the honor, I'd like to raise this baby with you. It'd mean the goddamn world to be his dad."

Her eyes well with tears, and they drop one after another. And this time, when she goes to pull her hands from mine, I let her. She bolts from the couch and starts pacing.

Back and forth, back and forth, back and forth.

After what feels like an eternity of pacing and tears, I stand, causing her to run smack into my chest on her return trip. However, instead of pushing me away, she wraps her arms around my neck and burrows her head into my chest. "Y–you mean that?"

"With all my heart, darlin'. I can't think of a thing on this earth that would mean more to me."

"You realize you're one of a kind, Cash Carson?" she sniffles and wipes her tears on my sleeve. "A dream come true."

"As long as I have you, I don't need to dream, because you're more than I could ever ask for." Bending low, I scoop her into my arms. "Which way to your room?"

She directs me, and I set off up the stairs. I push open her door and set her down. "Get undressed, Myla."

"Undressed?"

"Yup," I tell her, popping the 'P' as I make my way into her bathroom.

I set to work drawing her a bath but come to a dead stop when she steps into the room. She's completely bare and completely breathtaking. *Goddamn.* This may not be the first time I've seen her body, but with it constantly growing and changing, every time is like the first time, and I fucking love it...her.

Wordlessly, she makes her way to me, and I help her step into the tub. "You relax, darlin', and I'll start dinner, yeah?"

"Yeah, babe. No way am I gonna argue with that." I step out of the bathroom and rifle through her clothes for her phone. Finding it, I bring it to her. "What's that for?" she asks with a sweet smile.

"Just thought you might wanna tell Azalea the news."

"Well, you've just thought of everything, huh?"

She laughs but takes her phone from me, and not even two seconds later, it trills out her text tone. Her gaze grows hazy and distant as it beeps again. And again.

"Everything okay?"

"Uh...yeah, yes. Everything is f–fine." I can tell she's lying from the wobble in her voice, but I don't call her on it. We've both had an emotional day, and with all the resolve I'm capable of, I turn and head out to the kitchen to whip us up some dinner.

Even if it kills me, I have to trust that if those texts were important, she'd tell me. Especially after today.

Chapter Thirty-Six

Myla Rose

I SHOULD BE RELAXING.

I should be over the moon giddy.

All my dreams just became reality, but with a handful of text messages, it feels like the walls are closing in on me.

When my phone flashed with a text from an unknown number, I figured it was a new client or a referral. But as soon as my eyes scanned those cruel words, I knew it was Taylor.

In my heart, I know I need to tell Cash about the texts. And in my heart, I know he's who he says he is and that he's in this for the long haul. I know we aren't just playing house, but what if this proves to be too much? I know he says he wants my heart and that he can handle my baggage, but what if this breaks us?

It's one thing to say he wants to raise this sweet baby with me, but it's totally another to go toe-to-toe with

Taylor and all of his family's resources and connections.

Sinking lower into the water, I let the tears fall as I read his awful, hate-filled texts again.

Unknown: I may not want you, but there is no way that trash is going to have you.

Taylor: Mark my words, Myla Rose. Just because I don't want you doesn't mean I'm willing to share. I may not be yours, but you're mine.

Taylor: That baby is mine. I own you. Both of you.

Taylor: Expect to hear from my attorney. Maybe if you ask nicely, I'll give you every other weekend.

This feels impossible. Insurmountable. I need Cash. I love him. So very much. From the very second I heard his deep, rumbly voice and looked into those rain cloud eyes. He's haunted my dreams and occupied my waking thoughts since day one, and deep in my soul, I know we can weather this storm together.

He's my strength, my support, and I know he can only help me through things he's aware of. I also know that means I need to buck up and tell him about Taylor's texts. I just hate the thought of such a special night being tainted by such ugliness.

So, later. I'll tell him later.

I soak until my skin shrivels and prunes, which takes me back to the beach with Preston and Lucas. Those boys are such a joy, and thinking of them brings me the smile I need to head out and face Cash.

Dressed for comfort in ribbed sleep shorts and a matching tank, I make my way into the kitchen where I find Cash effortlessly plating our dinner. "Mmm," I moan. "Something sure smells good."

"Perfect timing. Hope you like alfredo?"

"Does a cow have spots?" I pick up one of the plates and follow him out to the dining room table. Sitting down, I waste no time digging in. I'm emotional and hormonal...and just plain hungry. "Oh-mah-gah," I say around a forkful of pasta, savoring the explosion of flavor. "This is so good. Like, so good."

"Glad you like it, darlin'."

We make it through dinner without any mention of the texts, which elates me. I'm thanking my lucky stars, thinking he's gonna let it drop. What a joke, and damn if I shouldn't've known better. Cash Michael Carson is nothing if not persistent.

After scrubbing the dishes and loading the dishwasher, Cash leads me to the bedroom. I fix my gaze on him, staring hungrily as he sheds his T-shirt, jeans, and socks before crawling into my bed and sliding under the sheets.

When he pats the spot next to him, I realize I'm still standing at the foot of the bed staring at him. "You coming, Myla?" I climb into the bed next to him, nestling my head on his warm, strong chest, and he wraps me in his arms, and it just feels so right.

Which is why my heart drops clear into my gut when he hits me with, "Myla Rose, you wanna tell me why that message on your phone got you all upset?"

My entire body tenses, and I know he feels it, but after a deep breath or two, I manage to relax...sort of. "Nothing to worry about, babe. Just a difficult client." Oh, God, I hate lying to him.

"You sure, darlin'?" His tone tells me he's suspicious. My belly feels like it's full of lead.

"Yeah, Cash, I'm sure." *Sure that I'm going straight to hell.*

"Okay," Cash says on a resigned huff. "If you say so." He threads his fingers through my hair, using my long strands as leverage to lift my face to his. His lips come down hard on mine, his kiss searing me. "Good night, darlin'."

"G'night, babe." I toss and turn restlessly. This baby boy already has me all kinds of uncomfortable, and adding another body to the bed is an adjustment. After a few more rounds of side-back-side-back, I find my sweet spot curled up on my right side against Cash's warm body.

I'm finally drifting off, wrapped once again in the arms I've dreamed about so many nights, when I hear Cash mumble oh, so softly, "Love you, darlin'." It's so quiet, I almost wonder if I imagined it.

But like Cash, I'm not one to let things go, so just as softly, I reply, "I love you too, Cash Carson." I sigh and snuggle closer to him, reveling in the feel of his rough hand palming my bump as we both succumb to sleep.

I wake the next morning to the scent of bacon and coffee, and hot damn, if that isn't the best way to start the day. Mid-stretch, I realize that delicious scent is coming closer, and when I open my eyes, Cash is standing in the doorway with a tray.

"How do you feel about breakfast in bed?"

"Is that even a real question?"

"No, ma'am, I just wanted to hear that sweet, sleepy voice of yours." I can feel my cheeks pinken at his swoon-worthy words.

"Well, get in here, babe." Setting the tray at the end of the bed, Cash carefully gets back into bed before passing me my coffee—with just the right amount of half-n-half—along with a plate of bacon and fruit. Maybe not the most balanced meal, but it's perfect to me. Just like the man who made it.

"Hey, Cash?"

"Yeah?"

I fidget, turning to face him a little more fully. "Would you wanna come with me to my doctor's appointment Friday? I mean, you don't have to, but—"

Cash silences me with a quick kiss. "Darlin', there's no other place I'd rather be. Text me the time and address, and I'll be there."

"You're something else, Cash. An entirely different breed of man. The kind my Grams always said they didn't make anymore, but I know she'd be gaga over you."

"Well, that's an honor, from what you've told me about her." Yep, he knows every right thing to say to make my heart pitter-patter. "Now, eat up. We both have busy work days."

Chapter Thirty-Seven

Myla Rose

Yup, my appointment's at ten, Simon," I huff out, struggling to hold my phone and get dressed. "Sim, hang on. Gotta put you on speaker."

"Do you want me to come with you? This is the big appointment, right?"

"It sure is. But, no. You don't have to come with. Cash is."

"Cash, huh? Y'all serious?"

"I–I love him. So, yeah, it's pretty serious."

"Well damn, girl. Look at you all grown up."

I can't help the laugh that topples from my lips. "I've been grown."

He responds with a deep chuckle of his own. "You keep telling yourself that, Myles. No matter what, I'll always see you as that scrawny little freckle-faced girl with knobby knees and braces."

His words transport me back to when we first met.

I was sitting on Grams' porch—like I'd been doing every day since Mama dropped me off a week ago, waiting for her to change her mind and come back.

I was staring down at my lap, drawing shapes in the dirt on the bottom step, when a raspy voice called out, "She ain't coming back. You gotta know that."

I looked up, only to come eye-to-eye with the most beautiful blue eyes I'd ever seen. Blue like a swimming pool on a hot summer's day. Far too pretty for a boy, but belonging to a boy all the same. "S–she might," I told him defiantly. I could tell he was older, but not by too much.

"Naw. She ain't. Heard your Grams telling my mom. She's gone." I burst into tears at his words, realization blanketing me. "Now, don't cry, girl."

But I can't help it. I devolved into a teary, snotty mess. She may not have been a good mother, but she was all I'd ever known.

"C'mon, please don't cry." The boy wrapped me tightly in his arms and held me until my tears dried. "You're better off without her."

"You think so?" I asked, taking the time to really look at him. He was scrawny, with matted hair and covered with dirt smudges.

"I know so. Now, what's your name?"

"Myla Rose," I told him, thankful to have a friend.

We both startled when from beyond the clearing, we heard a booming voice roar, "SIMON, YOU GET YOUR ASS HOME, BOY."

He jumped up like someone had lit a fire under him.

"Gotta go!"

From that day forward, Simon was my protector and I was his escape.

"Simon, I'm as grown as it gets. I pay my own bills, own my business, and I'm about to pop out a baby." My words aren't said with venom, and I know he can hear my smile.

"Yeah, yeah. Guess you're right. Well, I wanna see pictures from the ultrasound, 'kay? Gotta see with my own eyes that my nephew's growin' good."

"That I can do. Why don't you see if D wants to meet us for lunch, and I'll invite the girls?"

"Sounds good. See you later, Myles."

My fingers fly across my screen as I fire off a quick group text, asking the girls to lunch before tossing my phone in my purse and heading out the door. I'm so beyond ready to check on my little bean that I don't even wait for their replies. Twenty weeks is the appointment every mom gets crazy-anxious-excited for. There's something so surreal about seeing your baby on that screen, and this time, we'll get an in-depth look.

The tech will measure his little bones and give us an estimated weight, she'll count his fingers and toes, and I'll get to see his sweet baby face. I'm so damn ready. Not to mention, this is also the last time I'll see him before his grand arrival in September. And Cash will be there with me, by my side and holding my hand through it all.

Today is gonna be one for the books. I can feel it.

I pull into the parking lot, only to find Cash ready and waiting for me, coffee in hand. *This man—gah!* "Well, hello, handsome. That for me?" I nod, gesturing toward the coffee.

"Sure is. I read online that caffeine can help the baby be more active during an ultrasound." Oh. Oh, my heart.

"Well, look at you. All thoughtful."

"Always for you, darlin'. Now let's go. I'm ready to lay eyes on my boy." Seriously, I must have done something awfully right in a past life to have this man here and now.

After jotting my name down on the sign-in sheet, Cash and I take a seat toward the back of the waiting room. We're both anxious, all drumming fingers and tapping feet. Thankfully, we don't wait long before my name is called.

The nurse leads us back to the ultrasound room and instructs me the same as last time—on the table, shirt lifted, waistband rolled down. Belinda squirts the warm gel onto my belly and starts expertly shifting the wand around.

"All right, here we go." She moves the wand, applying pressure. "Ten little fingers. Ten toes."

The whoosh of my bean's heartbeat fills the room, and Cash sits up straighter. "Is that—"

"Yes, sir, that's your baby's heartbeat. A perfect one

hundred and thirty beats per minute."

"That's not too fast?" The worry in his voice tugs on my heartstrings, reminding me that I'm keeping secrets from him.

"No, sir, his heartbeat is one hundred percent within a normal and healthy range." Belinda continues about her measurements, but instead of watching the screen, I'm watching Cash. His cheeks are damp with happy tears.

"All right, Miss Myla, I have some images for you and Dad to take home. Dr. Mills—"

"I'm sorry, Doctor who?" Oh, Jesus. Guess I shoulda told Cash who my doctor is. Not that he's anything like his wife or his son.

Belinda's eyes dart between us uncomfortably. "As I was saying, Dr. Mills isn't quite ready, so y'all can head back out to the waiting room. A nurse will call you."

I grab Cash by the hand, tugging him along behind me, seating us as far away from other people as possible in the small space.

"Your doctor's related to Taylor how, exactly?"

"Don't get mad, okay?" His mouth is tight, but he nods. "Dr. Mills is his dad."

"His dad? You have to be kidding me, Myla. Really?"

"But he's so different from Kathy and Taylor, I swear it, Cash. I think he might love this baby too. I mean, he's never outright said that. He's never been anything but professional, but I just know it." Reaching for his hand, I take a trembling breath. "I promise, babe, I wouldn't come here otherwise. Trust me?" Those two little words almost make me puke, because why should he trust me? I'm a liar. He just doesn't know it.

"I know. Fuck, I know. Just don't like it. Can I come to the rest of your appointments?"

"Sure, if it'll make you feel better."

"It will. It so will." His features return to normal, and he relaxes back into his chair. His easy trust in me has me feeling lower than the floor.

Fifteen minutes later, the nurse calls my name again, and we head back with her. "Sir, you can head on to the exam room, and as soon as your wife finishes with the nurse, she'll join you."

I'm about to correct her, but Cash just smiles and thanks her.

Five minutes later, I'm joining him in the exam room, and shortly after that, Dr. Mills is knocking on the door.

"Come on in." He enters the room, seating himself on the swivel stool in front of his computer.

"Not alone today, I see, Ms. McGraw."

"No sir, this is Cash Carson."

His eyes widen at the name, and a barely-there smile graces his lips. "Nice to meet you, Mr. Carson. Glad to see someone's looking after these two." He clicks around my file for several minutes before standing. "Go on and lie back, and we'll listen to little man's heartbeat and double-check how he's measuring."

I follow his instructions, and he works in silence. Though it's not an awkward silence like you'd expect, just a calm kind of quiet. "All right, Ms. McGraw, you're measuring right on time. The girls at the desk will get your next appointment set up. Have a nice afternoon, and it was very nice meeting you, Mr. Carson." And just like that, he's out the door and on to his next patient.

"Well, he's..." Cash pauses, searching for the words. "Not what I expected."

"Told you so, babe. Now, wanna meet everyone for lunch?"

"Sure thing, darlin'." We walk hand-in-hand out to the parking lot. "I'll follow you?"

"Sounds good." I drop a quick kiss to his cheek before hopping into Bertha.

I guide the Land Cruiser to stop right outside Dilly's, a cute little lunch spot about a block from the salon. Cash pulls his truck into the spot behind mine before coming over to open my door for me.

"You ate here before?" he asks, helping me out of Bertha.

"A time or two. They're so close, but I always forget they're here. But the bean isn't feeling Dream Beans, and this is close enough for the girls to join. OH! You haven't met Magnolia. I hope she comes. Warning though, babe—she's shy. Like super shy."

"Well, we're at no risk for me scaring her away. Azalea though..." he trails off, knowing full and well that I'm catching his drift. Girl's a freight train gone off the tracks some days. Others, she's the Southern belle her mama raised her to be. The fun thing is that you never know which you'll get.

It seems we're the first to arrive, and since I'm not sure on how many are joining us, the hostess seats us at a large table in the back. Slowly but surely, our group starts to trickle in. First Drake, then Azalea.

"Hey, AzzyJo. Is Magnolia coming?" I ask her as she takes the seat next to me.

"Sure is," she tells me before turning to face Drake. "So you sure as shit had best be on your best behavior."

Drake holds his hands up in front of him. "Damn, Little Bit. Ain't been here five minutes and you're startin' in on me."

Azalea sighs loudly. "I mean it. She's...fragile. So be nice, and calm, and quiet. You know, all the things you aren't?"

"You wouldn't like me if I was all those things, Bit."

"I hardly like you now."

"Not what you said last—"

I can feel Azalea kick him under the table as she yells, "Can you just fucking agree to be nice?"

"Yeah, sure thing, Az," Drake says, his eyebrows drawn tight.

"Is Seraphine coming with Magnolia?" I ask, attempting to slice through their tension, because damn, it's thick.

"No, her dad's nurse called as we were leaving. I'm finished with my clients, so we just shut down the salon.

I made her swear she'd call if she needed us."

I don't like that, not one bit. That girl needs to realize that asking for help doesn't make her weak, especially when she has so many people who love and want to help her.

A few moments later, the door chimes and Magnolia walks in. Her head is down and her shoulders are hunched in, as if she's trying to make herself as small as possible. Briefly, she lifts her eyes to scan the restaurant before beelining for our table.

As she draws near, I realize she has tears in her eyes. "Mags?" I use the nickname without thinking about it. "Are you okay?"

"Oh, y–yeah, sure. I...b–backed into someone trying to park. I'm not the best driver, still fairly n–new." She looks down, embarrassed by her admission.

"Oh, well, that's no big deal, hun. Not to mention, that's what insurance is for."

"Y–yeah. You're r–right. H–he was just so m–mad," she laments, taking the seat next to Azalea. Over the course of the past week, Azalea, Seraphine, and I quickly realized Magnolia gets uncomfortable around men, so we try to always be present as a buffer.

Even now, Azalea quietly asks her to switch seats, ensuring that Mags is girl-locked on both sides. She's just gotten herself situated at her new seat when the door chimes again.

This time it's Simon, and he's fuming, muttering, and mumbling to himself as he heads our way. When he notices Magnolia, though, he comes to a dead stop. After forcing several deep breaths, he schools his features into what I call his calm mask.

"Sweetheart, you okay?" It takes me a moment to realize he's addressing Mags.

She nods, refusing to make eye contact. "You sure?" She nods again. "Good. I gave that jackass the what-for and sent him on down the road. Acting like a little paint swap is the end of the goddamn world. I swear, some fucking people."

Once we're all here, introductions are made, and Simon relays to us the altercation outside. Lunch is amazing, and the company is even better. By the time our checks arrive, we're all laughing, smiling, and passing around the pictures from my ultrasound.

All-in-all, today has been nothing short of magical. And I just know I'm the luckiest girl around because I have an entire lifetime of this on my horizon.

Chapter Thirty-Eight

Cash

I READ IN MY *WHAT TO EXPECT* BOOK THAT PREGNANCY can cause mood swings, but for the past month, Myla has been extra-super-moody. I don't wanna say crazy, but *damn*. She goes from hot to cold and back again in the blink of an eye.

Not to mention, these mood swings always go together with her text notifications. Reluctantly, I believed her the first time when she said it was a problem client, but come on. How many difficult clients can you have? Combine that with her conveniently forgetting to tell me her doctor was Taylor's dad—pregnant brain, she called it—and my doubts are building. I hate feeling this way, but I'm at a total loss.

I'm almost at the point of asking the guys if they know anything, but that feels like a violation of our relationship. Of her trust. Which is kinda absurd, since I'm ninety-nine percent sure she's lying to me.

Sliding my safety goggles back down, I shake off the negative thoughts fogging up my brain. This piece has a deadline, and these cuts have to be made to meet it, and distracted cutting leads to injury. No thanks.

I lose myself in my work for hours, measuring, marking, cutting, sanding. Again, and again and again. By the time I finish, the sun has long since set. I get so hyper focused when working that the outside world falls away, meaning I haven't talked to Myla Rose at all today. Not even once. *Fuck.*

Scrambling around the shop, I finally locate my phone on one of my work benches. Only there's no new notifications. *Double fuck.*

Unlocking my phone, I scroll as fast my fingers allow and dial Myla's number. Thank God, her sleepy voice comes through after the second ring. "Hey there, babe."

"Hey. Missed you today."

"Missed you too."

"Not to be that guy, but I was hoping to hear from you today..." I trail off, not wanting my agitation to upset her.

"I was so slammed at work today, and I remember you mentioning you *had* to get the piece you've been working on ready, so I figured you'd call me when you had time."

Her voice is raspy from sleep, and even if she's been lying to me, her words are a pang to my heart. "Fuck, darlin'. I'm sorry. Busy or not, I'll make time for you. Know that."

"Okay, Cash. Will you be mad if I go back to bed?"

"Not even a little. Sweet dreams, darlin'." I end the call and make my way home, feeling a smidge lighter.

I didn't sleep for shit last night. My mind was racing, all my thoughts centered on Myla Rose. Without bothering to check the time, I dial her number.

"Good morning, Mr. Carson," she chirps into the phone. Love that my girl's a morning person—after coffee, that is.

"G'morning to you too. You got another busy day?"

"Ugh, yes. We always get slammed right before summer really hits, then it slows down until fall."

"Can't wait for that slow time," I tell her, imagining all the ways I could keep her occupied.

"Though I'll probably stay busy, with little man coming in September."

"True. Didn't think of that. Well, I'm always here to help, darlin'. Any way I can."

"*Any* way, huh? I can think of a few." *Yeah, me too.*

"Why don't you share some of those ways with me?"

"Oh, come now, a girl's gotta have some mystery." Her voice is laced with humor, but damn if her words don't set me on edge. It's her mystery that's killing me. Like, I'm two seconds from going all Scooby-Doo on her ass.

"Guess that's right. Well, I gotta get going, darlin'. Talk later. Love you."

She releases a soft sigh. "Love you too, babe."

It's mid-morning when I finally give in to the urge to go see Myla Rose. I figure if I come bearing caffeine, I'll be an extra-welcome sight. Add a quick kiss in, and it'll hold me over until she's off for the day.

Whistling a tune, I pop into Dream Beans and grab her favorite brew, pausing only to jot a little note on the side of her cup before dashing across the street to the salon.

The instant I open the door, I can sense something's wrong. It's like the air itself is charged. "Good morning, Miss Seraphine," I say, my smile tight.

"Oh, C–Cash. H–hey! Is Myles expecting you?" She asks as she stands and dashes around the reception desk, placing herself between the main salon and me. Because that's not suspicious behavior...not at all.

Gesturing down to the coffee in my hand, "No, ma'am. Planned on surprising her."

"Right. Well...um. Lemme run and go get her?" She turns to go fetch Myla Rose, but I stop her movement with a gentle hand to her shoulder.

"I got it."

"I *really* don't mind. In fact, I insist." I'm getting fed up with this song and dance really fast.

"Nope, I'm good." I step around her before she can attempt to block me again. In the main salon area,

Azalea is frozen mid-cut, staring at me with a look that wavers between fear and sympathy. *What the fuck*?

Myla Rose isn't at her station, so I head toward the dispensary, but I don't make it further than the entrance to the shampoo area.

Because right there, not even five feet away, my worst fucking nightmare is playing out in front of my very eyes. It's like a goddamn train wreck. Even though I know the only end result is the carnage of my heart, I can't look away. Not when *my* girl has her hands on *his* shoulders. Not when *my* girl is leaning into *him* like he's all she'll ever need.

This is Kayla and Kevin all over again, only a thousand times worse. This is my world not only shattering...no, it's outright crumbling, disintegrating, and all that'll be left is ashes.

I watch, rooted, unable to move as he pulls her closer. Her eyes catch mine over his shoulder. "Ca–Cash. N–no—" Her words are cut off by the press of his lips, hot and hard on hers, and goddamn if she doesn't seem to melt into him like he isn't the devil fucking incarnate. Like he isn't a self-absorbed, piece of shit, broke-her-heart loser.

She finally pulls away from him, wiping the back of her hand across her mouth, before blinking up at me while still locked in his embrace. I hold her guilt-ridden eyes, totally frozen. *Just like before, I didn't see this shit coming, not from a mile away.*

"Mmm, Myla, *damn.* I forgot how good you taste,"

Taylor groans out, his voice chock-full of want and need.

I bolt, not wanting to stick around for her reply. I make a quicker than quick pit stop at her station, leaving her coffee and my heart. Because goddamn if it isn't broken.

"Tell her I'm done and not to call," I holler to whoever may be listening as I head straight back out the door and into my truck.

I slam the truck door before pounding my fist against the steering wheel a few times. *How could I have been so stupid?* Guess this explains her weird behavior—pregnancy mood swings, my ass. More like she was struggling to hide her ex from me.

I'm literally shaking with rage, far too unsteady to drive, but when I see her hauling ass toward my truck, shouting my name through her sobs along the way, I throw it in gear and floor it, leaving her and her bullshit excuses in my dust.

Not even two seconds after peeling out from Southern Roots, my phone starts ringing. I send the call to voicemail, not bothering to check who's calling. I know who it is, and I have no desire to even hear her voice.

Because I know myself. I'm crushed by her, and she still owns my soul. The second I hear her voice, laden with tears, I'll give in and believe whatever tale she spins.

My phone rings again and again, leading me to power it down. "Focus on the facts," I chide myself as regret trickles in for not answering her call.

"She's been keeping shit from you. Every damn time you give your heart to someone, they tear it to shreds." My bitter ramblings last the entire drive back to my house, though I don't stay there long because everywhere I look is a memory of her.

In the short time we've been together, there's not a part of my life she hasn't touched. She's met my entire family, minus my mom. She's scattered pictures of us all throughout my house and hers. Shit, she even brought one of her Grams' quilts over here to keep a piece of the woman who raised her close when she sleeps here.

Fed the fuck up with my warring emotions, I stomp back to my truck, and I just drive. Everywhere and nowhere. I drive for hours upon hours until finally landing at my workshop. Here, maybe I'll find the peace I need. Myla Rose has never stepped foot into this space, and thank God for it, because throwing myself into work may be the only way to scrub my brain of the events of the day.

I flip on the overheads, as well as my spotlights, only to come face-to-face with the crib I poured my blood, sweat, tears, heart, and soul into. "FUCK!" I roar before throwing a tarp over it. "Out of sight, out of mind." I repeat the mantra a few times before beginning the actual build of the project I've been working on.

With each swing of the hammer, a new emotion fights for control.

Sadness—*swing.* Anger—*swing.* Guilt—*swing.* Rage—*swing.* Jealousy—*swing.* Again and again, until my mind's a mess and the piece is complete.

Too tired to drive home, I pass out on the small couch in my even smaller office.

Done. I'm done.

Chapter Thirty-Nine

Myla Rose

I CAN'T BREATHE. I'M GASPING, BUT I CAN'T BREATHE. My heart is lodged in my throat, effectively cutting off my air.

Watching Cash's taillights, my brain keeps replaying the events that led me here, knowing deep down that this pain, this ache, is a byproduct of my own stupidity.

I woke up sporting the same perma-smile I've had since meeting Cash, and it only got brighter when his name flashed across my phone screen as I sipped from my second cup of coffee. Even though our call was brief, his voice was just what I needed to put me at ease about Kathy Mills being on my book today. That's just one more secret I've been keeping. Cash has no clue I'm still doing her hair, and I just couldn't bring myself to tell him.

When I walk into the salon, I'm met with the normal hustle and bustle of the day, but there's also a chill in the air. Upon closer inspection, the smiles AzzyJo and Seraphine are wearing look forced—contrite, even. "What's good this morning?" I ask to cut the tension.

"Not much, Myles," Seraphine says with a small shrug. "Please know I tried to stop him."

Her words have me on a wire's edge, and the second I round the partition to my station, I see the problem. My chair is occupied by none other than my ex. Why the fuck…

"Myla, Myla, Myla. Shame on you for keeping me waiting. You know how I feel about promptness."

Gaping at him, I hiss, "Why are you in—my—chair?"

"Use your deductive reasoning skills, doll face." I pale at the use of his pet name for me, words I'd have gladly paid a million times over to never hear again. Taylor lets out a loud, exasperated sigh. "Obviously, I need a haircut, Myla. And we need to talk."

"We have absolutely nothing to talk about," I bite out, my hands on my hips. "Less than nothing." I turn to walk away from him, but he reaches out and roughly grabs my wrist. His grip is hard, unrelenting. "LET ME GO!" I shout at him.

"Myla, really. You're making a scene." With his grip still firm on my arm, he all but drags me toward the shampoo area. "Shut your damn mouth."

With more bravery than I feel, I bark at him, "Thought you wanted a haircut?"

He lets out a cruel laugh. "Like I'd trust you to cut my hair. No, I'm here for us to talk." He tugs me further into the room, away from listening ears. "Well, I'll talk. You'll listen. Do what I'm saying, and maybe I won't take that baby from you."

Jerking back as if he's dealt a physical blow, my eyes glisten with unshed tears. Resigned, I stand quietly and listen to the bullshit he spews. He still has a tight hold on my wrist, and the more agitated he becomes, the harder he jerks me around by it.

I place my free arm to his chest to push him away, but he only pulls me closer. Muttering on and on about nothing. I think he's lost it. I glance up, hoping to be able to signal to Azalea to call someone.

Instead, I see Cash's eyes glaring down at me, clouding over with hurt. Next thing I know, Taylor's sealing his lips to mine, and I can't seem to get him off me.

With great effort, I remove his lips from mine. Cash looks murderous. "Mmm, Myla, damn. I forgot how good you taste." I move my eyes from Cash to Taylor, shocked at his vulgar words, and by the time I look back to Cash, he's gone.

All I had to do was talk to him. Open up about Taylor's texts and come to him with honesty. Instead, I lied, and now he's gone. *How can someone live without their heart?*

I'm still standing frozen on the sidewalk in front of the salon when Drake's truck slides into the spot where Cash's had just been. "Myles, I came as soon as Azalea called." His words are cautious, and he approaches me warily. "Are you okay?"

"Please make him leave." My voice breaks as I fall to my knees on the sidewalk. I can only imagine the way this looks to the townsfolk milling about—pregnant and having an emotional breakdown on the side of the street in broad daylight. I have no one to blame but myself.

"C'mon, Myles, let's getcha up off the ground."

"No! I'm not stepping foot in there until *he* is gone."

Without another word, Drake is off like a shot toward the salon. Several moments later, he stalks back out, all but dragging Taylor kicking and screaming behind him.

"Get your filthy hands off me!"

"If you don't want my hands on you, then don't come 'round where you ain't wanted." Drake accentuates his words with a shove to Taylor's chest. "Get gone, and stay gone."

"Please, Myla doesn't really want me to go." He sniffs, squaring his shoulders. "It's painfully obvious that her dalliance with that piece of trash was nothing more than a cry for my attention, and her lips on mine further proved it."

"So help me God, if you ever touch her again...and that 'piece of trash' is ten times the man you could ever hope to be," Drake tosses back, crowding Taylor's space.

"Yeah, so much of a man that he ran off, leaving *her* all alone, with *me*." Turning my way, Taylor drops down to his haunches and grips my chin, forcing me to look at him. "Guess he's just not that into you, baby do—"

Before that wretched nickname can pass his lips, Drake has him pinned on his back. "Say one more word to her, and *I swear I will end you.* Now, do as I said. Get gone and stay gone." Drake stands and extends a hand down as if to help Taylor up, and stupidly, Taylor accepts it. Once upright, Drake shoves him hard toward his little Mercedes coupe. Thankfully, Taylor seems to have gotten the message and gets into his car, speeding off away from us.

"C'mon, Myles, he's gone. Let's get you inside." I allow Drake to pull me up off the ground and guide me with a hand at the small of my back. I'm too humiliated to meet anyone's stare—and my God, are they staring. There's a small crowd of looky-loos gathered along the opposite side of the street, and Seraphine and Azalea are standing out front. The only person not accounted for is Magnolia, who turns up once we all head inside.

"Sister-girl, are you okay?" Azalea sweeps me into a tight hug, rocking me as she holds me.

"No. Not at all," I tell her honestly. She walks me over to my station, supporting me as I lower myself into my chair.

"Everything'll be okay, Myles. Just you wait and see." Bless her heart. I know Seraphine is just trying to be positive, but it only stands to make me feel worse. *This is my fault. I broke us.*

Snatching up the coffee Cash left, I notice there's something written on the side of the cup.

> Darlin'-
> The only thing hotter than this coffee is you.
> Love you, C-

My breath catches and a new round of tears starts,

causing the girls and Drake to spring into action. Azalea gently pries the now cooled beverage away from me. Seraphine retreats to the front desk, where she starts calling the rest of my clients for the day and rescheduling them. Magnolia busies herself at her station, trying to stay out of the way.

And Drake—thank God for Drake. He scoops me up and takes me home. He even carries me from his truck to my room and tucks me in. "I know it seems real bad right now, Myles. But just you wait. Shit has a way of getting sorted, and if I know Cash, he'll pull his head outta his ass and get this fixed. That man loves you. Now sleep, and I'll send Little Bit over when I get back to the salon." He drops a quick kiss to my forehead before retreating the way he came.

I'm out cold when I feel the bed dip behind me. For a second, my heart soars, thinking Cash is here, but my hope quickly deflates when Azalea's soft scent surrounds me. "It'll be okay, Myla, I promise," I hear her say, and then I'm drifting back to sleep.

Chapter Forty

Cash

THE SOUND OF SOMEONE POUNDING ON THE SHOP door wakes me. And goddamn if this isn't déjà vu. Only instead of an angry Kayla on the other side of the door, I find an even angrier Simon.

Disoriented from a night of restless sleep, I'm in no shape to deal with this shit. I attempt to shut the door, not caring one bit that I'm being rude, but Simon isn't having it. With the force of ten linemen, Simon knocks me back with his shoulder to my chest.

"You sorry motherfucker," he yells as we tumble to the ground. On the floor, he easily pins me. "I. Fucking. Told. You," he clips out, reinforcing each word with jarring shakes, slamming my upper body into the concrete floor.

"The hell are you mad at me for?" I demand, shoving him off me. Jumping to my feet, I put my workbench between us. "Your girl's the one you should be talking to."

"My girl? Thought she was yours? Thought you loved her? Thought you were good for her. What a goddamn joke." His fists are clenched, knuckles white from the sheer force of holding himself back.

"How are you coming at me with this? No. This is on Myla Rose."

"The fuck you say?" Simon advances, working his way around the bench.

"Seems to me she wanted to string me along as *Plan B* if shit didn't bounce back with Taylor," I tell him, my hurt coating each word like a poison.

"Are you that dumb? You can't seriously be that—"

"You bust into my goddamn workshop and have the balls to call me ignorant? Get out. The facts speak louder than whatever lies you're here to tell. Just get the fuck out, and tell Myla I'll drop her shit off later."

"Guess you are that dumb. Just know you're pissing away the best thing you've ever had over shit you don't understand." This whole time, I've been waiting for him to deck me like I know he wants to. And deep down, maybe I'm looking for a fight too. So I'm more than a little let down when Simon turns to leave without so much as a backward glance.

As my fight leaves my body, exhaustion crashes down hard. I stagger back to the couch and drop down onto it before falling back into the same restless slumber.

When I come to God knows how many hours later, I realize I never turned my phone back on. Patting around the couch and my pockets, it's nowhere to be found. *The truck*—it's in the truck.

Scrambling up from the couch, I rush out and plug my phone into the car charger before powering it back up. Mad and hurt or not, I want to know she's okay.

My phone takes what feels like forever to power up, and when it does, I'm bombarded with texts and missed call alerts from damn near everyone I know.

Sixteen missed calls from Myla Rose.

Four missed calls from Southern Roots.

Two missed calls from Drake.

One missed call from Simon.

Three from an unknown number.

Two from my brother and one from my mom—I really hope those are unrelated.

Swiping away the missed calls, I toggle over to my voicemail app, skipping the text messages altogether. Thirteen new voicemails, eight from Myla. Pressing play on the first one from her, I sink back into the seat, trying my hardest to safeguard my heart.

"C–Cash." The break in her voice just about kills me, "P–please call m–me. I–it's not wh–what you think." Being the glutton for punishment I am, I listen to the rest of her messages, each one less coherent than the one before it, with the final one being nothing more than the sound of her tears.

My heart is shattered, and the pain in her voice is

digging splinters right into my chest. I throw my phone down to the passenger floorboard without checking the other voicemails or texts because this shit is messing with my head. What right does she have to be upset? This is her fault. She's nothing more than a fucking cheater, just like Kayla, and it'll serve me well to remember that.

Chapter Forty-One

Myla Rose

My mom abandoning me? Yeah, it hurt, but eventually, I realized I was better off without her. My Grams passing away gutted me, but deep down, I knew she was in a better place. Taylor leaving me when that test came up positive tore my heart to shreds, but I found a way to paste it back together and came out stronger for it.

Cash shutting me out? Yeah, no. There is no positive spin, just a whole lotta pain, regret, and sorrow. Oh, and anger, too. Though that's directed mostly at myself.

"Myles, let's go, time to get up," Azalea says as she ties back my curtains and raises the blinds.

Immediately, I pull the duvet over my head to block out the light. What business does the sun have shining when my world is so, so dark? "C'mon, sister-girl. It's been four days. It's time to get it together."

"Nope. I'm fine right here, thank you very much."

"You say that, but you're not seeing what I'm seeing. Myles, you need a shower. You need to eat real food—if not for you, then for the baby. And Lord knows, you need to go rescue sweet Magnolia from your clients."

"Just go, Az. I'll rejoin the world tomorrow." I burrow further under the covers. "Yeah, tomorrow sounds good. Promise"

"No, ma'am. TODAY!" She rips the duvet from my body, leaving it in a heap on the floor before repeating the action with the sheets. "Get up, Myles, I mean it. I'll go start you a shower."

Opting to take the path of least resistance, I follow her. I can always get back in bed after my shower.

Standing under the hot spray, I can't help but cry. "You okay, Myles?"

"No," I choke out. "I just...I miss him."

"I know you do. Have you heard from him?" Her question causes my tears to fall faster, harder.

"N–no. He's finished with me."

"You don't know that."

"No, I do, and I deserve it. If there's one thing Cash hates, it's a cheater, which he thinks I am. I brought this on myself."

"Oh, Myla—"

"No, don't you 'Oh, Myla' me. I did this. I broke us, and you're right, I need to stop wallowing. Crying hasn't ever once changed shit, and it's certainly not going to now."

Azalea's cheeks split into a wide smile. "You opened

your mouth, and Grams came out, girl. Because that sounded exactly like what she'd tell you."

At that, I smile. My first post-Cash smile—something I wasn't sure was possible. Feeling a little stronger, I shut off the water and wrap myself in a fluffy towel. "Wanna grab something to eat?"

"Sister-girl, I thought you'd never ask."

After getting dressed, Azalea ushers me down the stairs and into the passenger seat of her little BMW Z4—a graduation gift from her mom and pops.

"Where are we going?"

"Late lunch and a movie. We gotta get your mind off he-who-shall-not-be-named."

Through my laughter I tell her, "While I appreciate the effort, you can say his name. We share friends, and I don't want y'all walking around on eggshells around me, okay?"

"You're stronger than me, Myles, that's for damn sure."

We spend the rest of the drive in a comfortable silence—me lost in my thoughts, and Azalea, well, Lord only knows why she's being so quiet.

I don't realize I've nodded off until Azalea puts the car in park. "Come on, we're here."

I take a few moments to get my bearings and realize she's driven us across the bay. "Why're we in Mobile?"

"Thought a change of scenery would be nice, and this restaurant is supposed to be to die for."

"Can't argue with that," I tell her as she links her

arm with mine, leading me toward the little bistro. It's unseasonably cool for June, so we opt to sit on the patio. Over the course of lunch, AzzyJo tries to distract my muddled brain and hurt heart with small talk, but it's no use. Cash Carson is so embedded into my heart that thoughts of him flow through my veins.

"Myla Rose, have you heard a word I said?"

"Honestly? No." I feel bad, but...

She lets out a frustrated huff. "I give up. Obviously, talking isn't the answer. So, let's move on to the distraction portion of our day. What movie you wanna see?"

"What's playing?" Azalea whips out her phone and pulls up the show times before sliding it across the table to me. I scan the list twice over before settling on the new *Pirates of the Caribbean* movie. Johnny and Orlando aren't a cure-all, but they're something good, and that's good enough.

By the time we walk out of the theater, the sun has set, and we can't stop talking about the movie. It was good enough that once my brain told my heart to shut it, I really got into it.

"Aren't you glad I pulled you outta the house today?" Azalea asks with a proud smile.

"Yeah, yeah," I say, pausing to dial Simon's number. I've watched all the rest of the *Pirates* movies with him, and seeing this one with Azalea feels like betrayal, and I need to confess.

"Oh, no, Myla, don't—"

Her words fall away when Simon answers on the

third ring. "Myles, hey. What's up?"

"I've gotta tell you something, Sim. Don't be mad, okay?"

"I could never be mad at you."

"Gonna hold you to that. I just saw the new *Pirates* movie with Azalea." I duck my head, waiting for him to give me shit about breaking tradition.

"Huh. Guess you'll just have to watch it twice."

"That I can do," I tell him just as there's a loud commotion in the background on his end. "What's going on, Sim?"

It's then that I hear it. Cash. He's with...Cash. "Simon, are you with Cash right now?" Azalea shakes her head, but she doesn't look the least bit surprised. Placing my hand over the speaker, I ask her, "You knew?"

"Yeah, I knew. Drake's with them too. It's not what you think though, Myla."

"Someone's gotta talk some sense into him," Simon tells me.

"Simon McAlister! No. Please, no. As much as I love y'all—and Cash—this is my battle, not y'all's. Please leave him alone. I've already caused him enough trouble and hurt. He doesn't need you going all *Big Brother* on his ass."

"Might be too late for that. Gotta go—talk to you later." He disconnects the call before I can say anything else, which pisses me off because I have a lot to say.

"Azalea Josephine, I can't believe you right now. You set me up!"

"We did this because we love you and we hate seeing you hurt. Please don't be mad."

With a frustrated shake of my head, I resume walking toward her car. "I'm not mad, AzzyJo, just annoyed."

"Well, hang on to that feeling then, because there's more coming your way." Her words are ominous, and I'm not quite sure what she means, but I'm too annoyed to ask.

God, I wish I would've asked.

Chapter Forty-Two

Cash

Four days. Four days without her smile. Her laugh. Her voice. *Fuck.* Four days without her touch. Four days, and I'm a goddamn mess.

I kept thinking she'd call again—praying she'd call again. But she didn't, and I'm too prideful to call her. No, instead, I keep listening to her voicemails on repeat. I've read her texts so many times I've memorized them. I miss her so much that I don't know what to do with myself.

But I'm also so fucking angry with her and hurt. She knows everything I went through with Kayla, and yet she so readily put me through it again. Makes me wonder if I ever even knew her.

My phone rings on the coffee table, and I lunge toward it, hoping it's Myla Rose. Mad or not, I ache to hear her sweet voice. She's like a sickness I can't seem to purge. I deflate when I see Drake's name on the screen, but I answer his call anyway. I've shut everyone out, and it's well past time to rejoin the rest of the world, broken heart or not.

"Hey, D, what's up?"

"Not much. You wanna drive out for lunch?" He sounds oddly hopeful, and I really do need to get outta the house.

"Yeah, I'll see you in twenty." I disconnect the call, hop in the shower, and throw on what I hope are clean clothes before hitting the road.

When I pull up to Drake's, I'm instantly on edge. There are familiar vehicles scattered throughout his yard. Doing a quick inventory, I see Simon's truck, Jake's SUV, and...my mom's Camry. *What the hell is going on?*

To ease my building anxiety, I reason that maybe it's just a big BBQ, and all our families will be coming. Yeah, that's it. Now if only I believed that.

I bypass knocking and let myself in. Shockingly, or maybe not, everyone is gathered in the living room as if they'd been waiting for me.

My mom is the first to greet me. "Cash, baby, I'm so glad you're here."

"Yeah, Mom, me too. Not to be rude, but why are y'all here?"

This time, it's Simon who speaks up. "We have shit to say, and you need to listen. Drake volunteered his house.

Figured you wouldn't step foot in mine." And he'd be right about that.

"Talk about what?" I ask, lowering myself into the only available chair. In the very center of the room. Seriously, I'm the middle of a goddamn circle. Yeah, this isn't a family BBQ. Not at all.

"About Myla Rose," Drake tells me.

Hearing her name has my spine straightening and my hair standing on end. "So, it's like that?"

"Yeah, Cash, it is," Drake says solemnly.

Glancing around the room, I feel caged and cornered. "Can't say I'm really feeling that right now."

"Oh, baby. You need to listen to your friends," Mom supplies.

"Do I? Why are you and Jake even here?

"I'm here because when I ran into Drake at the store the other day, I mentioned not hearing from you, and being the sweet boy that he is, he informed me as to why. I'm not gonna let you throw this girl and her baby away over some little misunderstanding."

"Yeah, because being lied to for a month and catching her lip-locked with her ex is some 'little misunderstanding'," I tell her using air-quotes. "And why are you here, Jake?"

"I'm just here for the show, brother." *Fucking asshole.*

"Of course you are." Shaking my head, I slump down, resting my elbows on my knees. "Let's just get this shit-show on the road, yeah?"

"Be glad everyone else favored talking sense into you.

My idea was to beat it into you."

"Thanks, Simon. Really, thanks." My sarcasm drips, coating the room.

Simon bolts from his chair. "I'd be more than happy to beat the shit outta you. Follow through on my promise—I told you not to hurt her."

I laugh a dry, hollow laugh. "Me, hurt her? Riiiight."

Simon lunges at me, and I'm up from my seat lickity-split. "You wanna go there?"

"Damn right, I do," Simon snarls, teeth bared.

We stand there, toe-to-toe, both ready and wanting for a fight. "It's not my fault Myla Rose lied to me and went behind my back with that ass. Not my fault she couldn't have her cake and—" Before I can finish my sentence, Simon decks me, the force knocking me back down into my chair. Rubbing a hand over my cheekbone, I wince from the pain. *Fucker hits hard.*

"Okay, boys," my mom says, her voice scolding and full of mirth all at once, "Let's all have a seat and say what we came to say."

"Think I said all I need to," Simon tells the group with a victorious smirk. As much as he pisses me off, and even though I'm still angry with Myla Rose, I'm glad she has him in her life. Such is the nature of the spell she's cast on me. She rips apart my very soul, and I'm worried about her. Talk about pathetic.

Drake clears his throat. "Well, I haven't. I'm not gonna say who's right or wrong or pick sides. Y'all both messed up. However, with that said, you need to listen to her. Let her say her side. You don't like what she has to say? Walk away. At least you'll both have some closure." I bristle at his words because I know—deep down—that he's right.

"Baby, you need to let that sweet girl have the chance to explain herself. I know Kayla"—I groan at the mention of my ex— "did a real number on you, but Myla Rose isn't Kayla. And even if this feels similar, that's just your brain overriding your heart. Listen to your heart, Cash." My mom, I swear. Such motherly advice, God love her.

"Listen, brother. You know how many times I almost lost Paige, but she was patient and stuck it out with me. Look at us now. Talk to your girl. You won't regret it."

Deep down, and I mean *way deep*, I know they're right. Even more than that, once I look past my hurt, I know Myla Rose. Regardless of what I saw, she's not capable of two-timing me. She's not Kayla. There has to be an explanation.

After a long pause, I cut myself a big ole slice of humble pie and address this group of people that loves us both so much that they ambushed me. "Y'all are right. I know y'all are right. Guess I'll give her a call."

"No need. She'll be here soon." Yeah, that edge I was on? Pretty sure I just fell from it.

special night, and I didn't want Taylor Mills tainting it.

"I know I should have told you the next day. Jesus, looking back, I should have told you right then. But everything just sort of snowballed. He would go days, sometimes weeks, between texts. Every time, I'd get lulled into this false sense of security. I'd convince myself that it was over and that his threats were empty." I risk a look at Cash and the vein in his neck is popping. He's so very angry.

Sinking lower into my chair, I pick back up. "The day at the salon was actually Kathy's appointment—and just so you know, I was planning to tell her that day that she needed to find a new stylist—but Taylor showed up in her place. I told him to leave, and he started to cause a scene. He told me he'd consider not stripping me of custody if I would listen to whatever he had to say. We had clients in the salon and I was desperate to get him out of there, so I gave in.

"I'll sure say you did."

I suck in a sharp breath. "Not like that. I listened as he droned on and on about the pressure he was under to do well in school. I listened to him lament about his mother pressuring him to marry 'up', like I fucking care, right? Anyway..." I laugh, but it's empty and hollow.

"He went on and on and on about nothing. Finally, I got fed up and told him to get to the point, and you know what he said? He told me he really didn't want anything to do with this baby. Said he should've made me get an abortion. Said he was only harassing me to watch me squirm. It took every ounce of willpower not to kill him. And this whole time, he's holding my wrist so tightly that it physically hurts." By this point, Cash is gripping the arms of the chair so hard his knuckles are a painful white.

"I was trying to get Azalea's attention, and there you were, with eyes full of dark clouds. And he hears me say your name, and that just sets him off all over again. Next thing I know, his lips are on mine and my world is slowly ending because you're hauling outta there like a fire'd been lit under your ass. I chased after you, but..."

"Damn, darlin'. I had no clue. I really wish you'd have just talked to me." His calling me *darlin'* has my hope soaring. That has to be a sign, right?

"I know, Cash, truly, I do. I'm only human, and I was so scared and so confused. I messed up. I get that. You have to know I'd never be unfaithful to you, right?" Mustering every bit of courage I possess, I clasp his hand in mine. "Remember when you said my heart was enough? Well, it's yours—take it or leave it." I release his hand and lean in, pressing a brief kiss to his lips before walking toward the back gate. From the edge of the deck, I turn and call to him over my shoulder, "Hey, Cash? I really hope you take it."

As I round the gate, I pull out my phone to text Azalea that I'm ready to leave. Only I never make it that far. Because standing in front of me is the sweetest-looking middle-aged woman I've ever seen.

"You must be Myla Rose," she states as she comes to

a stop directly in front of me. “I’m Sandra, Cash’s mom.”

“Yes, ma’am, it’s so nice to meet you.”

“Oh, sweet girl, I’ve heard so much about you that I feel like I already know you. Now, I expect to see you at our next Family Dinner Night.”

“Oh, no, Ms. Carson—Cash and I...we aren’t—”

“Maybe not right now, but I raised my boy right, and he’ll come around. Just you wait and see.”

Chapter Forty-Four

Cash

Turns out everyone was right. Talking to Myla Rose changed everything. Turns out she was as much the victim as me. Her only true crime was her silence. Talking to me would have literally changed everything.

But that's okay. Now that I know the truth, nothing is gonna keep me from her. Not one goddamn thing. Myla Rose and her baby are my whole life, and I can't wait to fucking prove myself to her. *Again.*

There's just one little thing I have to do first, though. A score to settle, so to speak. So, with a fire in my gut, I head back to the place this shit started. The Mills' residence.

I don't knock on the door. I pound on it, and when their butler answers, I skip the pleasantries. "Tell Taylor to come down." He doesn't put up any fight. He simply presses the button on the intercom and summons Taylor.

Smart man.

"What are you doing here?" Taylor seethes when he sees me.

"We need to talk." I step into his space, forcing him back against the front door. "You leave Myla Rose alone, you hear me? Ask me how many fucks I give about your old money and fancy lawyers. None. I give none. That girl's never done a thing to you, and your tormenting her ends *now.*" I'd love nothing more than to knock the smug look off his face, but I reel it in. He's not worth the jail time, not with Myla on the line.

"You may have been dumb enough to let her go, and that's on you, but she's mine now. Mine to worry about. That baby's mine too. Know that. He'll never so much as know your name."

"You're gonna raise my bastard?"

"Not. A. Bastard," I grit out. "My blood may not run through him, but my love does, and that's more than your sorry ass will ever be able to say. You stay. The. Fuck. Away."

"Whatever. I'm over this little soap opera anyway." He shoves me away from him and scurries back into his house, which is okay because I'm so done here.

Chapter Forty-Five

Myla Rose

Today's my baby shower, and this small, itsy-bitsy, teensy-tiny part of me is scared Cash won't show. Crazy talk, I know. It's been a week since Cash and I sat down and talked at Drake's, and a lot has changed. All for the better, too. We see each other most days, and we text and talk every day. It may've only been four days, but we had a lot of making up to do.

I even joined him at his mom's for Family Dinner Night. I'm now the designated bread bringer. The only thing better than Sandra's cooking is her ability to wrap you up so good in her love that you never wanna leave. She's everything a mama should be, and I know with one hundred percent certainty that Grams would approve of this family I've found myself a part of.

Though we haven't made up *that* way. Not from lack of trying on my part either. My hormones have me wanting him like never before. I'm damn near insatiable, but Cash puts the brakes on every damn time.

We haven't even spent the night together again, and it's literally killing me. Like for real. I'm ninety-nine percent sure Cash is planning something special for us, and I have a feeling that the waiting will be oh, so worth it.

Another upside to our patching things up is that I finally felt little man move! Even better, Cash was there for it. It was damn near magical, and while I was a sobbing mess, Cash just smiled and smiled like he'd won the damn lottery.

He's convinced that the baby waited for him and me to get right before landing any big kicks, though countless people have tried telling him that sometimes, first-time moms take longer to feel it. He's not having any of that, though.

"Myles, do you want me to curl your hair?" Azalea asks as she plugs in my curling wand.

"God, yes. I'm not even thirty weeks, and getting ready makes me feel like I've run a damn marathon."

"Well, sit down, sister-girl. Your shower is in less than two hours!"

Thirty minutes later, I'm primped and fluffed to Azalea's liking. My long red locks float down my back in soft waves, and my makeup is light and tasteful, nothing more than a little eyeliner and lip gloss. Azalea says I glow enough all on my own, God love her.

"All right, time to go!" Azalea chirps as she shuffles me down the stairs and into Bertha. I swear, I think she's more excited about my shower than I am. "I'll follow you there. Drive safe!"

I walk in to Drake's, and I'm immediately surrounded by all the people I hold near and dear, though as I make the rounds, I can't help but notice Cash's absence.

Knowing me just as well as she knows herself, AzzyJo pulls into the kitchen with Seraphine and Magnolia. "Myles, he'll be here."

"Why isn't he already here?" My voice comes out high and screechy, even to my ears.

Seraphine wraps me in a hug, "Hun, chill. Your shower started like ten minutes ago. Give the man some time."

While Mags doesn't have much to add to the conversation, she clutches my hand in hers, giving it a quick, reassuring squeeze.

Twenty more minutes pass, and still, no Cash. Feeling dejected and miserable, I excuse myself to the washroom. "Get a grip, Myla Rose." After splashing some cool water on my face, I make my way back out to the party.

I'm stopped in my tracks by the sight of Cash, dressed in a crisp gray button-down and dark-wash jeans, with his hair combed and gelled away from his face, standing next to my dream crib. It's everything I could've ever imagined and then some. Instinctually, I know he built it, and damn if that doesn't make me swoon.

With no hesitation, I rush to him, wrapping my arms

around him, holding him tight. "I love you, Cash Carson. I'm not sure what I did to deserve you, but my Lord, I'm not gonna question it."

He drops a kiss to my forehead and steps out of my embrace. "Speaking of questions, darlin', I got one for you." I gasp when he drops down to one knee. "Myla Rose McGraw, you are far and wide the best thing that's ever happened to me. You're the reason the sun rises and sets in my universe, and I need to know, darlin'...will you do me the honor of allowing me to be your husband and that sweet little boy's daddy?"

With tears streaming down my face, I nod and launch myself into his arms. "God, yes. Always yes. IloveyouIloveyouIloveyou."

"Love you too, darlin'. Both of you. Now and forever."

Epilogue

Cash

I'll never forget the way I felt watching Myla Rose walk down the aisle toward me. Time stood still. I was frozen, with my heart in my throat. Myla is beautiful seven days a week, but on our wedding day... she was fucking *radiant.* I'm talking a halo of light and a *Hallelujah* chorus surrounding her as she walked down the rose petal-strewn walkway.

I took my time, raking my eyes down her body from head to foot. Her red hair was spun up in a loose bun, and her lips were a juicy shade of peach. I couldn't wait to find out if they tasted as good as they looked.

Her dress was off-white because she said she couldn't wear white with her skin-tone, but what-the-fuck-ever—she'd look perfect in a paper sack. Either way, I just wanted her with my last name. Not gonna lie, though, it was the fit of the dress that had me feeling like I was gonna die, right there at the altar. The chiffon material clung to her ample chest and floated down her body, swooping over the bump that carried *our* son.

Our vows were filled with promises of love and trust and patience and to always put the other first, though we spoke them quietly, because they weren't for everyone else. No, they were for us, and only us. Once we exchanged rings and were pronounced husband and wife, I gathered her up in my arms and kissed her like never before.

Our kiss was searing, branding, a promise of forever in and of itself.

When Myla Rose pulled back and looked at me with tears in her eyes and a smile on her lips, my heart felt like it was boomeranging around in my chest. She was just so damn beautiful. In that moment, I thought, *life will surely never be better than this.*

Well, I was wrong.

Because the birth of our son? Yeah, that's right on up there with our wedding day. Brody Michael Carson—named Brody because Myla said he looked like one, and Michael so that he and I shared a middle name—came kicking and screaming into this world at eight A.M. on a Wednesday morning in late September. He weighed in at seven pounds, seven ounces and measured twenty-one inches long.

The first time I held him, my heart cracked. Not because it was broken, but because it was growing. That tiny baby boy became our whole world—I'm talking pure fucking perfection, swaddled in blue.

I don't know what our future holds, but one thing I'm more than sure of is with Myla Rose and baby Brody by my side, anything is possible, and everything is coming up roses.

The End

Acknowledgements

Wow, my first book. Never thought I'd see the day, and without the help and support of so many, I can truly say I wouldn't have.

Karin, we started this journey together, and you've quickly become one of my very best friends. Your belief and faith in me means the world to me. You're my hero, babe!

Lo and Heather, my twins. Love y'all to the moon and back. Two times.

Shawn, this book wouldn't be what it is, without you! You challenged me and never hesitated to ask "WHY?". Thank you SO much!

Cassie, love you boo!

Joy, thanks for letting me annoy the crap out of you!

Paola, thanks for believing in me!

To my amazing beta readers, y'all are legit the best around. Thank y'all!

To my Minxes, y'all are the coolest, most amazing group around. Thank y'all so much for always putting up with my endless questions. It means the world to me.

To the blogs and readers who take a chance on little ol' me! I hope y'all adore Cash & Myla Rose!

To my Mom. You always said you wanted to read this, and I always blushed and told you "No!". I take it back… I just wish you were here to read it. I love you, eternally.

To my family for their unrelenting love and support.

But most of all, to my husband and children. Without y'all, my life would be dull and gray. Y'all are my hope, my sunshine, my air, and more. I love you.

About The Author

LK Farlow (A.K.A Kate) is a small town girl with a love for words. She's been writing stories and poems for as long she can remember.

A Southern girl through and through, Kate resides in beautiful, sunny LA—that's Lower Alabama, y'all—with her amazing husband and three wonderful children. When she's not writing, you can find her snuggled up on the couch watching nature documentaries while she crochets or with her nose in a book.

All Kate really wants in this life is her family happy, strong coffee, a good book and more Happily Ever After's.

Facebook: @AuthorLKFarlow

Reader Group: LK's Darling's

www.authorlkfarlow.com

Made in the USA
Columbia, SC
14 April 2021